CRAZY LIKE A FOX

Center Point
Large Print

Also by Rita Mae Brown and available from
Center Point Large Print:

Let Sleeping Dogs Lie

**This Large Print Book carries the
Seal of Approval of N.A.V.H.**

CRAZY LIKE
A FOX

RITA MAE BROWN

CENTER POINT LARGE PRINT
THORNDIKE, MAINE

This Center Point Large Print edition
is published in the year 2018 by arrangement with
Ballantine Books, an imprint of Random House,
a division of Penguin Random House LLC.

Crazy Like a Fox is a work of fiction.
Names, characters, places, and incidents are the
products of the author's imagination or are used fictitiously.
Any resemblance to actual events, locales, or persons,
living or dead, is entirely coincidental.

The text of this Large Print edition is unabridged.
In other aspects, this book may vary
from the original edition.
Printed in the United States of America
on permanent paper.
Set in 16-point Times New Roman type.

ISBN: 978-1-68324-667-1

Library of Congress Cataloging-in-Publication Data

Names: Brown, Rita Mae, author.
Title: Crazy like a fox / Rita Mae Brown.
Description: Center Point Large Print edition. | Thorndike, Maine :
    Center Point Large Print, 2018.
Identifiers: LCCN 2017050418 | ISBN 9781683246671
    (hardcover : alk. paper)
Subjects: LCSH: Arnold, Jane (Fictitious character—Fiction. |
    Fox hunting—Fiction. | Large type books. | BISAC: FICTION /
    Suspense. | FICTION / Humorous. | GSAFD: Mystery fiction. |
    Suspense fiction.
Classification: LCC PS3552.R698 C73 2018 | DDC 813/.54—dc23
LC record available at https://lccn.loc.gov/2017050418

CRAZY LIKE
A FOX

DEDICATED TO
MY FAST LADIES

Maria Johnston, jt Huntsman

Whippers-in
Rebecca Birnbaum
Kristin Ford
Dee Phillips
Mary Shriver
Candace Waycaster

CAST OF CHARACTERS

THE HUMANS

Jane Arnold, M.F.H., "Sister," runs The Jefferson Hunt. MFH stands for Master of Foxhounds, the individual who runs the hunt, deals with every crisis both on and off the field. She is strong, bold, loves her horses and her hounds. In 1974, her fourteen-year-old son was killed in a tractor accident. That loss deepened her, taught her to cherish every minute. She's had lots of minutes as she's in her early seventies, but she has no concept of age.

Shaker Crown hunts the hounds. He tries to live up to the traditions of this ancient sport, which goes back to the pharaohs. He and Sister work well together, truly enjoy each other. He is in his mid-forties. Divorced for many years and a bit gun-shy.

Gray Lorillard isn't cautious in the hunt field, but he is cautious off it as he was a partner in one of the most prestigious accounting firms in D.C. He knows how the world really works and, although retired, is often asked to solve problems at his former firm. He is smart, handsome, in his early sixties, and is African American.

Crawford Howard is best described by Aunt

Daniella who commented, "There's a great deal to be said about new money and Crawford means to say it all." He started an outlaw pack of hounds when Sister did not ask him to be her Joint Master. Slowly, he is realizing you can't push people around in this part of the world. Fundamentally, he is a decent and generous man.

Sam Lorillard is Gray's younger brother. Sam Lorillard works at Crawford's stables. Crawford hired Sam when no one else would, so Sam is loyal. He blew a full scholarship to Harvard thanks to the bottle. He's good with horses. His brother saved him and he's clean, but so many people feel bad about what might have been. He focuses on the future.

Daniella Laprade is Gray and Sam's aunt. She is an extremely healthy nonagenarian who isn't above shaving a year or two off her age. She may even be older than her stated ninety-four. Her past is dotted with three husbands and numerous affairs, all carried out with discretion.

Anne Harris, "Tootie," left Princeton in her freshman year as she missed foxhunting in Virginia so very much. Her father had a cow, cut her out of his will. She takes classes at the University of Virginia and is now twenty-two and shockingly beautiful. She is African American.

Yvonne Harris, Tootie's mother, is a former model who has fled Chicago and her marriage. She's filed for divorce from Victor Harris, a hard-driving businessman who built an African American media empire. She built it with him. She is trying to understand Tootie, feels she was not so much a bad mother as an absent one. Her experience has been different from her daughter's and Tootie's freedoms were won by Yvonne's generation and those prior. Yvonne doesn't understand that Tootie doesn't understand.

Wesley Carruthers, "Weevil," was the huntsman for The Jefferson Hunt from 1947 to 1954 when he disappeared never to be found. As beautiful as a Greek god, bursting with life and humor, ladies threw themselves at him. Often he picked them up, married or unmarried. Consensus, over time, was that an irate husband killed him. The problem is that he does reappear in 2017, young and handsome. How?

Marion Maggiolo owns Horse Country, an elegant tack, clothing, silver, etc., store in Warrenton, Virginia. If there's a board, Marion sits on it as she is a powerhouse of good deeds and wonderful ideas. She and Sister serve on the board for the Museum of Hounds and Hunting. They get far more than they bargained for.

Alfred and Binky DuCharme are two brothers in their early seventies who hate each other so much they haven't spoken for over fifty years. This is because Binky stole and married Alfred's girlfriend.

Margaret DuCharme, M.D., is Alfred's

11

daughter and she's acted as a go-between for her father and uncle since childhood. Her cousin, Binky's son Arthur, also acts as a go-between and both the cousins are just fed up with it. They are in their early forties, Margaret being more successful than Arthur but he's happy enough.

Walter Lungrun, M.D., JT-MFH, is a cardiologist who has hunted with Sister since his boyhood. He is the late Raymond Arnold's son, which Sister knows. No one talks about it and Walter's father always acted as though he were Walter's father. It's the way things are done around here. Let sleeping dogs lie.

Betty Franklin is an honorary whipper-in, which means she doesn't get paid. Whippers-in emit a glamorous sheen to other foxhunters and it is a daring task. One must know a great deal and be able to ride hard, jump high, think in a split second. She is Sister's best friend and in her mid-fifties. Everyone loves Betty.

Bobby Franklin especially loves Betty as he is her husband. He leads Second Flight, those riders who may take modest jumps but not the big ones. He and Betty own a small printing press and nearly lost their shirts when computers started printing out stuff. But people have returned to true printing, fine papers, etc. They're doing okay.

Kasmir Barbhaiya made his money in India in pharmaceuticals. Educated in an English public school, thence on to Oxford, he is highly intelligent and tremendously wealthy. Widowed, he moved to Virginia to be close to an old Oxford classmate and his wife. He owns marvelous horses and rides them well. He thought he would forever be alone but the Fates thought otherwise. Love has found him.

Edward and Tedi Bancroft, in their eighties, are stalwarts of The Jefferson Hunt and dear friends of Sister's. Evangelista, Edward's deceased sister, had an affair with Weevil; although hushed up, it caused uproar in the Bancroft family.

Ben Sidell is the county sheriff who is learning to hunt and loves it. Nonni, his horse, takes good care of him. He learns far more about the county by hunting than if he just stayed in his squad car. He dates Margaret DuCharme, M.D., an unlikely pairing that works.

Cynthia Skiff Cane hunts Crawford's outlaw pack. He's gone through three other huntsmen but she can handle him. Sam Lorillard helps, too.

Monica Greenberg, a dazzler, rides sidesaddle and is organizing a sidesaddle exhibit for the Museum of Hounds and Hunting. She is patient and kind, just loves her horse.

Cindy Chandler owns Foxglove Farm, one of The Jefferson Hunt's fixtures. She's not much in evidence in this volume but, like all landowners, she is important.

Victor Harris is Tootie's father. Jerk doesn't begin to cover it.

THE AMERICAN FOXHOUNDS

Lighter than the English foxhound, with a somewhat slimmer head, they have formidable powers of endurance and remarkable noses.

Cora is the head female. What she says goes.

Asa is the oldest hunting male hound, and he is wise.

Diana is steady, in the prime of her life, and brilliant. There's no other word for her but "brilliant."

Dasher is Diana's littermate and often overshadowed by his sister, but he sticks to business and is coming into his own.

Dragon is also a littermate of the above D hounds. He is arrogant, can lose his concentration and tries to lord it over other hounds.

Dreamboat is of the same breeding as Diana, Dasher, and Dragon, but a few years younger.

Hounds take the first initial of their mother's name. Following are hounds ordered from older to younger. No unentered hounds are included in this list. An unentered hound is not yet on the Master of Foxhounds stud books and not yet hunting with the pack. They are in essence kindergartners. **Trinity, Tinsel, Trident, Ardent,**

Thimble, Twist, Tootsie, Trooper, Taz, Tatoo, Parker, Pickens, Zane, Zorro, Zandy, Giorgio, Pookah, Pansy, Audrey, Aero, Angle, Aces.

THE HORSES

Keepsake, TB/QH, Bay; **Lafayette,** TB, Gray; **Rickyroo,** TB, Bay; **Aztec,** TB, Chestnut; **Matador,** TB, Flea-bitten Gray. All are Sister's geldings. **Showboat, Hojo, Gunpowder,** and **Kilowatt,** all TBs, are Shaker's horses.

Outlaw, QH, Buckskin, and **Magellan,** TB, Dark Bay (which is really black), are Betty's horses.

Wolsey, TB, Flaming Chestnut, is Gray's horse. His red coat gave him his name for Cardinal Wolsey.

Iota, TB, Bay, is Tootie's horse.

Matchplay and **Midshipman** are young Thoroughbreds of Sister's that are being brought along. Takes good time to make a solid foxhunter. Sister never hurries a horse or a hound in its schooling.

THE FOXES

Reds

Aunt Netty, older, lives at Pattypan Forge. She is overly tidy and likes to give orders.

15

Uncle Yancy is Aunt Netty's husband but he can't stand her anymore. He lives at the Lorillard farm, has all manner of dens and cubbyholes.

Charlene lives at After All Farm. She comes and goes.

Target is Charlene's mate but he stays at After All. The food supply is steady and he likes the other animals.

Earl has the restored stone stables at Old Paradise all to himself. He has a den in a stall but also makes use of the tack room. He likes the smell of the leather.

Sarge is half-grown. He found a den in big boulders at Old Paradise thanks to help from a doe. It's cozy with straw, old clothing bits, and even a few toys.

James lives behind the mill at Mill Ruins. He is not very social but from time to time will give the hounds a good run.

Ewald is a youngster who was directed to a den in an outbuilding during a hunt. Poor fellow didn't know where he was. The outbuilding at Mill Ruins will be a wonderful home as long as he steers clear of James.

Grays

Comet knows everybody and everything. He lives in the old stone foundation part of the rebuilt log-and-frame cottage at Roughneck Farm.

Inky is so dark she's black and she lives in the apple orchard across from the above cottage. She knows the hunt schedule and rarely gives hounds a run. They can just chase someone else.

Georgia moved to the old schoolhouse at Foxglove Farm.

Grenville lives at Mill Ruins, in the back in a big storage shed. This part of the estate is called Shootrough.

Gris lives at Tollbooth Farm in the Chapel Cross area. He's very clever and can slip hounds in the batting of an eye.

Hortensia also lives at Mill Ruins. She's in another outbuilding. All are well constructed and all but the big hay sheds have doors that close, which is wonderful in bad weather.

THE BIRDS

Athena, the great horned owl, is two-and-a-half-feet tall with a four-foot wingspan. She has many places where she will hole up but her true nest is in Pattypan Forge. It really beats being in a tree hollow. She's gotten spoiled.

Bitsy is eight-and-a-half-inches tall with a twenty-inch wingspan. Her considerable lungs make up for her tiny size as she is a screech owl, aptly named. Like Athena, she'll never live in a tree again because she's living in the rafters of Sister's stable. Mice come in to eat the fallen grain. Bitsy feels like she's living in a supermarket.

St. Just, a foot and a half in height with a surprising wingspan of three feet, is a jet-black crow. He hates foxes but is usually sociable with other birds.

SISTER'S HOUSE PETS

Raleigh, a sleek, highly intelligent Doberman, likes to be with Sister. He gets along with the hounds, walks out with them. He tries to get along with the cat, but she's such a snob.

Rooster is a Harrier bequeathed to Sister by a dear friend. He likes riding in the car, walking out with hounds, watching everybody and everything. The cat drives him crazy.

Golliwog, or "Golly," is a long-haired calico. All other creatures are lower life-forms. She knows Sister does her best, but still. Golly is Queen of All She Surveys.

SOME USEFUL TERMS

Away. A fox has gone away when he has left the covert. Hounds are away when they have left the covert on the line of the fox.

Brush. The fox's tail.

Burning scent. Scent so strong or hot that hounds pursue the line without hesitation.

Bye day. A day not regularly on the fixture card.

Cap. The fee nonmembers pay to hunt for that day's sport.

Carry a good head. When hounds run well together to a good scent, a scent spread wide enough for the whole pack to feel it.

Carry a line. When hounds follow the scent. This is also called working a line.

Cast. Hounds spread out in search of scent. They may cast themselves or be cast by the huntsman.

Charlie. A term for a fox. A fox may also be called Reynard.

Check. When hounds lose the scent and stop. The field must wait quietly while the hounds search for the scent.

Colors. A distinguishing color, usually worn on the collar but sometimes on the facings of a coat, that identifies a hunt. Colors can be awarded only by the Master and can be worn only in the field.

Coop. A jump resembling a chicken coop.

Couple straps. Two-strap hound collars connected by a swivel link. Some members of staff will carry these on the right rear of the saddle. Since the days of the pharaohs in ancient Egypt, hounds have been brought to the meets coupled. Hounds are always spoken of and counted in couples. Today, hounds walk or are driven to the meets. Rarely, if ever, are they coupled, but a whipper-in still carries couple straps should a hound need assistance.

Covert. A patch of woods or bushes where a fox might hide. Pronounced "cover."

Cry. How one hound tells another what is happening. The sound will differ according to the various stages of the chase. It's also called giving tongue and should occur when a hound is working a line.

Cub hunting. The informal hunting of young foxes in the late summer and early fall, before formal hunting. The main purpose is to enter young hounds into the pack. Until recently only the most knowledgeable members were invited to cub hunt, since they would not interfere with young hounds.

Dog fox. The male fox.

Dog hound. The male hound.

Double. A series of short sharp notes blown on the horn to alert all that a fox is afoot. The gone away series of notes is a form of doubling the horn.

Draft. To acquire hounds from another hunt is to accept a draft.

Draw. The plan by which a fox is hunted or searched for in a certain area, such as a covert.

Draw over the fox. Hounds go through a covert where the fox is but cannot pick up his scent. The only creature who understands how this is possible is the fox.

Drive. The desire to push the fox, to get up with the line. It's a very desirable trait in hounds, so long as they remain obedient.

Dually. A one-ton pickup truck with double wheels in back.

Dwell. To hunt without getting forward. A hound who dwells is a bit of a putterer.

Enter. Hounds are entered into the pack when they first hunt, usually during cubbing season.

Field. The group of people riding to hounds, exclusive of the Master and hunt staff.

Field Master. The person appointed by the Master to control the field. Often it is the Master him- or herself.

Fixture. A card sent to all dues-paying members, stating when and where the hounds will meet. A fixture card properly received is an invitation to hunt. This means the card would be mailed or handed to a member by the Master.

Flea-bitten. A gray horse with spots or ticking that can be black or chestnut.

Gone away. The call on the horn when the fox leaves the covert.

Gone to ground. A fox who has ducked into his den, or some other refuge, has gone to ground.

Good night. The traditional farewell to the Master after the hunt, regardless of the time of day.

Gyp. The female hound.

Hilltopper. A rider who follows the hunt but does not jump. Hilltoppers are also called the Second Flight. The jumpers are called the First Flight.

Hoick. The huntsman's cheer to the hounds. It is derived from the Latin *hic haec hoc*, which means "here."

Hold hard. To stop immediately.

Huntsman. The person in charge of the hounds, in the field and in the kennel.

Kennelman. A hunt staff member who feeds the hounds and cleans the kennels. In wealthy hunts there may be a number of kennelmen. In hunts with a modest budget, the huntsman or even the Master cleans the kennels and feeds the hounds.

Lark. To jump fences unnecessarily when hounds aren't running. Masters frown on this, since it is often an invitation to an accident.

Lieu in. Norman term for go in.

Lift. To take the hounds from a lost scent in the hopes of finding a better scent farther on.

Line. The scent trail of the fox.

Livery. The uniform worn by the professional members of the hunt staff. Usually it is scarlet, but blue, yellow, brown, and gray are also used. The recent dominance of scarlet has to do with people buying coats off the rack as opposed to having tailors cut them. (When anything is mass-produced, the choices usually dwindle, and such is the case with livery.)

Mask. The fox's head.

Meet. The site where the day's hunting begins.

MFH. The Master of Foxhounds; the individual in charge of the hunt: hiring, firing, landowner relations, opening territory (in large hunts this is the job of the hunt secretary), developing the pack of hounds, and determining the first cast of each meet. As in any leadership position, the Master is also the lightning rod for criticism. The Master may hunt the hounds, although this is usually done by a professional huntsman, who is also responsible for the hounds in the field and at the kennels. A long relationship between a Master and a huntsman allows the hunt to develop and grow.

Nose. The scenting ability of a hound.

Override. To press hounds too closely.

Overrun. When hounds shoot past the line of a scent. Often the scent has been diverted or foiled by a clever fox.

Ratcatcher. Informal dress worn during cubbing season and bye days.

Stern. A hound's tail.

Stiff-necked fox. One who runs in a straight line.

Strike hounds. Those hounds that, through keenness, nose, and often higher intelligence, find the scent first and press it.

Tail hounds. Those hounds running at the rear of the pack. This is not necessarily because they aren't keen; they may be older hounds.

Tallyho. The cheer when the fox is viewed. Derived from the Norman *ty a hillaut*, thus coming into the English language in 1066.

Tongue. To vocally pursue a fox.

View halloo (halloa). The cry given by a staff member who sees a fox. Staff may also say tallyho or, should the fox turn back, tally-back. One reason a different cry may be used by staff, especially in territory where the huntsman can't see the staff, is that the field in their enthusiasm may cheer something other than a fox.

Vixen. The female fox.

Walk. Puppies are walked out in the summer and fall of their first year. It's part of their education and a delight for both puppies and staff.

Whippers-in. Also called whips, these are the staff members who assist the huntsman, who make sure the hounds "do right."

CRAZY LIKE
A FOX

CHAPTER 1

Leaning over the long glass display case, Marion Maggiolo squinted. "This glare drives me crazy."

Her older friend, Jane Arnold, "Sister," Master of The Jefferson Hunt Club, responded, "One only notices it at certain angles."

Once that was out of her mouth she realized she was talking to a perfectionist, one whom she loved, but a perfectionist nonetheless.

Marion pulled her cellphone out of her jacket pocket, placing it just to the left of the offending glare. "Look at that."

Sister dutifully bent down to look at the cellphone surface. "I guess the phone blocks the light."

Both women looked upward at the lighting.

"I wonder if we could change the light so it doesn't glare off the case." Marion placed her forefinger on her lips. "Well, we can, but we can't sacrifice brightness or clarity. People do read these displays. They especially like the photographs."

The two stood in the Museum of Hounds and Hunting located at Morven Park. This room housed the Huntsman Hall of Fame. Each inductee's life was written in easy-to-read type;

his horn was usually on display along with a coat, a cap, and other items germane to foxhunting and the inductee's personality. The photograph of each Hall of Famer had been chosen with care by the families as well as the Board of Directors. Only one woman had been inducted. An individual could only be considered for inclusion if he had carried the horn for twenty years. Most had hunted far longer than that, but often the photographs chosen were of the gentlemen and lady in their prime.

Sister and Marion stared at such a man, prime and in his prime, Wesley Carruthers. The photograph showed an impossibly gorgeous man, perhaps early thirties, raising a silver punchbowl, a hand on each handle. He had just won best-in-show at the Virginia Hound Show in 1951.

"Didn't they call him Weevil?" Marion asked Sister, who was about fifteen years older than herself.

"They did. I was just a kid when he won—I was at the show with Mother. I actually did hunt behind him once or twice. I was still in grade school. Mother wanted me to see as many packs and their huntsmen as possible. I'm forever grateful to her because I learned so much. Just soaked it up."

"You've bred a good pack. You must have absorbed something."

Sister laughed. "True. A pack is one thing

you can't really buy. Oh, people have, but they inevitably ruin the hounds because they don't know what they're doing and, worse, they don't know their bloodlines." She held up her hand. "Don't get me started. You know hounds are my favorite subject."

"I think there are others," Marion wryly commented, returning her gaze to Weevil.

Sister stared at the beautiful man as well. "A cross between Gary Cooper and John Wayne, when young."

Marion studied the strong masculine face, the wide shoulders, tiny hips. "The young John Wayne was wonderful-looking."

"As was Gary Cooper, a Montana boy."

"Was he?"

"Was, and Wayne was from Iowa. Now Weevil, he hailed from The Plains, Virginia. Grew up with everyone in Northern Virginia, worked his way up to being huntsman by whipping-in with other packs. Started at the bottom, third whipper-in, kennel assistant. In those days, clubs could afford a lot of help. I think he was First Whipper-in at Green Spring Valley in Maryland, before coming back here to carry the horn for Jefferson Hunt."

Hunt service, like any profession, contains stepping-stones. Certainly talent is a factor but so are drive, social skills, and physical toughness, especially physical toughness. Many whippers-in today express no desire to become huntsmen.

29

They are happy whipping-in, which means riding hard, knowing the hounds, and working on the edges of the pack. If there's a problem usually a whipper-in sees it first and tries to correct it, like keeping a pack from running onto a highway in pursuit of the fox that knows exactly what he or she is doing. A few rich hunts still have large paid staffs. Most hunts feel fortunate to have one paid whipper-in, the rest being honorary, which is to say, amateurs. And often those honorary people are fantastic but hold well-paying jobs or provide taxi service for the kids before and after school. This is the main reason so many current whippers-in don't aspire to being huntsmen. They can't afford it. Their jobs are too good. Few hunts could survive without honorary whippers-in, and this included The Jefferson Hunt where Weevil had been huntsman. Jane Arnold, "Sister," was the Master of Jefferson Hunt, had been for over forty years, but Weevil was long gone by the time she'd moved to central Virginia.

Marion sighed. "He was gorgeous. They never found him, did they?"

"No." Sister slightly shook her head.

"Murder. No one thought he died a natural death."

Sister heard footsteps. "Weevil managed to cuckold most male members of the Virginia and Maryland hunts."

"Let's go," Jake Carle, Director of the Hall of Fame, called to them. "If we don't go now we won't get a table." He then walked to the top of the stairwell, crossed to another room, climbed a few steps to the ballroom, and called to Monica Greenberg. "Leesburg."

"In a minute," she replied.

"You know where to find us." He turned, retraced his steps, meeting Sister and Marion.

The three left. Jake had finished his meeting with other board members. Everyone hopped in their cars to drive into Leesburg.

No sooner had they been seated than Monica was directed to their table. As she walked across the restaurant, all eyes followed her. Some recognized her as the sidesaddle rider on the fabulous Winter Party, a sensational team. She carried herself with perfect posture, head held high, attractive enough on the ground but on a horse the effect was pure beauty.

Paying no mind to people's reactions, she took the offered seat. "Were you talking about me?" she teased.

"We wondered how your history of sidesaddle is coming along." Jake liked anything historical, as did Sister and Marion.

"When I asked for photographs I had no idea how much material is out there. Most of it in black and white. I thought I'd receive about fifteen photographs. I have sixty-two."

"Bet the early ones are smashing." Marion couldn't wait to see the finished exhibit, pictures framed, biographies next to them.

"I have one from 1860 but quite a few starting in the 1870s and moving onward. Obviously men liked to take photographs of women riding sidesaddle. A well-turned-out lady turns heads." Monica smiled.

"You certainly did. Still do," Jake complimented her.

He thought of the three as "the girls" but would never say that. Given that Sister, Marion, and Monica knew exactly who they were, if he had done so they wouldn't have been offended.

Changing the subject, Monica asked, "Did you all take two cars?"

"We did," Marion answered.

"Thought so, as I heard three sets of footsteps on the stairs, first one then a few minutes later more."

No one thought anything of the observation at the time.

As with any group of people who know one another well, and work together, they talked about the museum, about Monica's efforts for the Washington opera, about Marion's planned fashion show of hunting attire to raise money for the museum come November.

"Seems far away but it's only ten weeks." Marion placed her small notebook by her plate.

"First question. Do we have the models wear garters?"

"Chorus girls wear garters," Monica mischievously said.

This provoked a discussion about achingly proper attire as opposed to comfortable turnout. Boots no longer actually folded over, which was what created the need for a garter in the first place back in the seventeenth century. Far be it from foxhunters to bypass a tradition whether useful or not.

Sister jumped right in. "I wear them on the High Holy Days."

Jake grimaced. "You would. If ever I have a question about proper turnout, I refer to you, madam."

She smiled at the good-looking former Keswick Master. "Is that a gentleman's way of saying I'm older than dirt and remember everything?"

"Sister, you will always command a room." He grinned at her, proving once again why women adored him.

The garter discussion pooped out. They finally reached what they were all dying to talk about, since it was mid-September.

"How's your season so far?" Joyce Fendley, who had joined them from her committee meeting, Master of Casanova Hunt, asked.

The table erupted. Everyone babbled at once. The dryness. The heat. Tons of game but the scent wouldn't hold. On they talked. A group bound by passion, by love of animals, for no one would kill a fox, and without realizing it, by love of one another.

Marion reached in her pocket for her cellphone, wanting to check the weather. Her face registered surprise. "I can't believe I did that."

"Did what?" Sister asked.

"I left my cellphone on the display case."

Jake, overhearing, suggested, "You know where the key is kept. Go back after dinner. It's a lot closer than driving up from Warrenton tomorrow."

Marion's shop, Horse Country, was located at 60 Alexandria Pike in Warrenton, miles away. Clothing, silver, hand-painted china, and horse furnishings could all be found therein. Marion's idea for a fashion show really was to raise money for the museum, but if seeing runway models encouraged people to come to the store, so much the better.

"Do you know exactly where you left it?" Joyce inquired, having spent time in her life on search missions.

"Right by Wesley Carruthers's artifacts."

Jake, overhearing, folded his napkin. "There were so many suspects in his disappearance, I think every man who foxhunted in Virginia and Maryland was questioned by the police."

"Wasn't Averell Harriman one of the leading

suspects?" Joyce mentioned the wealthy man who performed public service.

"Absurd. Averell would never commit murder." Jake spoke. "I was a kid at the time but I remember my father paying a lot of attention to this."

"Some women"—Joyce glanced around the table—"would never have been foolish enough to risk their position no matter how handsome the man."

"I agree," Sister added. "But the old gossip trumpets that plenty of ladies did."

"Well, the real scandal, the one that broke the camel's back, was when he was supposed to be sleeping with Christine Falconer as well as her daughter Madge." Marion suppressed a grin.

"No!" Sister exclaimed.

"You hadn't heard that?" Marion was surprised.

"Dear God," Sister thought out loud. "He must have been out of his mind."

"Or they were." Jake ordered an after-dinner drink.

"Wasn't Jim Falconer Undersecretary of State?" Joyce inquired. She thought a moment and answered her own question. "He was. All those men had served with distinction in the war, and when Eisenhower swept into office so did they."

"Did a good job, too. We'll never see public servants like that again." Sister's voice rose slightly. "Sorry. That was an editorial comment."

Jake waved the apology away. "I think we all feel that way. Look how many presidents we've had in the last few decades who have never served their country in uniform, never been in a war, not that I want people to go to war, but if they have to I think they are more reluctant to squander American lives."

"Hear, hear," all responded in unison.

As the meal finished, people stood up.

Jake called to Marion, "Look at Weevil's cowhorn. It's foxhunting scrimshaw. Quite something."

Driving back to Morven Park, Sister said, "How many times have I looked at that horn and wished I could pick it up and view the entire scene? All I could see was the fox, a few hounds behind."

Marion considered. "Maybe I should put mirrors around it."

She drove into Morven Park, the early fall air still warm. The mansion, a great white sepulchre, commanded a level rise above the one thousand acres. The massive Doric columns bore testimony to the power of the place, the solidity of it, the gravitas of Westmoreland Davis himself, a former Virginia governor who had lived there. Five chimneys poked up through the gray roof, multiple flues sticking above the white chimneys. Heating the mansion, always expensive, must have been near impossible before electricity.

Marion closed the door to her Jaguar, as did Sister. The two women fetched the key from behind one of the long green window shutters.

Flipping on lights as they walked in, they reached the Hall of Fame room quickly.

"Right where I left it," Marion rejoiced, snatching her phone.

Turning it on to see if she still had a charge, she noticed a small red circle by the camera icon.

Sister, looking over her shoulder, watched as Marion touched the camera.

Both women stared, speechless.

"What!" Marion, shocked, finally spoke.

Sister looked at the moving picture. "It can't be true."

Marion then looked at the case. The horn was missing. "Sister, it is."

There in front of them, taking a selfie video, was Weevil, smiling, holding up his horn. He wore a black turtleneck. They couldn't see what else he was wearing.

"This is impossible. He's been dead, we think, since 1954."

"And if he were alive, he'd be about ninety-five. I recall someone at the table saying he was thirty-two when he disappeared. This man,"— Sister pointed to the iPhone—"is in his early thirties."

Marion looked at the case. The lock wasn't

broken, but she knew it would be easy enough to spring. She pressed the camera on the phone again.

"There may be more."

There was. Weevil put the horn to his lips and blew "Gone to Ground."

Marion gasped. "It's impossible."

Sister put her arm around Marion's shoulder. "It may be impossible, but there is Weevil Carruthers blowing 'Gone to Ground,' telling us he's safe and sound. Cheeky devil. Handsome. Handsome. Handsome."

Marion swallowed hard. "A ghost?"

Sister inhaled deeply. "Marion, I want to find out and I don't."

CHAPTER 2

Comet, furious with himself, flew through the late-summer corn soon to be harvested at the western edge of Ed and Tedi Bancroft's large estate. The praying mantis clinging to a corn leaf dug its spikes in deeper as Comet brushed through the corn. The mature gray fox, a dashing fellow, zigzagged as Dasher, a hound in his prime, ran close behind, too close. The pack of The Jefferson Hunt, first cast at seven-thirty A.M. due to the September heat, had started from the covered bridge at the Bancrofts'. Noses to the ground, those hounds, hunting for their first season, darted about, finally settling down when Cora, the older head female hound, chided them. On they pressed, the day promising little. Heat already coming up, high 50s now. The scent would lift to dissipate quickly but that was cubbing, the beginning of every hunt season. As in any sport where there's been a layoff, foxes, hounds, horses, people need to slip back in the groove. The young foxes, like the young hounds, learned the horn calls, the ways to baffle hounds as well as where various dens offered a place to duck in. Often, the owner of the escape den complained loudly. The sound of the pack always shut up the fox, gopher, or whoever owned the den. Then again, once danger passed, the uninvited guest, with apologies, left.

Comet knew it was a Thursday, a hunt day for Jefferson Hunt. Living near the kennels, he knew the schedule, especially when the horses to be hunted the next morning were brought into the barn that night. No one wanted to chase a playful horse, risk being late to a hunt. In they came.

Keenly aware of the seasons, Comet figured the late corn would soon be harvested. Those wonderful corn patches burst with birds, mice, any creature wanting corn on the cob. Even after the harvest, the stalks, the corn left on the ground brought in so many tasty creatures. Comet had plenty to eat where he lived, but he felt like hunting. So he crossed the beautiful wildflower meadow between Jane Arnold's Roughneck Farm and After All, the Bancrofts vast, immaculately maintained estate. Passing through the large meadow, black-eyed Susans nodding, then into the cornfield, he could hear the chatter from the mice, the occasional chipmunk even before stepping into the slightly rustling corn.

The pack, moving westward, curling slightly south, baffled the whippers-in. Betty Franklin and Tootie Harris thought the hounds would sweep north toward the old Pattypan Forge, always a good spot. But noses down, silent, they pushed. The two humans knew they were working, but the scent wasn't strong enough to speak. Perhaps in time it would heat up and they would open, sing.

Shaker Crown, the huntsman, in his early forties, liked letting his hounds solve problems. Some huntsmen were always picking up hounds, moving them to a place considered by the human more favorable. Foxes cared nothing for what humans considered favorable, but the incessant fiddling with a pack of hounds made them dependent on the humans. Given human shortcomings, never a good thing.

Sitting in the big cornfield, Comet ate succulent corn. Why bother hunting? He'd started out thinking catching a mouse would be bracing, but the sweetness of the corn, those large lower ears just waiting to be plucked, proved so much better than running about listening to the mice scream bloody murder to one another. Those high-pitched voices could be irritating. Full, Comet had been sloppy. He'd left the farm before the hound and horse trailers had, so he didn't know where they were going. He knew it was a hunt day. He'd also seen the trailers, cleaned and ready to go. Sloppy. He knew perfectly well that After All was one of the hunt's best fixtures, a place where a club could hunt. He also knew it was cubbing, and Sister Jane never liked to take her youngsters too far from the kennels. If a youngster wandered off, a rarity but it did happen, they would find their way home. If an older hound, used during cubbing to settle and train the youngsters, began to tire, he or she could return to the trailers or wait to be picked up by a road whip, a person in a special hound truck ready for any task. Today it was Betty's husband, Bobby Franklin.

Well, the hounds nosed around the edge of the cornfield and by the time Comet heard them, Asa, the old gentleman with the basso profundo voice, opened.

"Gray!"

"Shit." Comet cursed as kernels tumbled from his jaws.

Giorgio, in his second year hunting, crashed into the corn close behind Dasher, who didn't mind as he was fast. The hounds strung out in the corn rows, the corn bending as they pushed through.

First Flight, led by Sister on Keepsake, a most sensible horse, skirted to the edge of the cornfield, following on the outside. No Master, or field member for that matter, ever wanted to destroy a farmer's crop. Hunts lost territory through such thoughtlessness.

Shaker also kept clear of the unharvested corn; ahead of Sister, he listened to hound voices, each of which he recognized. Betty Franklin, way on the other side of the cornfield, where it abutted the woods, also listened as did Magellan, her Thoroughbred. Hearing the corn swish gave him a moment.

"There's a monster in there." The rangy fellow wavered.

"Magellan, calm yourself." She patted him on his neck.

He trusted Betty, as most creatures did. He somewhat stopped tensing, but his ears swiveled all over the place.

Betty thought to herself that this was how a large prey animal survived. One should never punish a horse for being a horse. Instead, give him confidence. One did that by remaining calm, with a low voice, a pat, and just the tiniest picking up of the reins in case a buck occurred. Magellan, now past that, had been more than capable of launching you when younger.

Already over the hog's-back jump, waiting in the wildflower field was the second whipper-in, Tootie Harris, age twenty-two. Given that she couldn't go into the cornfield, she prudently galloped ahead, took the jump, turned her horse's head toward the horn calls, and waited. She especially did not want to turn the fox. Given his path of running, she was pretty sure it was Comet. They'd become well acquainted with each other, as the gray lived under part of the old stone foundation, laid in 1787, of her newly built, "old" cabin.

Sure enough, she watched the wildflowers sway mightily. He was out of the corn. She counted. By the time she reached thirty, Dasher was in the wildflower field. She could just see his handsome head and his stern. Within seconds the rest of the pack pushed on. The field, moving fast alongside the corn, kept behind Shaker, who had slowed slightly, fearing he would step on one of the hounds. Couldn't see a thing. The Bancrofts kept a riding path around all their crop fields, so Sister turned right, reached the midpoint of the field, checked Keepsake, turned left, and in two strides she was over the hog's back, a jump that scared horses not accustomed to seeing one. Fortunately, everyone in the field this Tuesday was a Jefferson member, so the jump proved no obstacle. Those in Second Flight, the one with no jumping, continued on to a large gate. As always, the dismount, the opening, and two people staying behind to close took time, but Second Flight did catch up just in time to see everyone standing in front of the authentic-looking cabin.

Comet, secure under the foundation, watched as Pookah and Pansy, two hounds in their second year, dug at the large stones.

"Give it up, girls," Comet barked.

"I knew it was you! I will get you. I will." Pansy allowed herself a moment.

"You're delusional. If you couldn't reach me when I fell half asleep in the cornfield, you'll never catch me. Never."

Asa, now nose to nose with the girls, his voice

44

mellow, replied, *"True enough, smartass, but we made you run for it."*

A pause followed this. *"Well, yes, you did."*

That pleased the hounds. Shaker blew "Gone to Ground," and praised his hounds. "We're home. We've been out for an hour and a half, heat's coming up. Why don't I just walk them to the kennels?"

"Good idea," Sister agreed.

The pack, terribly pleased with itself, walked smartly to the kennels, which took all of seven minutes.

The riders who were not staff parked at After All. They turned to go back, led by Ed and Tedi Bancroft.

Tedi called over her shoulder, "You'll be at the breakfast?"

Sister nodded to her friend and neighbor.

Hounds up, horses wiped down and turned out, Sister, Betty, Shaker, and Tootie piled into Shaker's aging Land Cruiser, which he'd bought used. He loved that vehicle; it could churn through anything, fit six people inside if needed. He could flop down a seat and put a few hounds in the SUV, too. The gas mileage was a trial, but other than that the Land Cruiser was made for country people.

Gray Lorillard, Sister's boyfriend, owned a new Land Cruiser. Just made Shaker's mouth water.

• • •

The back verandah, people talking, the table laden with food, the serve-yourself bar not being used hard as most people would leave to go to work, bore testimony to the endless hospitality of the Bancrofts. A few outsiders sniffed that given all that inherited wealth they could afford to be gracious. However, many a rich family exhibited robust ungraciousness. The Bancrofts liked people. True WASPs, they kept their good works to themselves, but for four generations the Bancrofts had helped thousands of people, most especially through their bequests to hospitals and educational institutions.

Kasmir Barbhaiya, who had moved from India, chatted exuberantly with Tootie concerning Asa's deep voice. The small group—it was a weekday hunt, so only about twenty people had come out—relived the hunt.

Sister kissed Tedi on the cheek. "When you were at Madeira you-all hunted around Virginia and Maryland, did you not?"

"What fun it was." The attractive woman, in her mid-eighties, beamed.

Sister, her cellphone in the inside pocket of her light tweed, pulled it out. Marion, a technical whiz, had sent Sister a copy of Weevil at the museum. Marion had also taken this to the police department, which found it marginally interesting. A missing cowhorn from Morven

46

Park appeared to endanger no one. Jake Carle, like Marion and Sister, was riveted. Marion and Jake decided not to send out a notice to museum members. Not that they would hide anything should someone notice a missing cowhorn, but better to wait. It was all too fantastic. Then again, the cowhorn could show up without undue detective work, which wasn't going to come from law enforcement people.

"Do you recognize this man?" Sister played the video.

Tedi smiled. "Weevil!" Then her hand flew to her breast. "Weevil at the museum?"

Sister explained what had transpired.

"Edward. Edward, darling, come here a moment." Tedi then leaned toward Sister. "He was at Dartmouth when I was at Madeira, but he'd come home for the holidays and we hunted around. By the time I was a junior in college we'd covered most of Virginia and Maryland."

Edward excused himself from Sam Lorillard, Gray's brother, who worked for Crawford Howard, a thorn in the side of Jefferson Hunt. Crawford, however, was happy to use the hunt to train his green horses, Sam in the irons.

"Honey, look at this."

Sister played the video.

"There were no videos when Weevil was alive," Edward, a man married to facts as well as to Tedi, remarked.

"Darling, this was three days ago."

"That's impossible." He looked again at the replayed images. "Impossible."

Sister stared up into Edward's eyes. She was six feet tall, and he was taller. "You were in your early twenties then. Is it possible you don't exactly recall how he looked?"

"Not likely." Edward half-snorted. "That s.o.b. romanced my sister, then took one look at Tedi and made a pass at her. I charged right up and said, 'If you so much as lay a hand on her, I will kill you.'" He smiled sheepishly. "I was a young man in love and now I'm an old man in love." He wrapped his arm around his wife's still-tiny waist.

"And you, Tedi, do you believe this is Weevil Carruthers?"

"Sister, if you ever saw the man in the flesh, you would never forget him. That's Weevil."

"Could it be someone made up to look like Weevil?"

Tedi stared at the video, then into her friend's cobalt eyes. "No. A man would have to be born that impossibly handsome. He was, you know. Did you ever see him?"

"From a distance. My mother took me to a hunt on our way down to Raleigh once. I was, I don't know, maybe ten. I dimly remember a handsome blond man on a steel gray horse. I think I was too young for a strong response."

Edward laughed. "Indeed. I remember when he disappeared. If you were a hunting man you practically had to take a ticket and stand in line at the Albemarle County Sheriff's Department. The department called on Richmond officers to help, I remember that. Too many suspects—they were overwhelmed. Never found him, of course."

"Until now, if you believe in ghosts," Sister simply stated.

Taken aback, Edward replied, "I don't. I don't, but that video is hard to explain and blowing 'Gone to Ground' is, well, very Weevil."

"People must have liked him despite all," Sister said.

"Oh, he was great fun, charming, a hard rider, and he could hold his liquor. Men liked him until he slept with their wives or daughters. After I told him I would kill him, he smiled at me, and said, 'She's worth killing for. I'm glad you know that.' Then he tapped his cap with his cowhorn, nodded to Tedi, and rode off. How could I not like him?"

"You?" Sister focused on Tedi.

"Yes, he was impossibly handsome but he was, oh, fifteen years older than I, so he seemed old. But I liked him. He was a rip-roaring huntsman, but you know, in those days more game, fewer roads. Thought today good hound work, by the way."

"Was." Sister loved a compliment, which she

49

always took to be for the hounds, not herself. "This video is so strange. I had to show you, as surely there's some kind of logical explanation. Although unlike you, Ed, I do believe in ghosts."

CHAPTER 3

Neat piles of papers on the right-hand side of Crawford Howard's specially built enameled desk reflected the blue light of the computer screen Crawford was studying. The L-shaped desk had a heavy glass insert in the section where he wrote letters. The desk itself, enameled in hunter green, dominated the room, as did the man himself.

Crawford, now in his mid-fifties, had made his first fortune in Indiana, building strip malls. Once secure, he moved to central Virginia, which he remembered, as a young man, visiting historic sites with his parents. He fell in love with the beauty of the state, and the strange romance of the battlefields, starting with Yorktown. He also fell in love with foxhunting. He began hunting with Trader Point Hunt near Zionsville, Indiana. As this was a drag hunt, he learned to jump because hounds always found the dragged scent. Once he moved to Virginia he encountered the vagaries of live hunting, as well as the difficult terrain of The Jefferson Hunt, where he started.

Accustomed to getting his way, thanks to his wealth, he felt, after a few years and large checks to the club, he should be appointed Joint Master to serve along with Sister Jane. However, riding and giving money is not the same as knowing hunting, and he didn't really know it. He knew real estate, he knew construction, he knew the stock market, but he couldn't tell the difference between an American foxhound and an English foxhound. While that can be learned, modifying one's behavior's to Virginia standards was too much for certain egotistical personalities. Crawford was such a one.

Needing, at long last, a Joint Master, Sister asked Walter Lungrun, M.D., in his early forties. She'd known him since he was a child. She also knew her husband had fathered him on Mrs. Lungrun. Neither she nor her husband referred to this, and Mr. Lungrun raised Walter as though his own. In theory, no one knew.

In a snit, Crawford withdrew from The Jefferson Hunt to start his own outlaw pack. Having blown through three huntsmen, it was not a success. He'd hired a young woman, Cynthia Skiff Cane. She could deal with his meddling better than the prior men, but there were days when even she had to walk away, diplomatically.

Having lost some weight, Crawford, in good shape, still with a full head of hair, proved attractive enough. His wife loved him. Someone did, thankfully.

He leaned back in his chair, letting out a long deep breath. "My God."

Then he picked up the phone to call an old

college friend in New York City who was a vice president at a large brokerage house. "Larry."

"Crawford, how are you?"

"Dismal. I've been looking at our dollar rising even higher today. The euro is about worthless."

After a pause, Larry replied, "Great for importers. Bad for exporters."

"My mat business is suffering. I'm losing money hand over fist."

Crawford, keeping his fingers in many pies, had bought into a wonderful business manufacturing car mats and truck bed mats to protect the paint and offset the slipperiness of a truck bed, especially in foul weather. You could break a leg back there.

"You fortunately are diversified. I have clients who really are going broke over this."

"I hate to lose money," Crawford grumbled. "And I believe I will lose more. Why did anyone ever think a European Union would work? They've been killing one another over there for centuries. Hell, if you go back to Julius Caesar and Vercingetorix, thousands of years. Absurd."

"Well now, Crawford, I'd like to think that World War Two truly woke them up. I'd like to think that the European Union will pull the chestnut out of the fire."

A long sigh followed this. "I'm not going to argue."

"That's a first." His old friend laughed. "Back

in the days of our Sigma Chi bull sessions, who could argue all night long, with or without booze?"

Crawford smiled at those days, how much he loved his fraternity, the sheer fun of it all. "You'd be surprised at how much I've learned."

"You married Marty. That was the best move you ever made. You make a mess, brother, she cleans it up."

A really long pause followed this, then Crawford assented. "You're right."

"I am drawing a red square around this day in my desk calendar." Larry laughed, as Crawford laughed with him. "It's good to hear your voice. I can tell you what our analysis is up here." He paused. "It's going to get a lot worse before it gets better."

"Yes, I think so, too."

"Can you develop new markets? I'm assuming the losses are with the mat company, Protect All."

"Are. Larry, it takes years, sometimes, to develop new markets. I'd always hoped Africa would build good roads. I'd love to expand there but even South Africa—hell, the elephants can't walk on those damn roads once you get out of the cities."

Larry laughed. "True, but I do love Cape Town. Melanie and I go once a year to visit Danielle, Nate, and the kids. I was worried when she chose to move there. Well, I was worried when she fell in love, but God, it is beautiful and seems stable enough."

"I don't know if any place is stable anymore. Truly. I'm even wondering about us."

"You're in a doom-and-gloom mood. We do this every eight years. We'll survive. You know history. You love history."

Crawford smiled. "You're right. Hell, we survived Buchanan."

"I know you've moved some investments out of Europe. You're fine. If Protect All's profits drop, even if they drop precipitously, hang on to the company. It's a damn good one, Crawford. You were shrewd as always to buy it. Gotta go, bro."

Crawford hung up the phone somewhat mollified, but the numbers were jarring. He returned to his enormous computer screen, built just for him at a cost of twelve thousand dollars. He loved it despite what he saw at this moment.

Marty popped her head into his office. "Sweetie, coffee? Tea? Coke?"

"No. Just got off the phone with Larry. Sounds great." He wrinkled his brow. "Wanted to talk to him about the strong dollar and"—he exhaled—"the faltering Euro. He thinks it will get worse."

"Let's take a ride. It's a perfect September day. That will restore your spirits. I'll call Sam and have him saddle up our babies."

He nodded. "You're right. Nothing I can do here anyway."

"Is everything else all right?"

"Yes, it is. I just sometimes think the world is going to hell."

"Honey, people have been saying that since B.C." She laughed.

Once at the stable, Sam brought out two immaculately groomed horses. "I didn't tell Skiff you were going out. She's out there roading the hounds."

"Ah, good." Crawford smiled.

Sam Lorillard, a reformed alcoholic, now in his mid-sixties, was an early recipient of a scholarship to Harvard, no mean feat for an African American of his generation. He blew it. His brother Gray saved him, literally pulling him off the streets down at the old C&O train station, throwing his sorry ass into rehab.

Crawford was the only person who would hire Sam, since most everyone in central Virginia had been disappointed, let down, or, if female, dumped by him, or the reverse.

Gray, now retired as a partner from a prestigious accounting firm in D.C., was Sister's gentleman friend. No one of their generation would say "lover." And as Crawford set himself against The Jefferson Hunt and Sister, it could get dicey. Sam loved Sister. He'd hunted with her since college, but he had to eat and he needed the self-respect of a job.

"How'd Ranger do yesterday?" Crawford

inquired of the young horse Sam hunted with Sister.

Crawford liked his horses trained. They couldn't really do it with his hounds. He was more than happy to use Jefferson Hunt for this.

"A little fussy at the checks but he's getting it." Sam held the offside stirrup, the right one, while Marty mounted, then performed the same service for Crawford.

Looking up at his boss, Sam said, "You know everything about technology."

"I wouldn't go that far." Crawford liked the compliment.

"My brother told me about a strange incident at the Museum of Hounds and Hunting." He proceeded to relate the story with detail, as Gray had seen the video.

"It's possible to do something like that with a hologram. We will soon see modern films with late, great actors in them, bit parts perhaps but quite believable. It would be possible to do this if there was original footage of—what's his name?"

"Weevil. A nickname, as he was called, behind his back, 'The Necessary Evil.' "

Marty laughed. "Must have been quite a character."

"So they say."

Crawford reconsidered the story. "Yes, it could

be done with a hologram." He paused, glanced down at Sam. "But no hologram could have stolen the horn. Has to be some kind of prank."

Some prank.

CHAPTER 4

The kennel office, a fifteen-by-twenty-foot room, enjoyed light from old paned-glass sash windows. The floor was granary oak from a torn-down grain storage building. The office was part of the original design in 1887. M. A. Venable, the founding Master of The Jefferson Hunt, shrewdly used whatever he could find that was inexpensive. Today those granary oak floors would be dubbed "repurposed" and cost a bloody fortune.

Sister kept the windows cleaned and shined, too. When she walked to her desk the floor, still tight as a tick, didn't creak. She did.

An attractive fireplace centered in the wall opposite the front door was simple; the surround was wood, and under the mantel a wonderful carved foxhunting scene unfolded. This had been done by a Czech, one of those early immigrants at the end of the nineteenth century who had superior woodworking skills.

Sister's desk sat opposite Shaker's, a rough sort of partner's desk arrangement, as the desks came from old schools when schools became consolidated in the late 1950s and early 1960s. The original desk used by Mr. Venable had been a Louis XVI, black with gold ormolu. Somewhere along the way it disappeared. Sister hoped the day would come when she'd walk into a room and there it would be.

Jefferson Hunt had fallen on hard times after World War I. Venable was dead by then. The place sat vacant until five years later, in 1925, Virgil Arnold, Sister's uncle-in-law, a confirmed bachelor as the phrase went, bought it. When he died he willed it all to Ray. Ray and Sister were young then, with the energy to transform the place.

The hunt limped along over the early years without Venable. Hounds were kept in the majestic brick kennels, each wing connected by a brick archway: girls to the left, boys to the right.

Despite her protests, Sister was elected Master in 1973, possibly because she modernized the kennels with electricity, etc., even before she and Ray focused on the house. Her love of hounds did not go unnoticed.

Everything in the kennels could be easily washed down, whether it was the feed room or the two large squares where the hounds slept on raised berths. Skylights allowed light in those rooms, which saved on the electric bill. On the bitterest days, the boys and girls had heat thanks to the wall heaters beside the metal inside doors. The solid outside door, also covered in tin, had a square opening to the outside, covered by a rubber flap. The hounds could go in and out without wasting heat.

In summer's heat hounds preferred being outside in their huge runs, huge as in an acre each. The doors would be open for breezes. They had sections of raised boardwalks so they could sleep off the ground if they liked that. They also had what Sister now called condos, special buildings with wraparound decks. In summer one entire side of the condos was removed. They could go in for shade but enjoy air circulation. In winter the side was closed with an opening.

The outside runs, with lots of shade thanks to old big trees, kept hounds happy. Like horses confined to stalls, hounds would prefer to be outside. Perhaps most people would prefer that, too.

Sister sank into her supportive chair. Damn thing had cost nearly a thousand dollars. She made a steeple out of her fingers and thought. This was the day after the After All hunt, the first time she had had to herself.

The late-afternoon warmth meant all the windows were opened. Raleigh, her Doberman, and Rooster, the harrier, flopped at her feet. Golliwog, the long-haired calico cat, reposed on the desk, thinking herself ornamental.

Sister reached to pet Golliwog who took this as her due. A mighty purr followed.

"Do you believe in ghosts?" Sister asked her friends.

"Yes," Raleigh and Rooster replied in unison.

"Piffle." Golly felt contrary.

"There are ghosts at Hangman's Ridge," Rooster hotly testified.

"Then why go up there?" the calico sensibly questioned.

Raleigh, now on his haunches, eyes level with the cat, put his head on the desktop. *"If Sister goes, we go. I hate it up there."*

"If you slobber on this desk, I will smack your nose," Golly threatened.

"I am terrified." Raleigh yawned, which made Sister smile.

"Eighteen people were hung up on that ridge. It's haunted. Crimes and sin." Golly liked expressing moral observations.

"What if someone was innocent?" Rooster's sweet eyes focused on Golly.

"Rooster, most people accused of crimes have committed them. Humans make rules which they use to keep other people in line. I suppose some of them are useful, like don't murder anyone, but then maybe some people just need killing." The cat pronounced this with vigor.

"Well—?" Raleigh was thinking about it.

"I seem to have provoked a discussion." Sister laughed at her beloved animals.

Opening the long center drawer, she rifled around for loose hound pedigrees. It was too early to bind this year's pack together in the annual book so she placed papers where she could easily study them. Sky blue editing pencil in hand, she began to read.

Golly batted the pencil. *"Gotcha."*

"Golly." Sister quietly reprimanded her.

Now the center of attention, the cat grabbed the pencil with both paws.

Raleigh, head still on the table, wisely shut up.

Sister pulled the pencil from the cat's paws which sent Golly straight up in the air; twisting as she came down, she grabbed the pencil again.

"Why do I put up with you?"

"You don't know the half of it. She shreds the toilet paper and blames it on us," Rooster complained.

"Careful. I'll get you when you're asleep," Golly threatened, then clamped her jaws around the blue pencil, yanked it out of Sister's hand, jumped off the desk, and raced around the room.

"You are impossible." Sister stood up.

Golly dropped the pencil. *"I am fascinating."*

"Oh, spare me," Raleigh moaned.

Sister bent over, taking the pencil from Golly, who had once again bitten into it and was loathe to give it up. Teeth marks now cut into the barrel. She ran her fingers over the pencil and opened the drawer, dropping it back in.

"That's a valuable pencil." Golly leapt back up on the desk and leaned over to paw at the handle for the center drawer.

"If you open that drawer, no catnip," Sister warned Golly while the two dogs prayed for punishment.

"Bother." Golly flopped down on the desk.

"I wonder." Sister walked over and opened the door to the library/record room.

Safe in old glass bookcases, the dark green leather books with gold years printed on the spines testified to the longevity of the hunt. The first book was 1887, the year's numbers printed in a typeface popular at the time, a typeface still used. Each book contained the pedigree for each hound, photos of each hound, a photo of the pack and the staff. Back then, labor being cheaper, the hunt could afford a professional huntsman, two professional whippers-in, and a kennelman. The huntsman also worked in the kennels. The administrative staff was also listed, the president, the vice president, secretary, and treasurer. They were honorary, unpaid.

Sister pulled out 1953. Opening the book she ran her fingers over the page. The typeface had been cut into the page, producing a clarity no amount of filmed print could match. Flipping through she found a photo of Anthony, an ancestor of Asa. Asa looked a lot like Anthony, which made her think of genetic persistence. Every hound breeder hopes to accentuate those good persistent qualities and minimize the not so good. People, on the other hand, breed indiscriminately; at least, that's what Sister thought.

A photograph of Weevil, cowhorn to his lips, calling his hounds, caught her attention. She scanned through for more pictures of Weevil, and there were a few. He really was divine-looking.

Then she put 1953 back in the case, pulled out 1954. She noted that Virgil Arnold was the vice president. There was a happy picture of Weevil, his arm around his first whipper-in, a young fellow, Tom Tipton. Snow sparkled behind them. Another photo of Weevil showed him in the kennels, puppies spilling around him.

"So he made it to the end of the season," she said to herself, shutting the volume and replacing it.

Back at her desk she called Sara Bateman.

Hearing Sister's voice, Sara teased her. "What do you want?"

"Your good company."

"Oh, right. Butter me up."

"No, really, I want your company."

"Dale and I have been up in Boston with the grandchildren. I'll be out. Both of our children are giving us grandchildren. I've never had so much fun."

"I can imagine, but you have fun no matter what. Do you think Dale would look at the treasurer's report for the hunt club from 1947 to 1954?"

"I'm sure he would, but why those years?"

"The huntsman from that time, Wesley Carruthers, disappeared never to be found. He was accused of stealing jewelry from one of his affairs, never proven. One of those spiteful rumors, I suspect, but let's look at the treasurer's reports anyway in case thieving attracted him. I'm curious if anything jumps out at Dale, curious numbers, so to speak."

"I doubt there are receipts kept from that time, but he'll look."

"Thank you. I'll get the reports to you next time you hunt. I have another favor."

"Boy, you're working me over."

"Well, I have to abuse someone." Sister laughed.

"Yeah, yeah. What is it?"

"Tom Tipton, whom you know, is ninety. I never see him but you tell me he's spry. Will you bring him to a hunt? I'll have someone drive him around."

"He'd love that, but, Sister, what is this about?"

"It's about Wesley Carruthers. I'll show you when I see you. Tom whipped-in to him."

"You know Tom will gallop down Memory Lane. He'll never shut up."

"That's what I'm hoping."

CHAPTER 5

The routine of hounds and horses varies somewhat due to latitude. The higher latitudes feel the cold earlier. The southern ones relish warmth longer but sooner or later Boreas, the north wind, blows hard on everyone. As to the light, that seems to affect animals and people even more than the cold.

Tootie, Sister, and Shaker, working in the kennels, were sweating. The clock read eleven A.M. The mercury climbed to the mid 70s.

Tootie power washed the feed room. The light spray soaked her shirt. Felt good. Power washing created such cleanliness. She felt real achievement. It was.

Sister checked a hound's paw. Zane, now in his third year, had snagged a claw.

"I don't want to stand still."

"Shaker, give me a hand, will you? He's antsy." Sister then spoke to the young hound. "I'm going to clip it at the end, put iodine at the root. You be a good boy."

"Torture." Zane dramatized.

Raleigh sat on the floor. All the hounds knew him. He accompanied them on all their walks. So did Rooster, willed to Sister by his late owner, Peter Wheeler. Peter had also willed Sister his

67

land, his house, and the stunning old mill, still running, on the property, Mill Ruins. He loved Sister, loved Jefferson Hunt, and loved Rooster. Having lived a good, full life, he left in peace.

Rooster, next to Raleigh, glared at the young hound. *"Suck it up."*

Zane, ears back, eyes wide, winced as Sister clipped the claw nowhere near the quick. The problem was where the claw inserted into the pad, as Zane had pulled the claw so hard.

"This will sting." Expertly, quickly, she dabbed iodine on the small wound.

"I'm dying."

Both house dogs looked at him with disgust.

"Can't wrap this. He'll chew it off and make it worse." Shaker stated the obvious.

"Well, let's keep him up in our recovery room for a few days. See if it begins to heal. If not, he'll need to go to the vet and she'll perform her special claw operation."

"Operation." Zane's understanding of human English was good.

"Your liver. The vet will take it out," Rooster mischievously reported.

"No!" Zane screamed.

Sister leaned toward him, hugging him to her chest. "Honey chile, calm down." She glanced down at Rooster and Raleigh. "You two are enjoying this far too much."

"Not me," Raleigh fibbed.

"He is, too." Rooster contradicted the sleek Doberman.

The creature deeply enjoying this was splayed on the office desk. Her marvelous ears could hear a rat piss in cotton. Golliwog relished it all. Her long, luxurious tail, a source of vanity, swayed gently. Her big smile revealed pearly white fangs.

"Dogs are such lowlifes." She sighed.

Tootie rolled up the power washer hose and pushed the large machine, an expensive one, too, back to the equipment closet.

"She start her night classes?" Shaker inquired as she passed the medical room.

"Last week," Sister replied.

Tootie, a graduate of Custis Hall, a private girls' secondary school in Staunton, had hunted with The Jefferson Hunt from ninth grade to graduation. From there she matriculated at Princeton along with another classmate, Val Smith. Excellent as her grades were, she hated being away from Jefferson Hunt.

She left Princeton, knocked on Sister's door, asked for a job. She'd whipped-in her last year at Custis Hall; good, too. Sister, after a long, long talk with Tootie, took her on. Tootie's day started at dawn with physical labor. The kid loved it. Her parents nearly suffered a stroke. She didn't budge, so her father, one of the richest African Americans in Chicago, pulled the money plug. Tootie didn't complain. Her mother, Yvonne

Harris, a former model, tried everything she could think of: wheedling, guilt, extravagant promises. Tootie held firm.

In her second year now as staff, she'd matured, topping out at about five foot six. Her best friend and former roommate at Princeton, Val Smith, stood at six feet two inches. Sister once was six feet two inches but she'd shrunk to six feet, half an inch. Tootie felt like a midget. Her mother leaned on Val, too, to bring Tootie around, but all that came of the Harrises' theatrics was that their daughter wanted nothing to do with them. She didn't want to hear about money, suitable marriages, wasting her mind. Her father, all ego, said he didn't care. Her mother did.

Sister and Shaker knew sooner or later the other shoe would drop or wind up in their asses. Both mother and father blamed Sister, the father more so.

Sister had nothing to do with it, but she wasn't going to turn away a college freshman with no skills other than hunting.

"All right, Zane, come along. My, that's a pronounced limp."

"I'm dying."

The injury was slight, but Shaker loved the young hound, so he scooped him up, all seventy pounds of him, carrying him back to the clean little room with a skylight, fresh water, and a wonderful bed.

Rooster and Raleigh stood at the open door. *"American Academy of Dramatic Arts,"* they said in unison.

Zane ignored them, placing his head on Shaker's shoulder, staring at his tormentors from that vantage point.

Sister unclicked the leash that she'd put on. "You'll be fine. You aren't the first hound to hang up a claw. Here." She reached in her pocket, giving him a dried liver bit.

"Hey!" Raleigh nudged her hand.

"Just wait, Greedy-guts," the tall woman commanded.

Tootie joined them at the room. "How is he?"

"Fine. Needs a few days for it to heal, and I think it will," Sister answered. "Done?"

"I'm going to ride two sets before the heat comes up more." Tootie smiled at Sister.

"Good idea." Sister turned to Shaker. "Let's all ride two sets. Knock 'em right out."

Sister rode Lafayette and ponied Rickyroo. Tootie rode Aztec and ponied Matador, while Shaker rode Kilowatt and ponied Hojo. He would still have one horse to work as he did not want to work the horse he hunted yesterday.

The fitness routine, strict, consistent, pleased the horses. Horses and hounds, both, thrive with routine.

Back at the stables, hosing down the horses,

71

Tootie asked, "I can ride Showboat if you're short on time."

"Why don't you ride Matchplay next to Showboat? The youngster will benefit from my old boy," Shaker suggested.

"Good idea," Sister called out from the wash stall. "I'll be in the house if you need me."

No sooner had she pushed open the mudroom door, Raleigh, Rooster right behind, than a huge furball shot past the two dogs and rocketed into the kitchen once that door was opened.

"Golly, you're nuts." Sister chastised the cat who'd left the kennels so obviously.

A familiar voice called out from the mudroom, boots knocking the boot scraper.

"Betty."

"Came by to sit down with you and do the fixture card."

"Oh, Betty." Sister's voice fell as she looked at her best friend. "Now?"

"No better time. Once we figure it out, we still have to call all the landowners and that can take weeks. People go on vacations; they don't know when they'll harvest their corn, hay, wheat. You know how much time it takes, then we've got to get it printed up, take it to Freddie Thomas, sit around and stuff envelopes, then send it off before Opening Hunt. I'm in the mood. Thought I'd get you in the mood." Beholding a less than enthusiastic face, Betty's voice hit the seduction register. "I brought a big bowl of my avocado, red beet, eggs, shaved turkey, parsley, and cheese salad."

"All those ingredients just for me?" Sister laughed, already opening the cupboard doors as Betty walked back out to her car.

"Sit close. We'll get some." Rooster beamed.

"I'll get some before you do. I can sit on a chair and even pat a folded napkin," Golly said.

The dogs stared at the braggart.

Raleigh warned, *"You'll get in trouble."*

"Uh-uh." The calico licked her paw.

Food on the table, Golliwog sitting just like a proper person in a chair, the cat did get a piece of turkey.

"I hate that cat." Rooster lay down, paws over his ears.

"Ta Ta." Golliwog licked her little dish, which Sister had thoughtfully put out.

"Why do you feed her at the table?" Betty must have asked this a thousand times.

"If she has a proper place setting, good china, she acts like a lady."

"Oh, my God." Betty rolled her eyes, then exploded into laughter.

"Betty, you wouldn't believe how Golly manipulates our mother. Shameful it is. Awful to behold." Raleigh cast his limpid brown eyes at the attractive Betty, perhaps ten pounds overweight.

The impromptu lunch group ate, the humans weakening and tossing bits to the dogs, Sister placing more turkey on the cat's plate. They talked about hunting, the weather, people, the subjects old friends visit and revisit.

"So she organized her classes around hunting?" Betty savored an avocado slice.

"Well, she did it last year. Tootie, thanks to her board scores and grades, had no trouble getting into UVA from Princeton. She doesn't want to go full time. If she does it this way, she's happy."

"And you said she's taking organic chemistry?" Betty leaned toward her friend. "As a freshman?"

"Well, she's half a sophomore. They accepted her first semester grades from Princeton, finally. So far she loves it."

"More power to her. I would hate it." Betty pointed a fork at Sister. "And you, a geology major."

"Like Tootie, I loved what I studied."

Betty put down the fork, pointed to her forehead. "Box of rocks."

"Never said I was bright." Sister laughed. "Or you!"

Table cleared, Betty pulled out paper and pencils. Doing a fixture card on a computer had proved counterproductive for both of them. Maps were spread all over the table. They kept checking them, studying the blue outlines signifying estates, farms, raw land where they had permission to hunt. Red outlines meant no hunting. Fortunately, there were few of those. Couldn't really do that with computers squatting on top of the topo maps.

Tedious as the chore could be, they compared notes about landowners, those wonderful people who gave the club permission to hunt over their lands, notes about terrain, and wind direction. Two heads bent over large colored maps from the U.S. Geological Survey.

What joy to work with a beloved friend. Neither woman could know that in twenty-four hours their world would be topsy-turvy. Fortunately, both had a good sense of humor. They would need more than that.

CHAPTER 6

A fine mist like a thin white veil covered Tattenhall Station on Saturday, September 16, at seven-thirty A.M. The temperature, 50°F, promised an hour of decent scenting given the moisture, but the morning would warm up, the mist would disappear, and with it, the scent.

Sister usually kept young entry near the home fixtures during cubbing. As they walked this country all summer, if a youngster wandered off, rarely, or overran the line way too far, the hound would know where it was and find the way back to the horn, the pack, or if all else failed, the kennels.

But this year's young entry and last year's entry, now second year, had worked together so well, so early, Sister thought to take a chance and go to this westernmost fixture, the former Norfolk and Southern railroad station. Across the road farther west reposed Old Paradise, once one of the most beautiful estates in Virginia, started by a very pretty woman right after the War of 1812. Thanks to her robbing British pay wagons and supply wagons, all that delightful money rolled in as Sophie Marquet kept the cash and sold the supplies to the American forces at a patriotic discount. Old Paradise, at five thousand acres, had been poached by Crawford Howard. He rented it from the two DuCharme brothers, neither of whom could keep up the place, neither of whom had spoken to the other since 1960, improved it, then laid cash on the barrel. They caved and sold.

When The Jefferson Hunt had Old Paradise as a fixture, that land, when combined with Tattenhall Station and some surrounding estates, plumped out at twelve thousand acres. What fabulous hunting, fabulous views. The DuCharmes apologized profusely to Sister. She said she understood. She did.

As Crawford painstakingly brought back the glorious huge stone stables, revived the fields, restored the fences, Kasmir Barbhaiya refurbished the old train station, allowing the hunt to use it as a clubhouse while he restored Tattenhall lands to fertility, building a surprisingly modest house, a true old-style Virginia center-aisle frame farmhouse with a wraparound porch. Crawford, knowing he couldn't outspend Kasmir, for a rich Indian is rich beyond most rich Americans, practically reeled back in shock when he beheld the pleasing, proportional light yellow clapboard farmhouse with Charleston green shutters. He felt it was a rebuke to his plans of grandeur, and it was. Kasmir had no need to show off. Indian he may have been, but he acted like a true old-blood Virginian.

Crawford sniffed that this was the result of the British ruling India as long as they did. The elite packed off their sons to Harrow, Eton, Groton, then university in England, so the boys became as upper-class British as the British, which is also to say, in many ways, Virginian.

What Crawford didn't say or realize was that he was vulgar. Everyone else said it for him.

This Saturday a field of fifty-nine people showed up, including Sara Bateman. Each week more Jefferson members joined the hunt as the excitement grew and the mercury slowly, too slowly, dropped. They also missed their friends.

They didn't miss much today. Shaker cast from the back of the train station; the hounds struck a line in a skinny minute, opened wide, and ran due east.

Sister, grateful that she rode Matador, a former steeplechaser, sailed over a stiff seven-board coop, stiff to keep out the cattle now on Old Paradise. Crawford put up fencing, but he didn't realize that some cattle are fence walkers and if they're not policed or put in pastures with stout fencing, those buggers will get out.

A seven-board coop is anywhere from three foot six inches to three foot nine inches, depending on the width of the boards. Taking such an obstacle at a gallop clearly was not for the fainthearted. A few checked their horses, waiting for Bobby Franklin to come up to a gate where they now joined Second Flight. Everyone else made it over the coop and the hounds were flying, just flying.

The huge pasture dipped down a bit toward a narrow creek running toward a much larger broad creek, which flowed easterly. As that creek fed into another, the waters eventually would find their way to the mighty James River and thence to the ocean a good one hundred fifty miles away, depending on the topography.

The creek itself proved no obstacle, but the additional moisture created slippery footing as the horses leapt over. Again everyone made it, but not without a bobble or two.

Betty Franklin whipped-in on the right while Tootie Harris performed this service on the left. Tootie, young and supple, seemed a part of Iota, her own horse. Part of her salary included Iota's board, since her father had withdrawn all economic support.

The fox, a half-grown son of Earl, the red who lived in Crawford's restored stone stable, had never been hunted before. Like the young hounds, he had to learn.

Dragon, in the lead, couldn't close the gap, for the little fellow had quite a start. Suddenly the scent evaporated. Hounds stopped.

"Noses to the ground," Diana ordered.

"Why does this happen?" Pickens, a second-year, whined.

"Happens more during cubbing," Trident,

older, answered. *"The temperature bounces around and so does the scent. Keep at it. We might pick it up again."*

Dragon, a braggart, announced, *"Lucky fox. I would have chopped him."*

The other hounds ignored this. No one was going to close that gap. The young fox ran like blazes.

The humans, grateful for the check, breathed heavily, leaned over to check tack, pull up their girth an inch if necessary, took a swallow from their flasks. Some flasks were incendiary. Others, like Sister's, carried iced sweet tea. Gray Lorillard, right next to her, imbibed something far more potent, then cheekily blew her a kiss.

"Worthless," she said under her breath, for one shouldn't talk while hounds are working.

He winked and nodded.

Steady old Asa, wise, walked toward a line of Leland cypress, some undergrowth beneath as Kasmir had not gotten to tidying up. Actually, Sister would have been thrilled if he didn't tidy up. More cover for foxes.

The hound sucked up the air, a slight snuffle as he did so. He walked with deliberation. His stern began to sway, then moved like a windshield wiper.

Diana, younger but she never missed a trick, watched her old mentor. She joined him. They walked along side by side. He stopped. Sniffed again. So did she.

"Here!" Asa bellowed, his deep voice filling the air.

"We're on," Diana commanded and the two hounds took off, the others quickly joining them.

Sister, Shaker, Tootie, and Betty loved watching hounds collapse on a line. Those in the field who liked good hound work were also impressed. This was textbook stuff, and with young entry, too.

Hounds moved through the undergrowth emerging on a trail in the woods, the old tire ruts pointing both north and south. Horses ran in the raised space between the tire tracks. By now Bobby Franklin had caught up to First Flight.

Freddie Thomas, an attractive woman, a strong rider, rode in Second Flight today as she was on a green horse. Better safe than sorry. She'd bring this mare along; she had her made hunter, so she could ride First Flight when she chose to do so. The riders checked again, the mist seemingly tangled up in the treetops, leaves still heavy on the branches, a spot of color here or there. The real color would explode mid-October. Out of the corner of her eye, half turning in her really expensive Tad Coffin saddle, Freddie caught a movement. The hunted fox quietly walked right behind her horse.

The rider behind her, Ben Sidell, the sheriff, counted under his breath, "One, two, three."

Freddie picked it up. "Four, five, six."

When they reached twenty both sang out, "Tallyho."

One must always give the quarry a sporting chance, hence the count to twenty. People forgot in the excitement of a view, but it really was bad sportsmanship.

Shaker swiveled around in his saddle. "Come along."

Hounds had heard the tallyho, knew what it meant. Happily they reversed field, forcing the riders off the road, horses' rear ends now in the woods, heads facing out. Otherwise, a nervous horse could kick a hound, or the huntsman.

Both Ben and Freddie had removed their caps, holding them in their hands, arms outstretched, pointing in the direction in which the fox was moving.

"Get 'em up." Shaker encouraged the pack.

Dreamboat struck first, then they all opened.

Shaker wove through the woods, twisting this way and that. The field followed. Gray bent low onto his horse Wolsey's neck, as a branch grazed his back.

Slowed them down.

The young fox burst out onto a meadow, heading for the county road that ran north and south dividing Tattenhall Station from Old Paradise. He ducked under the fence, blasted across the road, and ducked under the Old

Paradise fence, an old stone wall rehabilitated by Crawford at breathtaking cost. While people loathed his personal showiness, they all admired his restoring what was original about Old Paradise.

A herd of deer grazed in the field. The head doe lifted her head, hearing the horn.

"Bother. Let's go," she ordered her group.

The little fox headed for her.

She paused. *"Don't be scared, Sonny. Run in the middle of us. It will throw them off."*

Shaker came out on the road. The hounds soared over the stone fence. The huntsman looked at his Master.

"The MFHA says we can stay on a hunted fox even if it goes into another hunt's territory," he said.

Sister knew Crawford's was an outlaw pack. So did Shaker. The rules didn't apply to him, nor would Crawford have obeyed them. This flitted through her mind. She didn't want to start the season with a fight, because sooner or later he would hear about it. On the other hand, hounds roared on full throttle.

"The hell with it." She squeezed Matador, taking the fence in a graceful arc as Shaker, next to her, did also. They looked like a perfect pairs team.

Everyone followed. Poor Bobby had to ride a quarter of a mile to a gate to get in.

The head doe, now into a woods, rock out-croppings looming ahead, stopped.

The fox stopped with her.

"There's an old den in there. No hound can get into it but it will be easy for you. You'll be safe. It's a well-trained pack so they won't follow us, but if you jump up on that first rock, walk along the top, you'll see the den between the two boulders behind."

"Thank you." He did as he was told.

The head doe circled, going back toward the roar but far enough away from the hounds. She wasn't worried about the hounds. She was more worried about the horses. Once a horse had dumped his rider, run to the deer, and joined them. She never forgot that, and probably the horse hadn't either.

The young fox found the den. *How wonderful,* he thought, as it was very large with an exit in the rear. Best not to be in any den with only one way in and one way out. Best of all, leaves piled up from last year partly covered a rubber ball, a shiny toy truck, and a lead rope. Toys!

Parker reached the den after a scramble up the first covering rock.

"I know you're in there."

Feeling safe, the fox called out, *"I am."*

The hounds joined Parker but they couldn't even dig as it was all rock. The den was between two boulders that formed a crevice, but the den really was huge and tight as a tick. No rain or snow would get in.

Ardent, Asa's son, peered into the den as best he could. *"You did good for a kid,"* the hound complimented him. *"What's your name?"*

"Sarge."

"Well, Sarge, we'll see you again before this season is out." Ardent turned, walked back over the first large rock, and jumped down.

The rest of the pack took turns jumping up on the first large rock; only three could fit onto it at a time. Everyone sang.

Shaker rode up. Tootie quickly came to him, taking Kilowatt's reins as the huntsman dismounted. He walked to the large rock. "Good hounds. Good hounds."

"He's in there. If you just give me time, I'll figure out how to bolt him," young Pickens promised.

"Dream on," Cora, the matriarch, this probably her last season, replied. *"Nothing will get him out of there. He's a smart little fellow."*

"I could wait him out. Surprise him," Pickens, ever hopeful, said.

"Pickens, he can smell you just as easily as you can smell him. You'd have to hide about a quarter of a mile away," the older and wiser Delia, mother of the D hounds, advised.

Sister, standing perhaps ten yards back so the field could have a close view, looked upward at lowering clouds. Bobby Franklin arranged Second Flight right by First so everyone could appreciate the ritual.

Shaker put the horn to his lips and blew the warbling, satisfying "Gone to Ground."

Betty Franklin, slightly off on the right just in case the pack took a notion, turned her head.

Far in the distance, a mournful echo, deep, returned "Gone to Ground."

"Echo," Gray whispered.

The echo continued after Shaker ceased the distinctive notes. Deep, deep the sound seemed to linger forever.

Sister, intently listening, knew this was no echo. This was the call of an old hunting cow-horn, the timbre unmistakable. She shivered a moment.

Shaker interrupted her reverie, if that word could be applied to what she was feeling. "Master?" "Yes." She blinked.

"How about I hunt back?"

"Good idea. Shaker, you heard that?"

"Did. Curious what sound does." A crooked grin appeared on his rugged face. "Sounded like my old papaw blowing."

"I wonder."

"Madam?" He addressed her properly.

If a woman was your master it was either master or madam, if one was a hunt servant. Half the time they both forgot in the heat of the moment and he called her "Boss." She almost always properly called him "Huntsman" during a hunt if he called her "Boss," but she readily forgave him. They had worked together for years in such harmony as to make even the most trying of days a joy.

"Just thinking. A beautiful sound, that low call. Well, yes, let's go back. I'd like to get out of here before Crawford shows up, if he's around."

Shaker's grin widened. "He's not. If he were, he'd be here cussing us like a dog."

A half hour later, at a trot, no new scent, everyone was at Tattenhall Station.

Tattenhall Station's walls reverberated with the laughter, the chat. The breakfast was in full swing.

Kasmir asked Freddie, "How do you like your saddle? You look comfortable in it."

"I nearly died paying for it, I swear, but my riding has improved, and my horse is happier, especially this young one. It was worth every penny, plus the countless fittings." She smiled. "I never really believed a saddle could help one be a better rider, but I do now."

Alida Dalzell, a warm, highly intelligent woman in her early forties, dating Kasmir, talked to Sister. "Wasn't that something, the fox running with the deer?"

"They are so smart. He was a little guy with a big brain." Sister smiled. "Inexperienced whippers-in go after the hounds. They don't think to look for the fox."

"Half grown, you think?"

"Yes. He'll be looking for his own den if he doesn't already have one. By October or November, the fathers have pushed out all the sons. They have to make their way in life. I think the fox we ran is by Earl, the handsome red who lives in the stone stables at Old Paradise."

"You can tell?"

"Often you can. Like dogs, they have distinguishing features, family traits."

Alida laughed. "Like people." She paused, sipped her refreshing gin and tonic. "It's still warm enough for gin and tonic." She held up her glass. "Sister, I cherish your advice. I travel up from Carolina twice a month, Kasmir comes down. I am thinking about relocating here. What do you think?"

"We'd be lucky to have you, and Kasmir would be beside himself."

"There's a lot to think about. I've built a good business there. It's how Freddie and I met, at a conference. I gave a talk about forensic accounting, we discovered we both hunted, she invited me here, and I couldn't believe it. You all have been so kind to me."

Sister touched Alida on the shoulder. "Honey, it's easy to be kind to someone who rides as well as you do; you actually listen to people, and you make Kasmir laugh. You know how I love him. If they're all like him halfway across the world then it will be India's turn to conquer."

"He wants to take me there to see where he grew up. I think I will be overwhelmed. Just to think of how ancient the culture is, how rich the history, how mixed-up the politics." She laughed a bit.

"You don't have to go to India for that." Sister clinked glasses with her. "You come here. I will help in any way I can." She then called out over the heads of a small group.

"Sara. You had one of those Tad Coffin saddles made, too. Alida loves hers."

"After a few adjustments, I agree. Now what are you up to? I know there's more coming." Sara laughed.

Sister explained. Her phone was in the truck, but as Sara had never known Weevil, she offered to show her the video. Sara needed to haul her horse, Shane, back, and said she'd watch it later but not right now.

"Before you go, let me know. I brought the treasurer's reports that I copied for Dale."

"Without receipts I don't know what he can tell."

"Me neither, but I thought if something proved really amiss in the books Dale would know."

"You think this has something to do with money? From 1947 to 1954?"

"Well, don't most murders involve love or money?"

Sara smiled. "I think you'd know by now. That's sixty-three years ago."

Sister brought her drink to her forehead to cool off for a moment. "You're right. I don't know why this has gotten under my skin."

Sara nodded. "Love or money."

True enough, but in a way neither woman could have predicted.

Hours later, back at Roughneck Farm, horses cleaned, fed, and turned out, hounds the same, Sister and Gray had taken their showers and collapsed out on the verandah to drink and drink in the long, long twilight.

"How did Crawford take it?" He sipped his Scotch.

She pulled her sweater tighter over her shoulders. "Surprisingly well. It's dawning on him that he actually needs us."

"I wouldn't go that far."

"No, really. Maybe it's Marty." Crawford's wife. "Or Skiff. But I think he's beginning to realize we can divert the Master of Foxhounds Association from blowing this outlaw pack thing up. He thought he was bigger than the MFHA. Richer, yes. Bigger, no." She breathed in the delicious evening air. "It will take time to play out."

A brand-new shiny blue Lincoln Continental

crept down the farm road, slowed by the turnoff to the house, kennels, and barns, then moved forward. They heard the car stop, the door slam.

Tootie's small house couldn't be seen from the main house but one could hear, especially on a night like this.

A knock on the door and then, "Tootie!"

Sister sat bolt upright. "What?"

Gray now sat upright with her.

They heard the door open and Tootie's voice, her surprise clear in her tone, answer. "Mother."

"Dear God," Sister blurted out.

Dear God didn't cover it.

CHAPTER 7

*W*hat's going on over there?" Young Taz called from the boys' large play lot.

Tootie's house sat away from the kennels at a forty-five-degree angle, perhaps a quarter of a mile. Hounds could hear and smell everything. An unrecognizable car alerted everyone. They heard Tootie's voice, saw the limbs of the huge old walnut tree by the ruins of what had been the original cabin sway in a gentle breeze.

Gentle or not, it carried coolness as the twilight faded; night air brushed everyone.

Surprised, shocked really, Tootie opened the door wide. "Mother, come in. Do you need me to carry anything?"

"Later." The elegant, if drawn, Yvonne stepped into the pleasing cabin, a white clapboard addition looking old attached to the original cabin.

The job, well done, disguised the newness of everything. The stone chimney poked out of the slate roof. Another stone chimney was visible in the roof of the addition.

Striding as though still on the runway at the height of her modeling career, Tootie's mother walked into the big main room. Old cabins lacked either center halls or entrance halls. One walked right into the living space. The kitchens were usually at the rear of the big room. A summer kitchen was outside at a distance of twenty-five yards. All old colonial buildings in the South had summer kitchens. No one could stand the heat of cooking in June, July, August. Maybe they could in New Hampshire, but they certainly couldn't in Virginia. Those states farther south often used the outside kitchens for six months.

Tootie, recovering her wits, offered her mother a seat in an old comfortable wing chair.

Yvonne lowered herself onto it, crossing her impossibly long legs, legs she bequeathed to her daughter, which had made riding easier, at least when mastering the basics.

"Can I get you anything to drink? I have fresh eggs, but that's about it if you're hungry."

"I ate on the way." Yvonne looked up, swept her hand at the opposite old wing chair and Tootie dropped into it. "I didn't have time to call." She cast her eyes around the lovely little cabin. "Very nice."

"Sister and I rooted through old plans, visited original cabins. This is built on the site of the first dwelling this far west."

"Yes, you told me. Actually you showed me the ruins once when your father and I came to parents' weekend at Custis Hall. You and the girls were hunting. We met everyone, got a stable and kennel tour. You even showed us Hangman's Ridge."

"Would you like me to start a fire?"

"Not yet. It's still warmish. What kind of heat do you have?"

"I use the fireplace mostly. There's a heat pump. I keep the thermostat at sixty degrees. It saves money."

Yvonne's eyebrows zoomed up. "You don't pay the electricity here."

"No. I just don't like to run up bills if I can help it."

Yvonne studied her only child. How different she was from both her mother and father, neither of whom evidenced the least amount of restraint when it came to funds.

"Surely Sister can pay."

Tootie nodded. "She fusses at me, but I like to save."

"M-m-m. Aren't you wondering why I'm here, and here unannounced?"

"I know you'll tell me." Tootie allowed herself a sly smile not unnoticed by her mother.

"I am divorcing your father. Could not stand one more minute with his lying." She stopped herself. "I grabbed some of my clothes, all the credit cards, all my jewelry. Drove to the airport. Left the car forever, for all I care, got a ticket to Richmond, and here I am."

"He'll explode," Tootie replied, voice even.

"Good. Maybe he'll die of a heart attack and there will be no need of divorce proceedings."

Yvonne took a deep breath. "You don't have to say yes, but I'd like to stay with you, for a week at most. I'm going to look for a place to rent here. I'll be close to you, far away from him, and maybe I will learn to like some of these people you tell me about."

"You can stay here, of course. I work most of the day."

"Fine."

A long pause followed this. "Please be civil to Sister and Gray."

A flash of irritation crossed those perfect features, which then softened. "They were more your father's problem than mine. That and the fact that he couldn't understand why you wanted to work with animals."

"You never seemed too enthusiastic about it." Tootie said this without rancor—but she said it.

Yvonne shifted in her seat. "I can't say that I understand it. I don't. What upset me was when you left Princeton to come back here. You could have come home."

"This is home." Tootie's voice rose.

A very long pause followed this.

"I can't apologize for your father. I can't even apologize for myself. We haven't had the usual mother-daughter relationship. I was always off somewhere or hosting some enormous fundraiser. But when I was home, I tried."

"What you did was give me a nurse, then a

governess, then a dogsbody,"—she couldn't think of a better word—"all of whom spoke French!"

"Well, French is a passport to fashion, to elegance. Learning it from infancy is a huge advantage."

"I speak to hounds and horses." Tootie folded her hands together. "They don't care. You wanted me to want what you wanted. I don't."

"Fair enough."

This surprised Tootie.

Yvonne continued. "I was not warm and fuzzy. But I am your mother and I will make up for it."

"You want an ally against Dad."

"No, I don't. I hired Hart, Hanckle and Himmel as my lawyers. They'll take care of him. Plus when I was your age and married young, I didn't just fall off the turnip truck. I had my name put on everything, even the media business. He was so overcome with lust he agreed to everything. And I will give myself credit, I worked in our company. I actually liked it." She took a deep breath. "The bastard."

"Hart, Hanckle and Himmel." Tootie half laughed. "The hounds of hell."

"Well—yes." Yvonne laughed, too.

"Are you sure I can't get you anything?"

"A cup of chamomile tea. I'm tired. It will help and I'll just go fast asleep."

Tootie rose, walked to the kitchen and heard

the front door close. Her mother soon joined her carrying a Hunting World duffel, a bag known only to the cognoscenti. Everyone else bought Louis Vuitton. In the other hand, Yvonne carried a satchel.

"Let me show you your room. It's not much, Mom, but it's tidy and, well, you'll manage. What's in the satchel?"

"My jewelry. Every single piece. Here." She handed it to Tootie.

"Mom, this weighs a ton."

"Diamonds are a girl's best friend." Yvonne smiled.

The teapot whistled. Tootie left her mother at the room, a very clean room with a double bed, a comforter on it, and a nightstand with a light that swiveled so she could shoot the beam exactly where she wanted while reading.

As she poured the hot water into two large mugs, dropping in little silver balls filled with loose tea leaves, Yvonne returned and sat at the wooden table.

"Did you notice my car?"

"No."

"A brand-new Lincoln Continental Reserve. Seventy-five thousand, three hundred and twenty dollars. All-wheel drive. I guess I need that here. I had the cab driver take me from the airport to the Ford dealer—I researched with my phone, found one who had the Reserve—smacked cash down on the table, and walked out. At least I'll have decent wheels."

"Mother, people would notice you if you drove a Vespa."

"Very Audrey Hepburn." Yvonne gratefully took the tea, removed the ball, sipped the soothing liquid.

Tootie sat across from her with her own cup of tea.

"Mom, I'll be out of here at dawn, the kennels. We walk the hounds by seven but I have chores to do first. Shaker and I feed, wash down the feed room, all that stuff. Then we decide who we want to walk, off we go. Sister always walks with us."

"She's indestructible," Yvonne remarked with rueful admiration. "Proof that you've got to keep moving. How old is she now?"

"Maybe seventy-two or seventy-three. I can never remember. I don't think about it. I don't even know how old you are."

"Fifty-one." Yvonne held the mug tighter. "Fifty-one trying to dump a cheating, lying husband, trying to figure out what I did wrong, trying to find a better life."

"You made a great life, Mom."

"For everyone else. I did what I was supposed to. Everyone kept telling me how beautiful I was, break barriers, be one of the first black high-fashion models. So I did. It was exciting, but Tootie, I never really gave any thought to direction, to what comes next. Then Vic scooped me up. He'd already made the magazine turn into pages of gold. Together we built a media empire. It really was not without excitement, but I have never asked myself the questions you have." She blinked. "Well, I'm here. I know you think I'm a pain in the ass. I will try not to be, and I will try to find accommodations to get out of your way."

"I might be able to help. Because of hunting, I know this place very well and there are beautiful places to rent, to buy. Maybe not so many to rent, but we'll find them."

Yvonne stared into Tootie's light hazel eyes, so light they glowed almost amber green. Her eyes. She'd been a shitty mother. She'd been a shit to a lot of people. Haughty, demanding, ignoring anyone she didn't think was on her level or could help her. Here across from her sat her daughter, in many ways a stranger, and the child seemed more settled, composed than she had ever been. Her eyes misted. She caught herself. Finished her tea.

"I don't think I'll walk hounds with you tomorrow. I need to get my ducks in a row. But I will do it next day. I'd like the exercise."

"Okay."

Yvonne got up, leaving her cup on the table, kissed her daughter on the cheek, and retired to her room. No sooner had she pulled off her clothes than she fell into bed, exhausted.

Tootie washed the two cups, then threw on her Carhartt jacket—the Detroit model, four years old and holding up to hard chores. She walked out to the farm road, turned right, walked past the kennels on her right, the stables on her left, to the big house, a herringbone brick path leading the way.

The light in the den shone out. She stepped inside the mudroom, knocked on the door to the kitchen, stuck her head in as she opened it.

"Sister? Gray? It's Tootie."

Sister's voice carried down the long hall, "Come in, Sugar."

Golly, on the table forbidden to her, of course, opened one eye. *"Got any treats?"*

Tootie ignored her.

"Selfish." She closed her eye.

Tootie walked into the den, bookcases filled with books, a bar in one corner, and Sister's beautiful desk tucked under the paned-glass window, original blown glass.

"What's up?" Gray put down his *Wall Street Journal.*

"Mother's here. She's getting a divorce."

"I see." Sister told her to sit down. "We know. It was on the six o'clock news."

"What?" Tootie's eyes widened.

Gray folded the paper into quarters, placing it on his lap. "Celebrity report. Of course, the reporter cited your mother's career, your father's

100

career, and a brief interview with your father who had obviously decided to strike the first blow."

"He accused your mother of desertion," Sister quietly said.

Tootie snorted. "Asshole. Well, it won't do him any good, financially anyway. Mom's name is on everything."

"Your mother is an astute woman. It really will all work out, but it will be public and ugly for a while. The media wallows in scandal," Sister remarked with some bitterness.

"Yes, it does." Then Gray added, "But so did Procopius," referring to the sixth-century A.D. writer.

Sister smiled. "You're right. Bet we can go farther back than that. However, this isn't helping Tootie. Can you handle your mother?"

"I think so. She wants to find a place to rent. She doesn't want to go back to Chicago."

"Smart." Sister dropped her hand on Raleigh's head as he nudged her knee. "This will put some pressure on you."

"Well—maybe," Tootie agreed.

"How about if I alert Betty Franklin? She'll know the best real estate agent to help your mother."

"Okay." Tootie paused a moment. "She said she'd like to go on hound walks after tomorrow. I promise she won't be a pain."

101

"Even if she is, we'll deal with it," Sister reassuringly said.

After Tootie left, consoled, Gray slapped the paper on his knee. "What I'd like to do is slap that bitch in the face. Damn, she's treated us like dirt."

"Not as badly as he did," Sister rejoined. "We'll do what we can for Tootie, really." She leaned down to kiss Raleigh. "Gray, there's a sweet girl inside Yvonne. A girl sidetracked and abused because she was and still is so very beautiful. She trusts no one. Maybe Tootie a bit, and she hasn't been much of a mother. Perhaps the carapace will crack, fall away, and Yvonne can truly be Yvonne."

"Bullshit." He shook his head.

Sister didn't take offense. "Maybe only a woman can understand, honey."

CHAPTER 8

A list? Well . . ." A long pause followed this as Marion thought. "You make one for central Virginia, I'll make one for Northern Virginia. Actually, I'll start with Joyce Fendley. She knows everything."

It was late morning the next day.

"Good idea," Sister agreed. "No one is taking any of this seriously but you and I, and I would have placed it by the wayside if it hadn't been for hearing 'Gone to Ground' yesterday. I would have called you last night, but Tootie's mother showed up and pushed it all right out of my mind."

"I finally notified the museum board that the horn was missing. Reported to the Sheriff's Department. The board, while discomfited, just thinks it's odd."

"That hardly explains the selfie."

"No. Shrugged that off, too. As for the sheriff's office, polite, but a stolen cowhorn of some historical value doesn't merit investigation. Given the flood of new people, new money into Loudoun County, I do expect they face more pressing problems."

"So do we." Sister laughed. "Traffic, housing developments, and Yankees."

"I'm a Yankee and so are you," Marion teased her. "And don't forget, I came here as a child with my family. You came here for a job at Mary Baldwin College. You're getting above your raisins." She laughed as she used the old Southern expression.

Sister laughed, too. "You're right. Slap my face. But back to yesterday. Marion, I swear what I heard was not an echo. It was an almost exact copy of Shaker's length of notes. I might have accepted the echo because we were at the base of the Blue Ridge and we were on Old Paradise, which is filled with history, murders, fire, the severing of family ties, and never-ending stories of ghosts. Okay, I'll not argue the point. Old Paradise even in decay can haunt anyone, but Marion, it was the finish to 'Gone to Ground.' It lingered, a long, long statement, of what I don't know."

A sigh followed this. "Our cowhorn and yesterday's music may not be related. It's a far putt as they say."

"Not so far. He was the huntsman at The Jefferson Hunt when he disappeared. And he had been run out of Northern Virginia hunts for fornicating like a rock star. Well, he was a rock star. Huntsmen still are." She breathed in. "If we could find the cowhorn, that would be a start."

"I would hope Weevil's disappearance might

occasionally occur to huntsmen as they bed the Master's wife or whomever."

"It's the combination of hero worship and alcohol. Gets them every time. Not all of them, of course. There really are some sensible men out there. I am attached to one."

"How is he?"

"Gray? Wonderful as always."

"His brother?"

"Sam's doing well. They live in the old Lorillard place, as you know. Gray stays there maybe three days out of seven. There's still a lot of fixing to do. They work together. I think Gray finally believes that Sam's drinking is conquered, but Sam still says he is an alcoholic."

"They all say that. The clean ones, I mean. I guess you can never forget. Did you ever drink too much?"

"No. I don't much like the taste, although after a hard hunt and a hot shower, I might enjoy a Scotch or one of these new bourbons, you know, like Woodford Reserve."

"That's not a new bourbon."

"The old ones, the ones I remember from my youth, were all so sweet. Couldn't stand the sweetness."

"Some people can't let it go. I asked around after our adventure, for lack of a better word. Was Weevil a drunk? Hardly anyone left alive who knew him, but those in their seventies, eighties might have known him, young though some were at the time. No one recalled him drinking more than anyone else."

"Which means he was half loaded most of the time. Everyone drank." Sister thought. "But they knew how. Ray could put it away, but he held his liquor. Such a point of pride."

She recalled her late husband, gone now just over twenty years.

"You're right, they all did. Well, they might have held their liquor, but it didn't do much good for their inhibitions."

"Sometimes I think they all had more fun than we do."

"Oh, coming from your mouth!" Marion let out a whoop.

"Well—" Sister paused then remembered Monica's question at the restaurant. "Didn't Monica say she heard three sets of footsteps? The stairs aren't all that far from the ballroom where she was working. She could have heard things."

"You know, you're right," Marion responded.

"What if she heard Weevil coming up the steps? He could have ducked into the Huntsman's room at the top of the stairs, she could pass it and not see him. You only see a small part of the room from the open door anyway."

"It's possible. You think the third set of footsteps was Weevil's?"

"Just a thought."

"I thought ghosts could walk through walls," Marion lightheartedly remarked.

"Well, we know drunks walk into them." A sigh followed this. "Why blow the horn? Why steal it? I need to find out more about that cowhorn," Sister said with conviction.

"All right. Send me your list of possible amours for Weevil. I'll send you mine. And the sheriff hunts with you, right? Ask him to go back into the old files." Marion waited a moment. "And lest you forget, all huntsmen are possessive of their horns. It is his horn. Anyway, talk to your sheriff. Maybe he'll be more helpful than the one up here."

"Good idea. I'll be back at you but I want to go on record. You can talk me into anything. You talked me into serving on the board of the Museum of Hounds and Hunting. You talked me into focusing on the Huntsman Hall of Fame. Then you talked me into going over there to check out the glare on the display case. Wait, actually, first you worried about a fingerprint. We never got to the fingerprint. I want to go on record: If anything goes wrong, it's your fault."

This caused an eruption of laughter. "I feel your pain." Then Marion added, "I didn't forget the fingerprint. I asked the Sheriff's Department to take a copy of the fingerprint, which was still there. Jake Carle's. His fingerprints were everywhere. He's determined to refresh things and he's right."

"Well, let's get to it."

"Right. One last question since it's all over the news: Tootie's father, I mean, accusing Yvonne of desertion. He's a piece of work. Is Tootie okay?"

"Yvonne is at Tootie's, for how long I don't know."

"Poor Tootie."

"Tootie has dealt with them all her life. Poor us." Sister laughed, for she did love Tootie and wished all to be well, but she didn't especially want to be around her mother.

Sitting in the den, she replaced the phone onto the cradle. Given the location of the house, cell service was iffy. If she walked out to the stable, clear signal. But the landline stayed clear, when it worked.

A knock on the kitchen door sent her down the hall. "Just a minute."

Opening the door, she found Yvonne standing there. "I know I'm intruding. I should have called and I did, but the line was busy."

"Yvonne, please come in. I can offer you just about any libation you would prefer, plus a sandwich, a piece of coffee cake?"

"Tea. I've grown so fond of tea. Green tea." Yvonne noticed Golly glaring at her as Sister flicked on the stove burner after filling the teapot.

"I accept all tribute."

"She's chatty."

"She wants a treat." Sister opened a cabinet drawer, plucked out a sealed bag, then dropped it in front of Yvonne. "If you don't buy her off she'll make your life miserable."

Yvonne, not an animal person, knew everyone at Roughneck Farm was. Best to believe them. She offered Golly, now next to her chair, a rather large meaty treat pressed to look like a fish.

"Thank you."

"You can leave now, Golly."

"No." The cat sassed Sister by ignoring her and patting Yvonne's leg.

Sister scooped the offender up, opened the kitchen door to the mudroom, opened the mudroom door, and put her out, ensuring she'd stay out by sprinkling a bit of shredded catnip kept in a closed bucket on a shelf. Had the desired effect.

The teapot whistled, Sister pulled out the Brown Betty, measured out the tea leaves, put them in the pot, put the pot on the table, and pulled out two very old, elegant teacups and saucers.

"These are delicate."

"My great-grandmother's. I find I like old china, old silverware better than the newer things. Probably because it brings back memories. While that steeps, I do have some moist coffeecake. Won't spoil your dinner. That's far off."

"Given Tootie, that's nonexistent." Yvonne smiled. "I'm taking her to dinner tonight. She never would learn how to cook, but I noticed last night she's learned to make a proper pot of tea."

"Has." Sister checked the pot, then carefully poured out steaming tea into the fine bone china cups through a silver strainer. "Forgot to ask. Half-and-half? Sugar?"

"None, thank you." As Sister sat down Yvonne started. "You and I got off on the wrong foot when we met at Custis Hall years ago. Not much improved since then, but I was always with Vic. He blamed you as an impediment to Tootie's future. He wanted her to take over the empire, as he put it, or at the very least become a doctor or lawyer."

"He made that abundantly clear. What do you think?" Sister leveled her cobalt blue eyes at Yvonne, who had light hazel ones like Tootie.

"At first I agreed, but over time I saw how unhappy his demands made Tootie. She's not cut out for corporate life. Am I happy that she left Princeton and came here? No. I'm upset, confused. Everyone is so"—she paused—"white." Then she added, "She could have hung on for four years."

Sister, not a green tea drinker although her cupboard was filled with all manner of teas, took

110

a sip. "We all thought that. I asked Gray to speak with her, given his success and the fact that he knows some of what she will encounter."

"All my husband thinks about. He has reduced everything to race, cast it all on her, and while I know exactly what he's talking about—I was a pioneer, after all—times are different for her. Easier in some ways. He resents that. I'd say, 'Isn't this what we worked for? What we all fought for and marched for and threw ourselves into elections for?' Got nowhere, of course. Vic always has to be right."

"What do you think now?"

"Tootie loves you. She loves this life. She takes her classes and I believe she will go to veterinary school, then return here."

"But do you blame me?"

"Not anymore. Do I look at you and see my oppressor, a white woman of a certain class, education, and privilege? I used to. Were you raised with more privilege than myself? Yes. Do you have more privilege now? In some ways, yes, but I have made my way and I'm damned proud of it." Her eyes flashed, her back straightened. "But to be brutally honest, I need you. I want to make amends."

"Need me? For what?"

"To help me understand my daughter. I think she loves you more than me."

"Yvonne, no. You've been far away. You stuck

111

by your husband, and Tootie, well, there's no other way to say it, Tootie hates her father."

"So do I. That bastard. All those years in the magazine and then the talking heads on our TV shows, all of them talking about how African American men should stick with our women, *our women,* and, of course, we were to stick with them. Well, the bastard has been having affairs with white women half his age, beautiful, dumb, and blonde."

"Perhaps not so dumb, Yvonne." Sister couldn't help but smile.

"That hypocrite."

"Undoubtedly, but so many men think they are only as old as the woman they are sleeping with."

"It's beyond that. He's set one up as his primary mistress. He gives her twenty thousand a month for spending money! Her apartment is in one of the best buildings in Chicago, overlooking the lake. Well, half of that twenty thousand is mine and, fortunately, my name is on everything."

"Do you want to sue him for what he's spent on the women?"

"I've thought of it. I want half of the empire now. I'll sell off my half. Of course, I want half of what's in the bank. He can keep our apartment, the summer house in Door County, he can keep the goddamned cars. I want what's mine and I want out. If I fight for what he's blown on those women it will take longer."

"What about Tootie?"

"He's disinherited her."

Sister frowned. "I knew he threatened, but I didn't believe he would do it."

"His own daughter. Why? Because she won't bend to his will. She actually has a will of her own. And I would argue with her about that. My daughter was smarter than I was."

Sister touched Yvonne's hand. "Tootie is smarter than most of us. Sure, she has a lot to learn about life but she knows who she is. What can I do for you and for her?"

"Teach me to ride?"

"I beg your pardon."

"Teach me to ride. Tootie loves hunting. I want to learn about it and be out there with her. Well, I know she has a special job out there. She's told me about whipping-in but I don't really know what she's talking about."

Regarding this, weighing her words, Sister replied, "What I will do is send you to Sam Lorillard, a wonderful teacher. You're coming to horses in your middle age, a beautiful middle age but you will have more fear than if you were eleven. He will shepherd you through the fear, teach you about horses and hunting. If I do it then I'm the authority. Sooner or later you wouldn't like that. Sam will be perfect, and you will like him."

"Lorillard?"

"Gray's younger brother."

"Is he as handsome as Gray?"

"Same strong face. It's the maternal blood, the Laprades. Sam is thinner. Harvard. Bombed out due to drink and probably drugs. Cleaned up after years of self-destruction. He's so damn good on a horse and he truly is a good man."

"Are you sending me to him because he's black?"

"No. I'm sending you to him because he is that good, because he's part of the family, and because Tootie respects him. He works for a man who is ever competitive against me, but that won't affect you. If you meet with Sam, feel he's not for you, then I suggest Lynne Beegle Gebhard. She's fabulous. The only problem with riding with Lynne is you will fall in love with her father, Dr. Chuck Beegle. Every woman does."

Yvonne's eyebrows lifted, the corners of her mouth turned upward. "Really?"

"He's eighty-six, handsome as the devil, and just sweeps women off their feet. He's also the kindest man I've ever met and a marine. My hunt is filled with military people, but we do seem to be heavy on marines."

A pause followed this. "How do you know I won't fall in love with Sam?" Then she quickly added, "I am through with men. I'm not falling in love with anyone."

"We all say that." Sister let it lie. "More tea?"

"Yes, please. Thank you, too, for putting me in touch with Betty Franklin. We spent most of the day looking at rentals. As many times as I have visited Tootie when she was at Custis Hall, I never appreciated how extraordinary this part of the world is. I do begin to understand why she came back to Virginia."

"Any ideas?"

"I love Chapel Cross. All those wonderful places and the names, Old Paradise, Tattenhall Station, Mud Fence, Orchard Hill, Tollgate, and then if we turn left at Chapel Cross, Beveridge Hundred, Little Dalby. Betty mentioned other fixtures in other parts of the country, also charmingly named, all historic. Let's see, Mill Ruins, she showed me that. Impressive, that old huge mill with the wheel turning just spraying water everywhere. Close Shave. Loved that name. Litany Brook. Prior's Woods."

"Our ancestors pretty much named things as they were. Mud Fence really started with mud fences back in the mid-eighteenth century. Couldn't afford anything else."

"Yes, Betty told me all that. I've rented a what-do-you-call-it, a dependency at Beveridge Hundred. I'll be smack in the Chapel Cross area."

"Good. That was fast."

"I'm not wasting any time."

"You are in the perfect position to see the resurrection of Old Paradise, finally bought by

Crawford Howard. Sam will either give you lessons there—the stable is spectacular—or at Crawford's Farm just down the road from mine. Or both. If you like Sam, that is."

"I hope I do. I'm eager to ride."

"Do you need help moving in? Furniture, towels, all that stuff."

"It's fully furnished. I'm close to Tattenhall Station, so I assume if I need a cup of sugar I can borrow it from Kasmir. I do remember him."

"Such a sweetheart. He's given Jefferson Hunt so much. He says we brought him back to life. He visited here shortly after his wife, much beloved, died. One of our family members came from India, and Kasmir and Vijay met at public school in England, thence on to Oxford."

Yvonne breathed deeply. "I think I have a lot to learn."

"Well, riding and hunting takes some time."

"No, about people. I assumed everyone here was a redneck. Not you and Gray, that was obvious, but I really did think this was the sticks."

"It is." Sister smiled.

"Some sticks."

CHAPTER 9

Roughneck Farm, a sizeable holding although not nearly the two thousand acres of Tattenhall Station nor the vast five thousand acres of Old Paradise, offered beautiful views of the Blue Ridge Mountains, with one northern interruption. The lands included Hangman's Ridge, a nine-hundred-foot ridge, flat on the top. The north side dipped down to wild meadows lapping Soldier Road. On the other side of this road reposed Cindy Chandler's Foxglove Farm. Had it not been for the ridge the two neighbors and dear friends could have observed the lights at night in each other's homes, although those homes were actually miles apart. Light travels as does sound, especially the sound of wind.

The hounds, walking briskly at seven-thirty on Wednesday morning, September 20, heard the trees groaning as they bent on the ridge. Depending on the ferocity of the wind, you could tell how long before the wind, the rain, or the snow would hammer down the south side of the former execution spot. The enormous hanging tree, a trunk so thick now it would take four men to reach around it, stood where it always had, close to the middle of the flat top.

"Five minutes," Dasher predicted.

"Never good for scent, wind," Asa grumbled.

The long slanting rays of the just risen sun cast a reddish gold glow on everything. You might think that sunrise is the opposite of sunset but no, the quality of light is different. Hounds, foxes, horses were sensitive to light. Some people were, too.

Shaker walked in front of the pack, Sister on the left, Tootie on the right, with Betty and Yvonne about fifteen yards in the rear. Betty chatted with Yvonne from time to time, explaining why they walked hounds, the different hound personalities, and how gifted her daughter was. Betty never mentioned the divorce or the subsequent publicity.

Yvonne, coached by Tootie, wore sturdy walking shoes. Mother and daughter had the same size foot, 7½. Her designer jeans, too expensive for this activity, nonetheless were jeans. A thin cashmere sweater was pulled over a crisp white blouse. Yvonne was walking hounds, but she still looked like a model.

Sister made a mental note to tell Marion. If Yvonne truly stuck it out in Virginia, how perfect the former star would be for Marion's annual brochure, always printed on expensive paper, designed as a magazine with vivid color production. Yvonne in a shadbelly, a top hat, perhaps even a veil rolled up on the hat crown, would have ladies flying to the store or buying on the Internet. The woman could make a burlap sack appear chic.

Tootie, although a heavenly beauty, lacked her mother's incredible sense of fashion. Tootie was truly happiest in her Timberland boots, Wrangler jeans with holes in them, heavy socks rolled over the top of the work boots, a T-shirt tucked into her jeans, with an old Shaker-stitched sweater pulled over that.

The morning, coolish, proved invigorating. The wind made it down to the bottom of the ridge; fallen leaves swirled about, limbs bent over.

Fortunately the hounds were returning to the kennels.

Betty remarked, "Twenty miles per hour, I'd guess."

Sister called over to her, "Enough to knock you sideways."

"You. You're lean." Betty laughed. "You, too, Yvonne."

"Zumba." She smiled, naming the musical workout.

"Zumba! Rumba." Twist, a second-year youngster, with no idea of what either word meant, wiggled his butt.

"Boom Ba Ba Boom!" Giorgio, the handsomest boy in the kennel, giggled.

The rest of the pack babbled in happiness, winds at their tails as they passed the apple orchard, small trees heavy with red apples.

"You are all mental." Inky, head popping out from her den in the apple orchard, taunted them.

"And you don't provide good sport," Dasher chided her.

"Why should I give you a good run? I'm happy with my housework." A black fox, a variant of the grays, Inky was a born organizer, unlike Comet, the male gray who lived under Tootie's cabin.

"Did you take Raleigh's green-and-orange canvas duck?" Pansy innocently asked.

"He shouldn't leave toys lying around the yard. He's a spoiled brat," came her answer, which meant she took it.

Yvonne stopped, speechless. She pointed to the fox. "Tally—what do you say, Tootie? I can't believe I'm seeing a fox."

"Tallyho. You have to count to twenty, Mom. Supposed to give the fox a sporting chance, but that's Inky. She visits the kennels at night."

"She's not afraid?" Yvonne, astonished, stood in one spot until Betty waved her on.

"No. I think she can read the fixture card. She doesn't come out when we hunt here or at After All. She's a funny girl."

"Black. There are black foxes?" Yvonne, still astonished, asked, as Shaker opened the draw-run door to the kennels.

"Black, white, silver. Arctic foxes are white. Go on in there, Zandy." Betty gave a young hound the evil eye so she scooted right in.

120

"And silver must be commercially raised. I mean for silver fox coats, not that anyone buys furs anymore," Yvonne added quickly.

"I have always assumed that blacks or even silver foxes are a variant of the gray fox, or one whose breeding from the original stock has been tampered with by humans," Sister chimed in.

"You don't see silver foxes out hunting, do you?"

"No." Betty smiled. "Reds, grays, the occasional black—as well as the occasional black bear."

Yvonne's hand came to her breast. "I sincerely hope not."

Sister and Tootie walked back out of the kennel's main door having walked in through the draw-pen door.

"Your first hound walk, Mom." The leaves swirled.

"Good exercise, and Betty informed me a little bit about the hounds. Asa is the oldest and wisest and"—she thought for a moment—"Diana figures things out. I can see there is a lot to remember. Betty said if a hound needs correcting, you"—she looked at her daughter—"should say the name. So you have to know all the hounds. How do you know who they are from up high? I mean, darling, you're on a horse. You're looking at their backs, or they're far away."

"You learn over time. I watch the way a hound

moves. Most of The Jefferson Hunt Hounds are tricolors, so I can't always identify them by coat. If I get close I can. And then, yes, Betty's right. First say the name. If they don't listen, warn them, and if they still don't listen, crack the whip. Scares them."

"Do you have to crack the whip often?"

"No, thank heavens." Tootie handed her mother her whip with the long kangaroo thong, kangaroo being the best leather, costing about $350 for a staff thong, four feet longer than a field thong. Pricey, but it lasted for years. The other leather thongs wore out in two seasons if one was staff.

"I think I'll have to work up to this. You do it." Yvonne handed it back.

Tootie hopped on a mounting block, placed at the kennels in case anyone had to dismount there, then hop back up. She easily swung the thong in front of her, flicked her wrist and a rifle shot went off.

"What a sound." Yvonne stepped back a bit.

Sister smiled. "Generally does the trick."

"Can you do it?" Yvonne artlessly asked, then remembered she was speaking to the Master. "I'm sure you can."

Sister took Tootie's whip, stepped up onto the mounting block. She swung the whip in front of her. *Crack!* She swung the whip behind her. *Crack!* Then she shot the thong straight up, a twist of the wrist. *Crack!* Didn't say a word.

Tootie received her whip, laughed, then said to her mother, "Only Sister can do that."

"Show-off." Betty then took the whip.

She could crack it in front and in back but not overhead. "Just kills me that I can't do that and I've been trying for, oh, thirty-some years."

"Forty," Sister teased her.

"Don't tempt me," Betty teased right back. "Yvonne, my beloved best friend wants to tell you I'm older than dirt, which I am—but I can still ride her into the ground."

"Oh, you cannot. You're a better rider than I am, but I can keep up." Betty imploringly looked at Yvonne. "Honey, you have no idea what you've gotten yourself into."

"I'm beginning to understand that."

"Sister, I told Mom I'd look at the cottage she's rented. Okay?"

"Of course. Yvonne, let Betty or me know if you need anything."

"Yes. I can finally get rid of that lampshade with the fringe on it." Betty giggled.

As mother and daughter walked back to the cabin, Betty noticed the new Continental but said nothing.

Turning to her Master and friend, she did ask, "What do you think?"

"I think she's game. I actually do." Sister smiled.

"I hope so." Betty inhaled. "For Tootie's sake.

123

This wind isn't going to stop and I need a restorative cup of tea. Ask me to the house and let's gossip."

That afternoon, Gray returned from a meeting in Charlottesville with Derwood Chase, a high-end investor. The two had struck up a friendship decades ago on the tennis courts where Derwood was a power. Gray worked hard to improve his game. Neither man was cut out for golf. Both realized it helped business; they just couldn't do it.

"Hey. How was Derwood?"

"Just like always." Gray smiled.

"Johanna?" She mentioned his glamorous wife, an opera singer as well as a consummate hostess.

"Good. Ready?"

"Honey, you're monosyllabic but, yes, I am ready."

"Prepared?"

She closed the door behind her. "Is anyone ever prepared for your aunt Daniella?"

Well, Aunt Daniella, having recently turned ninety-four, was ready for them. No sooner had Gray and Sister entered her charming if overstuffed house than she gave orders. She wanted her pillow fluffed behind her. She wanted her drink. Of course, Gray and Sister were welcome to libations, too. She wanted her ebony cane laid across the small table by her comfortable chair. She wanted to know exactly what he thought of the economy. Were her funds safe with Derwood?

Gray patiently did as bid. Told her he'd just seen Derwood, who would never divulge anything about a client, but told her he knew Derwood paid special attention to her portfolio, which he did, by Chase Investment standards. They dealt in millions. Daniella's finances proved slim but Derwood nurtured her account. It grew. The old lady would never have a worry in the world. Her son Mercer had died within the last two years and she had inherited his funds and his house. He was a bloodstock agent and he'd done quite well for himself.

Gray sat in a wing chair by his aunt. "You look wonderful."

"Liar. I look like Hecate, an old crone."

"Never."

"He's right, Aunt Daniella. You look like a woman perhaps in her late sixties, if that."

Daniella eyed Sister, shifted in her seat. "You flatter me, but I still walk a mile in the morning, one in the evening. The secret is to keep moving."

"Thank you for allowing us to call on you." Sister reached into her bag, retrieving a cell-phone.

Daniella's eyes widened. "You aren't going to use that device, are you?" Then just as quickly she changed the subject, held up her glass. "Bourbon. A double."

"Of course." Gray took the glass, hurried to the bar, poured out the bourbon, then handed it to Daniella, who did look good for her years, her fortification, quite a fortification.

"I am going to use my device. I want you to see something."

"Porn?" The white eyebrows twitched, a little grin appeared.

"Later." Sister gave it right back. "When it's just us girls."

"Quite right."

Gray took a deep breath; the old dragon was in a good mood. Better remember to bring her a full bottle of special cask bourbon tomorrow.

Sister rose, then knelt by Daniella. "Please look at this and tell me who it is."

Daniella reached for her reading glasses on the table by her chair. Sister hit the button and boom, Weevil appeared.

Daniella sharply breathed in, her eyes huge now. Then he blew "Gone to Ground."

"Good God, Weevil! Weevil Carruthers. Whoever took a film of him?"

"Look again, Aunt Daniella." Sister replayed the video that Marion had sent to her phone.

"It's Weevil Carruthers. I'd know him anywhere." She stopped, looked at the video for the third time. "Morven. Morven." Then she looked at Sister in confusion, a flash of fear in her eyes. "It's impossible!"

"Yes. It should be." Sister told Daniella what had happened. "We can't believe it, but how can we not believe our eyes?"

"He's been dead since I was thirty-three!"

"Was he dead?" Gray quietly asked as he sipped his own drink.

"Granted no one ever found the body. Oh, there were rumors that he ran off to Paris, or London or even Istanbul. Some perfect ass said he became a Muslim. The rumors died down. Sooner or later we all believed he was dead."

"He had many enemies?" Sister stood up, a knee creaking.

"Irritating, isn't it?" Daniella smirked.

" 'Tis."

"The man exuded charm and sex. Perfectly heterosexual men felt the pull. I have never ever met anyone like him. Given that he slept with other men's wives, yes, he had enemies. But this?"

"It's dumbfounding. And then blowing 'Gone to Ground.' A thumb to the nose, you know."

Daniella, knowing the horn calls, nodded in agreement as Sister returned to her seat.

"I was hoping you might remember some of his affairs." Sister took out her Moleskine notebook, the grid pages before her.

Knocking back all of her drink, glaring at Gray, who quickly refilled the glass, this time putting in two ice cubes, Daniella sighed. "How do I know what was true and what was not? So much loose talk."

"Well—" Sister boldly pressed but with a compliment. "Did he approach you? You and your sister were famed for your beauty, your sparkling ways."

Daniella pushed back into the pillow, a sly smile on her lips. "Oh, everyone wanted us."

"So he did?"

"He did. I was married at the time. Husband Number Two. Was it Two? Well, no matter and Graziella"—she named her sister, Gray and Sam's mother—"she was always with Number One. How she loved that man. We politely spurned Weevil, of course. But, oh, my God, was he divine to look at, to hear his voice, a deep baritone rumble. Even the hair on his arms was golden. Everything about him was golden."

Sister wondered if she did spurn him. However, she was a woman of color, light as a white person but still. Neither one could have been open and Daniella, nobody's fool, would never have risked publicity. In fact, every man she married was richer than the last one, after she disposed of the first one, which had been pure physical attraction according to her.

Gray leaned forward. "You have always had sex radar, Aunt Dan. Admit it."

"Well—"

"You must have an idea of any affairs he had that were serious."

"Yes, I do, but I don't want to name names."

"They're all dead, surely?" he countered.

"Oh, they are, but their children aren't. Most of them are in their seventies, late sixties."

"Yes, of course. Do you think any of these people might be his? The husband didn't know?"

She shook her head. "No. He would have stamped his get." She used the horseman's term. "He must have been careful, or his lovers were. Any woman with a blond baby with a killer smile would have aroused too much curiosity."

"I assume he had quite a few flings with Deep Run ladies." Sister smiled, for the Richmond Hunt, a big fences hunt, always was famous for its good-looking women. Sister then continued, "Aunt Daniella, we have to get to the bottom of this, and we have to find that hunting horn."

"There are ghosts, you know. You should know. Your house is at the base of Hangman's Ridge. They still moan up there, the hanged men."

Neither Gray nor Sister disputed this.

"I believe there are ghosts, I do. But why would Weevil's spirit come back, take his horn from the Huntsman Hall of Fame, and then blow it? Yes it is in keeping with his cheek. Oh, he was full of the Devil." She laughed, then considered the request. "Well, this is what I know, what I am pretty sure about, and I rely on your discretion.

Edward Bancroft's older sister, Evangelista. Sybil looks just like her," she mentioned Ed and Tedi's daughter, visiting her son at college. "Wilder than Sybil, but a decent girl. Anyway, Evie fell head over heels. The family was horrified, broke it up. Sent her to London for the season." Daniella thought some more. "Florence Randolph. Married with two children. She was seen leaving the huntsman's house one night. Covered it all up."

"Shaker's house?"

"The very same. He might have had affairs with some northern hunt ladies, Green Spring Valley in Maryland. He hunted around, was always in demand, made the most of joint meets—but when he disappeared, he disappeared from here, so this is where the mystery began and may never end. If it hasn't been solved or resolved since 1954, I wouldn't get my hopes up."

Sister pressed the button again, turned up the sound so "Gone to Ground" rang out. "It's different now."

Daniella sipped a bit of her exquisite bourbon; the damned bottle cost over three hundred dollars, which Gray knew, since he would be replacing it. "Quite right." She waited a long, long time. "There was one other. Serious, I mean. I hesitate."

Both Sister and Gray leaned forward, holding their breath in curiosity.

She waited a bit more, ever the dramatist. "Margaret DuCharme." Pause. "Alfred and Binky's mother. Dr. Margaret is named after her grandmother. Doesn't look a bit like her, not that Margaret DuCharme—today's Margaret—isn't attractive, but she looks like her grandmother's people, the Minors. Acts more like a Minor, too. Intellectuals. Lawyers. Doctors. The DuCharmes were rich plantation men, gentlemen, ferociously conservative. I wouldn't be surprised if the original Margaret's husband didn't toast the king, even though they made their fortune during the War of 1812 robbing British supply trains. A fortune, all created by a raving beauty, Sophie Marquet, who beguiled the Brits, found out where the pay wagon and the supply trains were going, then later, with a small group of men, robbed them. It was said the good lady sold some of the goods to our troops but never relinquished the stolen cash, of course."

Sister and Gray had heard the history of Old Paradise, built by Sophie as was Custis Hall, the private school, many times. Daniella relished the victory of this early nineteenth-century woman so much it was delightful to hear her tell the tale.

"This state bursts with incredible people, past and present." Sister nodded to Daniella, indicating she was an incredible person. She was not always an easy one to be around, or to be related to.

"Where was I? Oh, Margaret. Elegant woman married to a crashing bore. Margaret's mother, the Minor, seethed with financial ambition. Margaret's marriage was arranged by her mother—not exactly on a par with Consuelo Vanderbilt's arranged marriage to the Duke of Marlborough, but just as bad." Daniella knew her history, social and political. "Brenden DuCharme didn't mistreat her. He took good care of her financially. When a man owns a huge place, thousands of acres, outbuildings, dependencies, all that, he doesn't pay but so much attention to his wife. He just bored her. Take it from me, he was boredom personified." She tapped her forehead. "Dumb as a sack of hammers. Brenden inherited everything. Never really had to work hard, solve problems, learn to get along with others. I wouldn't call him rude, especially, just dense. Very dense."

"Good-looking?"

"Are Binky and Alfred good-looking?" A pause. "I rest my case. Weevil zeroed in on her. She didn't have a chance."

"And you say she was lovely?" Gray asked.

"Was. Titian-colored hair. Blue eyes. Classic WASP features. Wonderful figure, full bosom, small waist. And, the best part, she could ride. They had opportunities to meet—and then again, there were fewer ways to catch someone then. If you had half a brain you could have an affair undetected."

Now Sister believed Daniella had indeed enjoyed the delights of Weevil as well as those of other men. For one thing, her collection of jewelry was suspicious. A few husbands, yes. That much jewelry, no.

"What happened?" Gray finished his drink.

"Oh, like Evie Bancroft, sent to Europe. Paris for Margaret. Spoke perfect French. Then again, she did evidence a strong interest in fashion. Brenden said she was going to bring back a collection of the latest high fashion, which she did." She shrugged. "Who is to say?"

"Aunt Dan. What do you think of that video? Truly?" Gray softly inquired.

"I think it's Wesley Carruthers. It frightened me a little and yet,"—pause—"and yet it made my heart leap to see him." She breathed deeply. "I miss old friends. I have outlived almost everyone of my generation. I have outlived my son. Losing friends, that's the hardest thing about aging." She stopped, remembered Sister's past. "Forgive me if I have brought up a painful memory."

Sister smiled. "Aunt Daniella, I quite agree. My son was killed in that farm accident in 1974. I think of him every day. Big Ray died in 1991. I don't think of him quite as much, but we mostly got along. People I started out with once I was

133

on my own are dying now. The generation of foxhunters in front of me from whom I learned so much are mostly gone. My old horses, my old hounds. I know exactly what you mean, but we go on. You certainly have."

"Life is to be lived. We all have sorrows." This was said with dignity. Daniella rolled the cold glass in her hand, then stopped. "Should you find anything out about Weevil, tell me. Ghosts don't drink, but how I would love to offer him a perfect brandy. To remember the old folks, friends. The laughter. How we laughed. I can still hear your mother's laughter, Gray. We were close, you know." Then switching gears. "How is Lucinda?"

Lucinda Arnold, Sister's mother-in-law, was alive, in her high nineties, in Richmond, Virginia.

"The same."

"Which is to stay she's still a bitch. Only the good die young," Daniella remarked.

Gray looked at her. "Indeed."

She reached for her ebony cane to crack him, stopped, threw her head back, and laughed.

CHAPTER 10

L ieu in," Shaker called in his singsong voice.

Cora, head female, standing by the huge waterwheel at Mill Ruins, took the lead, trotting down the farm road winding behind the mill. This road had no ruts because Walter Lungrun, M.D., scraped it; it divided two huge pastures. A half mile down the road, forests rich in hardwoods awaited them.

The water sprayed off the turning wheel, tiny rainbows spraying color at seven forty-five A.M. The meet started at seven-thirty but there was always someone rushing to put on their tack, or Sister's announcements took time. As there were no fixture cards during cubbing, information was transmitted before each meet or later by email. Even though it was September 21, Thursday, twenty-five people moved off behind the hounds. This goodly number in the middle of the week pleased Sister as well as her younger Joint Master, Walter Lungrun, sitting in his Tahoe converted to pick up hounds if need be. Next to him sat Yvonne Harris, looking as though she'd stepped out of a page of England's *Country Life* magazine.

Walter informed her, "That little toodle you heard on the horn is really for the people. It's to alert them to shut up, to keep them behind the hounds. 'Lieu in' is Norman French. Came into our language after 1066. He called that to the hounds telling them to search for the fox, to go into the covert."

"Norman French?" she inquired in her modulated voice, a voice cultivated to suggest just that, cultivation.

He grinned. "When William the Conqueror defeated King Harold in 1066, everything changed. We're still living out those changes. Latin, as in Norman French, intertwined with Anglo-Saxon. The French brought their ways with them and suddenly sauces appeared on long, well-appointed tables. Expensive, different furniture, really expensive architecture. Well, they brought their form of hunting as well. And we continue to use their terms."

"Was Harold that rough? I mean, was England before the conquest that primitive? I'm not much of a historian until you get to the Paris of the Belle Époque—the beginning of mass fashion, in a way."

"You'll have to teach me. About all I know is your coat sleeve should show just a bit of shirtsleeve unless you're hunting. Then the sleeves are longer. Oh, I know the best coats have buttons that really work so you can roll up your coat sleeves."

"Very good." Yvonne laughed. "My husband,

my soon-to-be ex-husband, had all his clothing tailored in Jermyn Street. He swore we still can't tailor men's furnishings."

"I've got a lot to learn."

"So do I. Norman French. So the hounds are bilingual."

Walter grinned again, a wide one. "Yvonne, you'll make a houndswoman yet. And so to answer your earlier question, Harold and his people weren't that rough, but Italy and France were more refined. They never let us forget it back then."

Driving the Tahoe, which Walter referred to as "The Beast" since it would go through anything, he followed the last of the field, Second Flight staying behind so as not to press horses or make riders nervous. Enough of them in Second Flight were nervous anyway.

Noticing this, Yvonne asked, "These people go slow?"

"No. They don't jump. They might jump a log, but they go to the gates. Often they run harder and faster than First Flight because they have to catch up. Second Flight is for green riders, green horses, to train them both. Sometimes a person just doesn't want to launch over jumps anymore."

"I see. So that's where one would start or finish."

"Yes. On big hunt days, days when we have over fifty people, sometimes Sister will allow a

Third Flight, people who go much slower and often stand on hills to watch the hunt unfold. Hilltoppers."

"I thought that's what Second Flight was called. I'm trying to learn and I've worn out my daughter with questions. I'll try not to prevail too much on you." She smiled, teeth gleaming.

"Don't mind a bit."

"Thank you for escorting me. I know you hunt up front."

"Sister may not have told you, but I just returned from a conference in Phoenix, plus I've pulled my back out. A little physical therapy will take care of that. I'll be out in two weeks tops."

"It's a passion." Yvonne smiled.

"A passion. An education, a chance to be with other people not riven with all manner of fears, and really, a way to imbibe beauty." Walter heard a deep voice, then another. "We've got a line."

He moved up, although still giving Second Flight plenty of room. Tootie, on the left, soared over a stout coop in the fence line on the left. Yvonne had never seen her daughter at work, so to speak. Her jaw dropped. Then Betty Franklin took the coop on the right, both women intently watching hounds as Tootie flanked them on the left.

"Why isn't Betty over there with Tootie?"

"If the fox turns right, hounds will follow. No one will be there. So Tootie is covering the left side. If hounds go into that thick wood up there and turn farther left, then Betty will jump back over and get on their right side in the woods or wherever they go. But right now, she needs to be just where she is."

The fox, a clever gray who had come to sneak by the red fox who lived behind the mill, realized the red fox wasn't going to be the problem, as that big fellow would fuss since the gray was in his territory. The droppings of grain in the barn proved too enticing, so the younger fox figured he could easily outrun the older. Now he had to outrun the pack.

The mercury, not yet at 50°F, cooperated in holding scent, but the low cloud cover really helped. The sun wasn't going to burn off anything and the temperature might stay down. Perfect hunting weather usually occurs with a low cloud cover and the temperature between, say, 38°F and 48°F. But good runs could be had in the 50s and 60s, especially down low by creek beds. The fox knows this, so on a sunny day he or she goes out into a pasture or onto a dirt road, sometimes even a macadam one, boogies along, and by the time the hounds reach the spot the scent has either evaporated or is rising over their heads.

Not today.

Sister, up front riding Aztec, her TB/QH cross, took the coop into the large pasture, then soared over the large log fence at the end of the newly mown field. She landed on a good wide path, good footing in the woods. Hounds at full cry tore up ahead of her. Betty had jumped back out onto the farm road and followed the pack on the road. If they turned farther left, which would be north, she could easily find a path into the woods, not as wide as the center path but she could get around. She knew the territory. Staff knows the territory often better than the people who own it.

"The creek," Parker shouted, and put on the afterburners hoping to reach the swift-running creek before the fox, who was far ahead moving fast to faster.

Walter fastened his seat belt. "You'd better do the same. Once we leave the hayfield the road is rutted. If you have any loose fillings they'll come out."

"Thanks." She looked for the Jesus strap and grabbed it.

Sure enough the fox headed straight down, for the land began to steeply incline to the creek. He jumped in and swam at a diagonal, crawled out on the other side, and took off.

Dragon reached the place where the fox entered the creek. Sniffing, he leapt into it, water breast high. He reached the other side. No scent.

"Move up or down," his mother, Delia, ordered him.

Hardheaded though he was, Dragon listened to his mother. Staying in the water, he moved

140

upstream first, up along the bank, sniffing. Twist, knowing older Delia knew her stuff, leapt into the creek and duplicated Dragon's efforts moving downstream. Twist was a weedy hound—no matter what Sister and Shaker did, they couldn't get much weight on the smallish fellow. Young, still learning, he could move with blinding speed which irritated Dragon, who wanted to be in front.

"Here!" The slender hound sang out, which really pissed off Dragon, who clambered out of the creek, flew to the spot, and opened before Twist could climb out.

The pack, in the creek, hurried out.

Thimble, Twist's sister, now alongside him, praised him, *"Good work."*

"I hate him. I really hate him." Twist indicated Dragon now ahead of them all.

Shaker, on tried-and-true Showboat, jumped straight down into the creek, holding onto the mane as Showboat leapt up in the air to get out. He was such an athlete he hit the top of the bank, water flying off his legs, as Shaker sat deep and tight. Off they ran.

Tootie, already ahead, had the presence of mind to think the fox would cross, so she went to an easy crossing, as did Betty on the south side. Finding a decent path proved more difficult. If both whippers-in remained in the woods they'd be dodging trees and bramble, and really fall behind.

Betty, having hunted this territory since childhood, swerved hard right, found the well-trod deer trail, and kicked on. Tootie moved into the wide cleared path and thundered ahead of the huntsman. She hoped she'd see a cross path so she could move farther left. She needed to be on the outside of the pack, not behind them.

Meanwhile, Yvonne thanked heaven for the seat belt and Jesus strap. Otherwise, her head would have smashed up into the roof of the old 2008 Tahoe. Walter rolled down the rutted dirt road, the incline not giving comfort. Finally at the bottom, they roared across a ford, and Yvonne gave thanks they weren't stuck in the creek bed. Walter knew what he was doing and moved along, his tires now creating mud tracks. Windows rolled down, he and Yvonne could hear the hound music as well as Shaker blowing "Gone Away."

The huntsman also let out an encouraging scream to his pack.

Walter laughed. "We tell him he sounds like a girl when he does that."

"It is high-pitched."

"A high pitch excites the hounds, but that doesn't mean we won't torment Shaker."

"I doubt anyone would mistake him for a girl." Yvonne laughed, too.

"He's the manly type. Huntsmen are, except for the lady huntsmen—but they are tough as the men."

"I guess you would have to be to do this." She shut up as he encountered another rut.

Walter pulled ahead as Second Flight followed Sister in the woods, where the sound ricocheted off the trees, the leaves muffling some of it.

Reaching open fields, uncut, he drove to where the rutted road intersected another rutted road, then turned around so the nose of the Tahoe faced the field and the woods, which were about a half mile away. The glorious sound came closer and closer.

"There." Walter pointed to some broomstraw bending.

Sure enough the gray popped out of the field, ran right toward the Tahoe, passed it, and flew to a huge old storage building down the road. He ducked into his den, dug under and into the outbuilding, a perfect site for coziness in all kinds of weather.

Yvonne, thrilled to have seen the fox, twisted around to follow his progress. "He doesn't look frightened."

"He knows he's got us beat. They usually do. Ah, here come the lead hounds."

Dragon, Dasher, Twist, and Thimble shot by, immediately followed by the rest of the pack, Asa bringing up the rear. Being the oldest, Asa wisely would stop from time to time to check and make sure the fox hadn't followed them and cut across the road or, worse, doubled back. Convinced the line was still true, he picked up speed, joining the rear of the pack.

Sister came out, reaching the road. She moved by Walter and Yvonne, for Walter had parked to the side to give everyone room. Within about five minutes all of First Flight had gathered by the storage building. Then Second Flight joined them.

Shaker, already on foot, blew "Gone to Ground."

"I was first." Dragon pushed forward.

Shaker patted the braggart's head, reached to each hound, praising, patting. "Good hounds. Well done."

Parker and Pickens, still young, about wiggled themselves to death, they were so excited.

Easily swinging back up in the saddle, Shaker tooted a few notes, then moved down the road toward where the creek in the woods poured into a deeper, rougher creek. His idea was to draw back to the mill.

Walter followed. "We're on a part of the land called Shootrough, because Peter Wheeler, who formerly owned all this, would bring out his cronies and they'd bird hunt. It's pretty good bird hunting, which I'm sure our fox knows."

"Tootie told me foxes are omnivorous."

"It's a good survival mechanism. We have it as well. Foxes are good hunters; they hunt much like cats do. But any animal will take the easy way out if you give it to them, and game gets scarce in winter, which is when we fill up all the feeder boxes. We have so much land, so many big fixtures that the kibble bill just for foxes can run about a thousand dollars a month, which is why we wait until winter. Clubs with smaller fixtures—which is to say most clubs north of the Mason-Dixon line, or even the Northern Virginia hunts these days—they might be able to feed year-round." He turned to her. "Development. It's a hunter's curse, any hunter."

"I read in one of the papers that the English are creating new villages. They have a housing shortage and they're trying to make the new places look like old places, I guess. But it sounds environmentally forward."

"Does. I expect some very smart young developers here will figure that out, but right now it's just divide up the land into squares and slap up houses, even if they're five-hundred-thousand-dollar houses. Not much thought goes into it."

She nodded. "We're so spoiled. We have so much land we forget to take care of it. I can't say as I thought of that until we sent Tootie to Custis Hall. Visiting there, walking the grounds, actually going to some of the teachers' lectures during parents' weekend. I began reading." She looked back at him. "There are greens in Chicago and people who want to protect the environment, but it's not the same as here. Here you live it."

"We try."

A deep boom rang out. Then a higher squeak.

Walter beamed. "Asa. The squeak was a young entry honoring Big Daddy, so to speak. What a joy it is to watch a hound learn its trade. Well, kind of like being a parent, I guess."

"I'm seeing Tootie in a new light."

"She's good, Yvonne, very good. Has the instinct for it as well as the physical ability. In truth, a whipper-in must ride better than anyone, better than the huntsman. However, most huntsmen started out as whippers-in so they can ride, and ride well, but you're riding behind the hounds. It's a different skill."

"I had no idea foxhunting was so complicated. When did you learn?" She grabbed the strap again as they reached the deep creek.

She also prayed they would not be crossing it. She had not brought water wings.

"In 1984. I was twelve. We hadn't much money but Sister and her husband, Ray, allowed me to ride their horses. Sister gave me lessons. I loved it from the first, and I loved her, too."

"I can see why." And she could.

Hounds would speak, then fall silent. Speak again as Shaker hunted them back toward the mill, which was anywhere from two to five miles depending on which way one rode.

Hunt and peck, hunt and peck. Hounds cut up

turning toward the higher woods. Walter backed out, got on the road, turned left this time when he hit the intersection, then sat at the edge of the woods. Hounds moved through it. Opened again, and this time it stuck.

Walter crept along. They reached the edge of the fenced pastures. Betty jumped in from the woods while Tootie leapt first over a coop forty-five degrees away from Betty. The two whippers-in waited for the hounds to appear, then Betty took two o'clock and Tootie took ten o'clock. Hounds came out working slowly, noses to the ground, but speaking.

Walter informed Yvonne, "It's a fading line. They're working steadily. If it heats up we'll have a good run. If not, the field will stay at a trot or walk, but this is good hound work."

She watched attentively.

The line never heated up but it did hold, and the pack returned to the mill, going behind it to the den of the red fox.

"Buzz off, blowhard. I could hear you for the last forty-five minutes." A voice wafted up from one of the den openings.

This so startled Pickens, Parker's littermate, that he stepped back.

Cora stepped forward. *"Rude."*

"You're disturbing the peace. Go to the party wagon and leave me alone."

The mill fox knew the drill inside and out,

calling the hound trailer by the name the hounds and humans called it, "party wagon."

"Come along. Good hounds. Good work." Shaker sang out, they turned and followed.

"He didn't have to be so rude," Pickens complained.

"He's a red fox," Dasher said. *"They think they're the center of the universe."*

The breakfast, held in the old house that Walter, renting it for a ninety-nine-year lease, had rehabilitated, kept everyone eating, drinking, talking.

Walter introduced Yvonne to Margaret DuCharme as a colleague. She was a sports doctor, he was a cardiologist. He left the two women to talk while he made the rounds as host and Joint Master.

"DuCharme." Yvonne thought. "Old Paradise. Tootie has told me about it. Very romantic."

Margaret shook her head. "Yes and no. Crawford Howard has finally bought it from my father and uncle, who don't speak, by the way, just so you know. At any rate, Crawford played a waiting game." She took a deep breath. "It's for the best. Since Tootie told you a bit about it, why don't I give you the tour when you're available?"

"I'd love that."

They moved on to others. Sister came up to Margaret, who had taken up hunting only two

148

years ago. As she was a natural athlete, it came easily. "Looking well."

"As are you, Master."

"How's it going?"

"It's really interesting. Of course, neither Dad nor I live in any of the dependencies anymore, but I can't stay away. The old foundation of the big house, as you know, withstood everything because it's cut stone, heavy thick stone, fitted together. Crawford has had it wrapped in heavy plastic, that awful blue stuff, and he's dug around the outside."

"Really?"

"He's pouring in goo, for lack of a better word, to seal it. No water will ever seep through."

"I'll be damned."

"He'll be glad to do it." Margaret teased her.

"Crawford thinks of everything."

"I bet they've found stuff in the walls."

Margaret nodded. "Pack rats."

"Binky," she mentioned her uncle, "now that he has money again, is being impossible. Bragging about how much the DuCharmes have done for the county since 1812."

"Well, snobbery hasn't done either your uncle or your father much good, has it?" Sister got right to the point.

Margaret laughed, then looked serious for a minute. "I'm tired of being the go-between. Now that they've sold Old Paradise, have gobs of money, the hell with it. I love Daddy but he's set in his ways. Hates change."

"A lot of old people do," Sister said.

Margaret smiled. "If I ever get like that, Sister, shoot me."

"Ditto." Sister changed the subject. "Think the lost treasure of Old Paradise will be found with all this digging, rebuilding? Is there any old estate in Virginia that doesn't have a story of lost treasure, murder, woe, perfidious Yankees? Ever notice it's rarely perfidious Southerners?"

"We do no wrong." Margaret clinked glasses with Sister, as she'd picked up her drink.

As Sister walked over to chat with Kasmir and Alida, visiting for a long weekend, she thought about wrongdoing. Yes, there were old murders, thefts, family feuds of which the DuCharmes were a leading example, but what Virginians excelled at, reveled in, were sexual peccadilloes. Wrongdoing. Yes, but so very fascinating.

Daniella Laprade, a fountain of old war stories, of scandal and sin, knew more than she was telling. Sister thought she'd wait a bit, then revisit the intrepid lady.

CHAPTER 11

How do you like it?" Yvonne asked Tootie as they walked through her rental.

"I really like the stone fireplace. You'll be glad you have it when the cold comes."

"Why? This place has central heat." Yvonne smiled, pleased with herself. "I inspected the heat pump and it's five years old so it ought to be good."

"I'm sure it is, but, Mom, these old places don't have insulation. They might have horsehair in the walls, hair from the tails, but not what you're used to, plus the windows will get ice cold." Tootie walked to a window putting her hand on the single pane. "Wavy, see?"

"Yes."

"That means it's original. Beveridge Hundred was built in the 1790s. Least that's what Sister says. She likes historical research, especially old buildings."

"You live in a new old building." Yvonne put her hand on the wavy glass, which, even though the temperature that Friday was 64°F, felt cool.

"The foundation was dug in 1787, the stone foundation under the front part of my cabin. It was one of the first settlements that far west."

"Really?"

"Most people didn't come out this far until after the Revolutionary War. Anyway, so many of those homes still stand. Like this one."

"I love the old names. Sister gave me one of last year's fixture cards and I never heard of such names: Mousehold Heath, Close Shave, Mud Fence. They're fanciful."

Tootie smiled. "Usually the name involves some feature, like Mud Fence. They didn't have enough money in the beginning for fences so they made them out of mud. Mill Ruins you saw. Was the first big mill this far west. Tattenhall Station used to be a stop for Norfolk and Southern railroad. Uh—" She thought a minute. "After All Farm was named by Edward Bancroft's grandfather after 1865. They came down from New York City, made a fortune during the war. After All. Sister teases the Bancrofts and says it's just beginning, no after all at all."

"People know one another well here, don't they?"

"Pretty much."

"When you finish vet school I assume you'll return here."

Tootie looked out the window. "I have to get into vet school first. Mom, there's a UPS truck coming down the drive."

Yvonne walked to the front door, opened it, and stepped outside to greet the driver, who introduced herself and handed over a UPS envelope. Tootie, outside now, too, waved at the driver.

"You know the UPS driver?" Yvonne was surprised.

"Karen Allison. She covers our territory."

"I see."

What Yvonne was beginning to see was that people did know one another. It wasn't like Chicago, too huge for that to be possible, but a city, like most American cities, where one could stay in one's glitter ghetto. You need not see or speak to anyone terribly different from yourself, especially different economically. You might know some people in your city block or blocks.

Yvonne opened the large cardboard UPS envelope and pulled out papers, a legal firm's address at the top center.

Scanning the papers, she laughed. "According to your father's legal firm, I'm not entitled to half. If I press this, I will be attacked by killer zombies." She threw the papers on the little table by the front door, laughing as she did. "If he pushes this into court, he will regret it for every day that he lives thereafter. You'd think he'd know by now that my IQ is above a good golf score."

"I'm sorry, Mom. I guess there is no such thing as a good divorce."

Well, she thought, *out of the mouths of babes.* Then she answered, "No, but some are better than others. I haven't provided much maternal advice but I can tell you when you marry get your name on everything. Absolutely everything. That way when you divorce, your husband's lawyers can't play Starve the Wife." Tootie remained silent so Yvonne continued. "You aren't seeing anyone?"

"No."

"Ah. Someone will come along."

"Mother, I am never getting married."

Yvonne laughed. "Every young woman says that, I swear. Granted, your father and I haven't left you with much of an example."

Tootie shrugged, then offered, "I'll stack wood for you. Sister has a lot of downed trees. Gray and I can cut them up. You'll need wood. It will really help, plus a fire in the fireplace is, I don't know, kind of perfect."

"All right. I will pay you and I'll pay Sister."

"She wouldn't take anything and neither will he." Tootie paused. "How did UPS know how to find you?"

"I hopped online, gave them my address the minute I signed the rental contract. Otherwise, you would have been inundated by things like that." She pointed to the papers on the table.

Tootie nodded, then smiled. "I like your place. It's cozy, and better yet, it's in the middle of our hunt country. We call all this out here the Chapel Cross fixtures 'cause where the roads cross is the old chapel. Still in use."

"I'm beginning to understand that everything is still in use. I expect to see Robert E. Lee walk around the corner."

Tootie considered this, then countered, "Mr. Jefferson."

"But of course," Yvonne agreed.

Sister, over at After All, showed Edward the video. As Daniella had mentioned Edward's late sister, she thought it worth a try.

He looked at it. "Mother and Father were upset with Evie but I didn't really know the scope of it. I was in my junior year at Dartmouth. Evangeline was not a student by any means. My sister was a party girl. She was intelligent but like most girls at that time, her job was to marry well, produce children."

"She never said anything?"

He shook his head. "Not really. Again, I was in college. We weren't that close. All I knew was that she infuriated our parents and they packed her off to London for the season. And there she stayed because she met Nigel."

"Ah." Sister took the phone back. "I don't know why I'm determined to find that cowhorn. Find out what this is really about. It can't be that much, really, and it was a long time ago."

Tedi poured Sister more tea. "People are still fascinated by the bizarre affair and that was what, the beginning of the nineteenth century?" Tedi

155

named a scandal of illicit love, the possibility of infanticide. Still no one knew what happened but, despite the accused man—a Randolph, no less—being cleared in the court, the scandal greatly reduced the power of the Randolph family. The name still held cachet but the political and economic power had faded over the ensuing two centuries.

"Who can resist a good mystery?" Sister smiled at her old friend.

"Did Louis the Fourteenth have a twin?" Edward added. "And for decades people believed the Czar, the Empress, and the children still lived. The bones weren't found until fairly recently. God, what an awful story."

"That it is." It flashed in Sister's mind that perhaps old bones would be found again. She kept this to herself.

"The pack's doing so well." Tedi beamed. "You know the day we elected you Master of the Hunt was a good day and what, over forty years ago?"

Sister groaned. "I've lost count but thank you."

"Foxglove." Edward named the place they would hunt tomorrow. "Aren't you glad you don't need to print up a fixture card for cubbing?"

"Am." She put down her cup. "Just gives me fits. You never know what's going to happen with weather, with a landowner. Well, there isn't a Master in the United States or Canada that doesn't deal with this."

"England, Australia, New Zealand, and are they still hunting in Scotland?" Tedi inquired.

"I should know and I don't. What's so funny is that banning hunting in England now means more people are hunting than ever before. Can you imagine Congress in the middle of the Iraq War spending so much time on foxhunting? It just makes one wonder, especially as I have always looked up to England."

"Let's not congratulate ourselves." Tedi laughed. "I'm sure we can descend into irresponsibility and silliness as easily as Parliament. We pick different issues, or better yet, we make them up to cover the real issues."

"Tedi, you cynic." Sister laughed.

"Old age." Tedi laughed back.

The Bancrofts had about ten years on Sister, Edward being a bit older than his wife. Perhaps there's a point at which one has seen it all.

Driving home, Sister called Ben Sidell from her cellphone.

"Master."

"Sheriff. Are you going to hunt tomorrow?"

"Wouldn't miss it."

"Good. Give me a few minutes after the hunt. I have a favor to ask."

"Anything."

When Sister got home she parked, walked to the kennels, and opened the door to the office where Shaker was pouring over pedigree papers.

"Studious."

"Trying."

"Well, we do need to think about breeding. It looks as though we have a good number of hounds but, as you know, if you don't keep up you soon lose out."

He nodded, for any hunt loses about ten percent of its hounds a year. Usually this wasn't due to death but to older fellows needing to be retired, and a few hounds that would be drafted to another hunt—especially if that hunt needed some of Jefferson Hunt's bloodlines, which had remained, for more than a century, well-defined, well-documented, and proven in the field. This was no easy task. Then again, a hound might become injured, pull a ligament, and its hunting days were over; usually, the hound would be claimed by a hunt member, where the lucky girl or boy flopped on the couch in the house.

"Mind if I sit across from you?"

"No."

The club, when it refurbished the kennel back in the seventies, had created a large storage room for past documents, photograph albums, even filing correspondence, some going back to 1887.

Flicking on the lights, Sister scanned the shelves, pulling down a leather-bound book, an expense the club still fielded. Each year's hound list was documented, a pedigree per page, photographs of each hound and perhaps a comment or two concerning each. Each year also contained hunt staff photos. Some prior masters kept meticulous hunting diaries, also filed. Sister did not do that, much as she admired the practice. She just didn't have time, plus she never felt she was a good writer, wouldn't properly describe the hunts. So far she hadn't been able to bribe anyone to do it for her, although some members maintained their own diaries.

Walking the shelves, the years embossed on the spines of the dark green Moroccan leather, shining in gold, she pulled out 1954 and joined Shaker.

She pored over the pedigrees, the notes written by Wesley Carruthers in a fine, masculine script, in black ink. People cared about such things then, and a man's hand was usually different from a lady's, hers having more flourishes; often she used a finer pen nib.

"H-m-m."

"H-m-m, what?" Shaker smiled at her as he noticed it was an old book, although he didn't know the year.

"The writing changes after February." She read some more. "Now it's Ralph Franklin, Bobby's grandfather."

"Did he hunt the hounds? I never heard that."

"No. He was the first whipper-in. Maybe Weevil was training him." Sister looked up at

159

Shaker. "Not a bad idea to have more than one person who can keep records."

"And then Weevil vanished?"

"1954. Anyway, I'll check with Ben Sidell tomorrow and ask him to allow me to look at the county records. A date of disappearance has to have been recorded."

"Boss, sounds like a good story."

"I think it might be but it doesn't have an end. He was never found. I'm just checking to see if he kept good records, which he did." She read more, flipped more pages. "The only criticism I can level at Weevil, as he was known, is that he was a little loose about naming hounds."

"How so?"

"Well, most hunts use the first initial of the mother to name the children. So we have Dasher, Dreamboat, and Dragon out of Delia, the father being Middleburg Why. He has named some of these hounds willy-nilly. Let's say the mother was"—she looked down—"Rachel. The puppies are Roger, Regina, Christine. See what I mean?"

"H-m-m. Odd."

Sister had before her a clue, but she didn't know it.

CHAPTER 12

The Sunday twilight finally gave way to darkness by eight-thirty. Athena, the great horned owl, over two-feet tall with a four-foot wingspread, wings folded, would have dozed off except for Bitsy's gossip. The screech owl, all of eight-and-a-half-inches tall, should have been named Town Crier. Her wingspan, at twenty inches, suited her little body. This unlikely friendship had begun when both were owlets born in Pattypan Forge, the large abandoned forge at After All Farm. This well-built foundry, first stone laid in 1792, served generations of After All's owners. People came from all over central Virginia to have iron things fabricated. The foundry fell into disuse in the 1920s as cheap axles, wagon rims, and small hooks were being made elsewhere, some even out of the country. Steel had become easily available and it was lighter than iron. Those war-torn nations after World War I produced many things cheaper later, too.

The building, interior intact, but old windows broken, had served as lodging for many creatures, Athena and Bitsy being just two. Once mature, both owls had left the forge to establish their own nests. Athena borrowed that of a great blue heron near Roughneck Farm. Bitsy made a wonderful nest up in the rafters of the stable at Sister's farm. Neighbors and friends, they would often cruise over the pastures together, the screech owl flapping many times to Athena's one great swoosh. She kept up, though.

Tonight, stars bright, they sat in the apple orchard.

Comet left Tootie's cabin to begin hunting.

"Maybe we should follow him. He'll push out mice," Bitsy suggested.

"In time. No hurry. I'm not hungry." She turned her majestic head. *"You?"*

"No. Tootie left part of a ham sandwich on the tack trunk in the aisle. I pulled out the ham. I really like ham."

Athena chortled. *"Well, you'll have to kill pigs to get it."*

Bitsy didn't reply as a figure quietly approached, almost creeping down the worn path to Hangman's Ridge. Athena followed Bitsy's gaze.

Both birds of prey observed while remaining immobile.

The human, unknown to them, reached the apple orchard, going no farther. Whoever he was, the light shining in Tootie's cabin, as well as those in Shaker's little clapboard house, stopped him. He studied them. He was smart enough not to get too close to the kennels as he would have set off the hounds, many lounging outside on this lovely night. The temperature, just dipping to the high 50s, felt wonderful to the hounds, as it did to the owls.

Except for the stars, the moon wouldn't rise until about eleven-thirty and it was just a few days after a new moon, so darkness prevailed. The human pulled a paper from his jean jacket, clicked on a tiny flashlight, studied it, looked up at the surroundings again, then turned, heading back up to the ridge.

Curious, the birds followed. Their flight, silent, allowed them to spy without being noticed. They moved from tree to tree, finally stopping at the top of Hangman's Ridge. They kept just to the edge of the wide expanse. The human never knew they followed him.

Glancing at the huge old hangman's tree, he shivered, hurried to the path on the other side.

Athena spoke. *"Never saw him before. Strange that a human would come down the ridge, then go back up again."*

"Young. Walks young," the little owl noted.

A light wind swept across the ridge, a low moan with it.

"They never leave, do they?" Bitsy's golden eye focused on the tree.

"Well, we will." Athena lifted off, opening her wings, gliding down the path back to Roughneck Farm.

Bitsy, next to her, opined, *"Being hanged. Imprisons them, I think."*

"They should have the sense to shut up."

"If they'd had sense they wouldn't have been hanged in the first place," Bitsy said about the ghosts.

Athena didn't argue, instead offering, *"Let's shadow Comet. Will drive him crazy."*

As they reached the gray fox just working across the pasture, crouching low, he looked up. *"Don't spoil my hunting."*

"You aren't going to get anything," Athena taunted him. *"You're spoiled eating all the leftovers from the cabin."*

"Gotta keep my skills up." He stopped, crouched flat to watch three does emerge from the woods that marked After All's property line.

Athena hooted, noting the deer, *"You aren't that good."*

As the owls and Comet bantered, Crawford walked into his office.

"You aren't going to work, are you?" Marty, DVD in hand, asked. "I thought we were going to watch *La La Land.*"

He smiled at her. "I'll be right there. Just wanted to check some data."

"I've heard that before."

"No, really. I'll be right there."

As she left for the small, comfortable media room, he clicked on his computer, sat down. Scrolling along, he suddenly stopped. An icon of a devil thumbing his nose appeared. The drawing, probably nineteenth-century, was familiar to him, but he didn't know where he had first seen it. What was it doing in his files?

He read on. The icon appeared again, with a cartoon puff coming from his mouth, a sentence inside: *Got two years of files. Many thanks.*

"Marty!"

Hearing the tone of his voice, she came right in. "What?"

"Look."

She walked behind him, bent over as he showed her the devil, kept going, then read the final message. "Whoever this is even got your blueprints"—she paused—"all the drawings for Old Paradise, the ruins, the outbuildings. Why would anyone want your files?"

She thought, then answered her own question. "To see if they can figure out what comes next. Perhaps. To find a pattern in your investments, your land purchase."

"For the last two years?"

"You've done a lot in the last two years. And you've been investigating sites for a satellite campus for Custis Hall. If someone happens to buy land you and the school are considering, that will be a nice profit."

He flopped back in his leather chair. "Yes, it would."

"Are you close to anything?"

"Well, I've looked at land around Zion Crossroads. Too expensive now, so I'll keep looking east. As for land across the James, Buckingham County—nothing. This is all the very early stages."

"True, but if someone had enough money to gamble a bit, early is better. But how did they get into your files?"

"I don't know, but I need better security. Christ, I'm paying enough as it is."

"Crawford, the Pentagon's been hacked, the Democratic National Party has been hacked. No one is really safe—I don't care what our government says."

He exhaled loudly. "You're right about that, but why would whoever did this taunt me? A devil thumbing his nose."

"Well, he has a sense of humor."

CHAPTER 13

"Yom Kippur," Betty said, riding a set with Sister and Tootie. "September thirty, Saturday's hunt is Yom Kippur."

"I'm afraid I have much for which to atone." Sister patted Rickyroo. "Fortunately, as a Christian maybe I can get away with it."

"Ha." Betty noted a startled woodcock flying up out of the wildflower field. "You can do better than that."

"Well, what is a Christian but a Jew with a life insurance policy?" Sister came back at her, then turned to Tootie. "You might want to ride ahead of us in case there is a lightning strike."

Tootie smiled. "Matchplay and I will stick it out. It is something, isn't it, to think that a religious observance is thousands of years old?"

"That it is," Sister agreed. "Impressive. Beautiful and binding. I'd like to think that Christians would be aware that September thirtieth is Saint Jerome's Day, one of the church fathers born, m-m-m, born 342."

"Didn't he go suffer in the desert?"

"Good for you, Betty." Sister beamed at her dear friend.

"Catechism. Amazing what sticks up there."

She tapped her cap with her everyday crop, applewood with a knob end.

" 'We are by nature sinful and unclean.' " Tootie began the Nicene Creed.

"Tootie, catechism?" Betty was astonished.

"Yes, ma'am. Chicago has an enormous Catholic population, and it's not just the Poles and the Irish. So I was packed off every Saturday for two years to study catechism."

"But I thought you all were confirmed at seven?" Sister, an Episcopalian, wondered.

"We are. Not Tootie." Betty answered. "The serious stuff comes later for Episcopalians. I mean, yes, you have baby catechism to become confirmed, but usually in your teens they throw the book at you, for lack of a better term."

"I never hunt without my rosary beads." Tootie laughed at herself. "But as you know I'm not much of a churchgoer. All that dogma." She stuck out her tongue.

"Do you think that's what's responsible for people falling away from the church? The numbers are ever growing," Sister, curious, wondered.

"Well, it hasn't helped." Betty spoke right up. "But think of it, Sister. When I was a kid, crèches could be displayed in front of public buildings during Christmas. We said a prayer to start each day in school, along with the Pledge of Allegiance. I never felt that these things were being forced down my throat. It was just the way things were."

"I can't imagine that. If my school, Custis Hall, had put up a crèche they would have been sued," Tootie noted.

"Times have changed and as you know, I sit on the board for Custis Hall. It's getting worse. Here's the thing—" Sister picked up a little trot as they moved through the wildflower field filled with yellows and reds, oranges and lavenders, the fall colors. "Why not celebrate everyone's faith? Yom Kippur, Eades. You name it. Maybe we'd all learn more about one another."

"The atheists would have a fit." Betty ducked a swirl of swallowtail butterflies. "Wow."

"Beautiful, isn't it." Sister watched the rising cloud wings fluttering. "Seems to me, Betty, the atheists could learn from these holidays, ceremonies, too. After all, religion has been one of the strongest forces throughout history, so they can take it as a history lesson. Other people can take it as an expression of faith."

Tootie, riding out a playful buck from the three-year-old Matchplay, laughed, then added, "Kind of a good idea. I'm not going to sit down and read about religion—I'm not really interested in it—but even I'd learn from these kinds of events."

Sister kicked into an easy canter. They loped along for a half mile, slipped down to a trot then to a walk, popped over the hog's back between

Roughneck and After All, turned, popped right back, a good lesson for the horses, especially young Matchplay, then back over to a walk.

Betty turned to Tootie. "It's a lot easier if he's out with older horses."

"He's willing, but he wants to see everything. Midshipman is a little calmer." She named the other young Thoroughbred, both of them had come from Broad Creek Stables as yearlings.

"With a bit of care, I think they can both be started in Second Flight once we survive Opening Hunt, the cast of thousands." Sister laughed.

Everyone who could attended Opening Hunt whether on horseback, on foot, or in a car. This day begins formal hunting, which means clothing changes. One wears a black frock, or scarlet if one is a male who has earned his colors. Tails, called shadbellys for the ladies, weazlebellys for the gentlemen, turn even someone not blessed by Nature into a dazzling specimen. Every master, every huntsman, and all the whippers-in just pray to get through it. All those people plus all those not riding presented some very quick judgment calls, like "Do I kill him now or later?" Or, "I've got to remember to thank Jennifer for pulling the chestnut out of the fire."

Jefferson Hunt's Opening Hunt was Saturday, November 4, enough time, one hoped, to have the pack working well together, as well as staff.

Fortunately, Jefferson Hunt excelled in both

170

departments, and the staff all liked one another. Hounds loved their master and the huntsman. The staff horses really loved their job. Ears forward, eyes bright, maybe a little wiggle before takeoff, hunt horses were born to hunt. There's a deep joy in being with an animal doing what it was born to do. Quite the reverse of seeing a Saint Bernard, the most loving of dogs, in a big city.

Walking back, the warmth chasing away those pains one accumulates with age, Sister and Betty nattered away. From time to time, Tootie would chime in. No aches or pains just yet.

"So Tootie, has your mother had her first riding lesson? Sister told me she wants to ride." Betty could hardly believe this.

"She did. She met Sam Tuesday at Beasley Hall," she said, naming Crawford's estate. "She was shocked that he made her clean the horse first." Tootie laughed. "But then she said she got into a rhythm and liked it. Her first lesson. A walk with Sam on the ground: success. Actually, going there will be easy as she passes the place on her way to Beveridge Hundred. She'll be all moved in tomorrow."

"Wednesday. That was fast." Betty whistled.

"She said she'd stay with me a week. She tipped a few days over," Tootie matter-of-factly added. "That was okay. The place is really nice. All the furniture was there, so she only had to buy food, special things that she wanted. She has to have six-hundred-count Egyptian cotton sheets. Stuff like that."

"Well, I noticed the new car. It's beautiful." Betty liked the Lincoln.

"She wants to buy me a new car."

"Let her," Betty fired back quickly.

"I don't know."

"Oh, Tootie, she's trying to make up for lost time and your Toyota has the flu. Find a good used car. That ought to diminish the guilt." Betty laughed.

Sister piped up, "She's right, Tootie. Winter will be here soon enough and that car is a hazard. How many times last winter did Gray or I make you take one of our SUVs?"

"I know. I just couldn't take his new car. Your Tahoe"—she grinned—"okay."

Sister's six-year-old Jeep, hard used, had been traded in for a Tahoe. She thought it was too big but the dealer, not far, could be easily reached in an emergency. All her friends who drove Tahoes liked them. She'd thought all these damn SUVs guzzled gas like a drunk grabbing a bottle of Ripple. However, she flipped down the two back rows, piled Raleigh and Rooster in, turned on Sirius radio, a first, and realized she liked it a lot. She could also drive hounds if need be. *Now I'm a carbon criminal,* she thought to herself.

Saint Just flew overhead, the large raven casting a glance down at them.

"Damn, he's big." Betty shielded her eyes from the sun.

"Gives me the creeps when the hanging tree is full of crows or ravens." Sister shuddered. "Hey, did I tell you we're hunting Old Paradise Saturday with Crawford?"

"What?" Both women nearly bellowed.

Rickyroo's ears swiveled. *"Humans make such awful sounds."*

Outlaw laughed. *"At least they aren't singing."*

Matchplay said, *"I like it when Shaker sings."*

Rickyroo agreed. *"A soothing deep voice. Anyway, looks like Saturday is going to be a big one."*

"Should be." Outlaw nodded his head once, then looked back at Betty, whom he dearly loved.

"When did this happen?" Betty wanted to know.

"After yesterday's hunt." Sister went on to explain her conversation with Sara Bateman Sunday. "She called after Tuesday's hunt to ask if she could bring Tom Tipton to Old Paradise Saturday. He wanted to see Old Paradise more than he wanted to have lunch in Richmond. So I called Crawford, explained everything, and do you know, he readily agreed? All he wanted to know is who would hunt the joint packs."

"That's a shock." Betty leaned back in her saddle, an old Prix de Nation, which fit her.

Sister, on the contrary, rode in a sixteen-and-a-half-inch Hermès, fifty years old, for the same reason: It fit her. "I said Shaker and Skiff could work together. They seem to like each other. Anyway, I was pleasantly surprised."

"There's got to be a hook somewhere." Betty's eyes narrowed.

"Maybe hearing Tom Tipton's background did it."

Tootie asked, "Who is Tom Tipton?"

"Sorry, honey. I should have told you straight up. He whipped-in to The Jefferson Hunt starting when he was in his twenties, pretty sure it was that, and left in 1959. He carried the horn from 1954 to 1959, then was offered a bunch more money to carry the horn for the Richmond Hunt, which he did. Everyone who ever worked with him was better for it. This was before my time. Anyway, I've chatted with him a few times when I visited Sara in Richmond. A real character." She paused. "Forgot to tell you, I wanted to take him to lunch to ask him about Weevil."

"Ah." Betty exhaled.

Tootie knew a bit of the story. Her curiosity wasn't aroused but then she was dealing with her mother and the divorce. Her father was really hitting up the media. Her mother remained unusually calm. Tootie knew Yvonne had a card up her sleeve.

CHAPTER 14

Two white heads, leaning together, reflected the light in Daniella's living room. Gray listened as his aunt and Tom Tipton galloped down memory lane. Daniella, a few years older than Tom, had formerly dazzled the young man. As her people were in the Thoroughbred business, they knew each other. Often if a horse didn't make it to the track it was trained as a foxhunter. Daniella, thanks to her great beauty, was used by her father to attend the meets and comment on how glorious a client looked on the potential sale. This worked a treat if the client was male. If female, not quite so much.

"Remember when Brenden DuCharme got hung over the tree branch? Oh Lord." Tom laughed, his voice still strong, not wavering at all.

Daniella clapped her hands in delight. "Damned fool. Turning around to look back at his wife during a hard run. Didn't see the tree looming ahead, the branch caught him right in the middle and there he dangled."

"And Margaret rode right by him!" Tom, overcome with mirth, wiped tears from his eyes.

"I happened to be driving Daddy's truck— he liked it if I could make specific comments about the hunt to the client. Saw you ride toward

Brenden to help him and heard Weevil cuss you like a dog."

" 'Hounds are more important than Brenden. He'll fall down eventually.' So I left him suspended there and hurried to the hounds to evade sulfurous speech. Tell you what, Weevil always put hounds first."

"Do you remember the time that buyer from Boston—rode with the rich hunt right outside of Boston—asked me if I was colored? Said I was whiter than white women he knew."

"Yes, I do, and I remember it was at the breakfast afterwards at Skidby. Could have heard a pin drop." Tom nodded.

"And Weevil came over and punched his lights out." Now Daniella had tears in her eyes.

"Those were the days." Tom smiled.

"And the nights."

They both laughed.

Gray interjected. "Tom, Skidby is being restored. By Helen Lutrell's granddaughter. She married a rich doctor."

"You don't say. Helen was a good woman. Always gave hunt staff a gift at Christmas. I reckon people don't do that anymore."

"They do." Gray jumped in again. "Sister gives hunt staff a bonus, but club members pitch in so it's one check from members as opposed to lots of small checks."

A knock on the door interrupted the reveries.

Gray got up, opened the door, whispered, "They're ready."

Sara had dropped Tom off so the old acquaintances could catch up. She'd brought a small cooler, then brought another one as she would drive Tom, while Gray would drive his aunt. Once Daniella heard Tom Tipton would be at the Saturday hunt at Old Paradise, she wanted to go. However, each of these nonagenarians should sit in the front passenger seat so Gray elected to give up his Saturday hunt to drive his aunt. After the hunt they could all join in at the breakfast.

Daniella, dressed in a long suede skirt, a tweed coat, and a white open-collared shirt with an Hermès scarf tied around her neck, looked every bit the non-riding follower.

Tom, also in a tweed, wore his old breeches and boots. He said that in case anyone needed a hand, he'd mount up, but really he wanted to show he could still fit into his hunt kit.

Just because they were in their nineties didn't mean all vanity had fled.

Sara had bought single-cask bourbon for Daniella and rye for Tom.

"Gray," she whispered in his ear. "I've got special stuff for your aunt. Cooler's in your car. Oh, two crystal glasses. God forbid Aunt Daniella's lips should touch plastic."

The two rounded up their charges as Tom and

Daniella argued that either one would be happy to sit in the back. A lie, of course.

As Sara drove Tom to Old Paradise, she filled him in on Crawford's shrewd waiting game. How he had bought out the brothers, how the two non-speaking men had agreed without needing to see each other.

"H-m-m. What's he going to do?"

"Bring it back. Right now he's got cattle on some of it. Has already restored the stable."

"Rich. Rich. Rich."

"M-m-m, with the personality trait of a man who has made his own money."

Tom shrugged. "At least he's given people jobs."

"That he has. Every time I go by there more men are working, and that's just what I can see in the fields. Fence repair, some stone fences, fertilizing, hay along the roadside. Cut now, of course. And he's got the old house plans."

"You don't say. With digging maybe they'll find the Old Paradise treasure."

"Wouldn't that be something?" Sara smiled.

Within twenty-five minutes, the Chapel Cross area slowed them due to the horse trailers. Sara turned down the main drive to Old Paradise.

Tom, hand gripping the handrest, stared. "I haven't been back here in thirty years. One of the last times I rode with Sister. Great day!" He saw the stables.

"Incredible, isn't it?"

"They're beautiful. Now—oh, Sara, the people who have gone on, the people who I wish could see this."

"Peter Wheeler?"

"For one. Big Ray. Well, I reckon I'll see them soon enough."

"Tom, only the good die young." Sara shot that at him, and he laughed at the common phrase.

Daniella hadn't seen the foundation work at the house ruins, the four majestic Corinthian columns, guardians to survival despite all. Even the Virginia creeper had been cleaned off just as it was turning red for fall.

"I can't wait to see the house when it's finished. Years, I bet."

"He has over forty people just working on the house alone." Gray told her about the packing around the foundation—what Sister called goo—the backfill, and now the prep work for rebuilding.

Sister, wearing her bespoke tweed, resplendent on Lafayette, her gray, drew all eyes to her. Next to her sat Crawford on Czpaka.

As this was a cubbing hunt, individual tastes showed more than during formal hunting. It was coolish this September 30 morning, for which both Masters were thankful, as were the two huntsmen and hounds. People donned tweeds in various colors all suitable for them, happy for the temperature. Kasmir wore a sleek beige tweed with a subtle thin green-and-magenta windowpane check. A perfectly tied green tie, matching the thin stripe, set off his look. His boots, peanut brittle in color, and his cap, brown, marked him as a man who had grasped all the subtleties. Alida, next to him, shone in a simple blue herringbone, brown field boots, and an understated dark blue tie with a white stripe. As her eyes were clear blue, one couldn't help but notice them or their effect on others.

Every single person really made an effort. Their horses gleamed, their spurs, whether Hammerheads or Prince of Wales, sparkled. Their gloves, paper thin as it would warm up, were usually mustard. A few were a light, handsome brown. The bridles and bits shone as much as the boots and spurs.

Crawford, having learned proper turnout when he hunted with The Jefferson Hunt, like Sister, wore a bespoke coat in a light green, lighter than Keeper's tweed, with an expensive old army green tie enlivened by thin orange stripes edged in gold. Understated, he made a good showing.

All gathered in the huge European courtyard at the stables. The workmen couldn't help themselves; they'd drifted over to admire the pageant. One young man with a bushy black moustache tipped his ball cap to the ladies.

The two packs stood together looking at Shaker

and Skiff. They shone. They wanted to go.

After the Masters thanked everyone, Sister especially thanking Crawford for having the hunt at Old Paradise, they walked off.

Sam Lorillard winked at Aunt Daniella.

Yvonne, in Margaret DuCharme's car, as Margaret thought this would be the best way to see Old Paradise, noticed how much Sam looked like Gray. In her one lesson, she hadn't focused too much on the man. Her attention had been riveted on the horse, which seemed so big. Sam looked as though he was born on a horse. Poor though he was, his turnout was impeccable. Hunt clothing is made to last. His jacket, seventy years old if it was a day, a houndstooth pattern much preferred in the 1940s, fit him like a second skin. Crawford had bought him a pair of Dehner boots last year, as his old boots had finally disintegrated. He wore a robin's-egg-blue silk four-in-hand tie, mustard gloves. Passing Margaret and Yvonne, he tapped his brown cap with his crop.

"You're the model. Think of the damage you could do to the men if you were out there," Margaret teased Yvonne.

The spectacle, not lost on Tootie's mother, secretly inflamed her. She would be out there, and she would look divine.

She smiled. "I am off men."

Margaret, who knew of the divorce thanks

to Vic Harris's stupid media attack on his wife accusing her of deserting him, simply said, "Every woman says that at some time in her life. Ah, there's my fella." She waved to Ben. "He's the sheriff."

Yvonne blinked. She'd heard about the DuCharmes. Tootie had filled her in as best the young woman could. Here was someone from a once powerful family, a family that made its fortune in 1812, dating a sheriff?

She couldn't help herself. "I thought Virginians were, well, Tootie went to Custis Hall and—"

"Snobs." Margaret shrugged as she cut on the motor. "You can find them anywhere. Things have changed here. I've seen a lot of change and I'm in my early forties. Dad talks about it. Says it really started after World War Two. Mostly it's for the good."

"I hope that's true everywhere, but I don't know. All this divisiveness."

"Media. All media-driven, I swear." Margaret then gulped. "Sorry, you and your ex own a magazine, TV channels."

"You don't have to apologize. Bad news sells." She half smiled. "There's something in the human animal that loves misery, so long as it's happening to other people."

"Ain't that the truth!" Margaret crept about fifty yards behind Sara Bateman's and Gray's cars. "I know you know a little bit about hunting because of Tootie. But I'll give you my running commentary, and as we pass things I'll tell you what they are or were. When the hunt is over I'll show you the big house—well, the foundation for the big house—and I'll show you the dependency where Dad and I lived and the duplicate where my uncle and his wife lived, not close together but you'll get the idea. In the nineteenth century, up until the 1920s, this place had two hundred and fifty people working on it."

"Dear God. I can't imagine the payroll."

"Fierce, but you could make money in agriculture then. People were housed as part of their compensation. Now that doesn't count. Minimum wage is as though everyone works in cities. Most of the workers lived in clapboard houses scattered around the five thousand acres. And given that Norfolk and Southern eventually came through this area, that just bumped up business."

"The 1920s?"

"Depression after World War One. And the influenza epidemic. Hurt everyone everywhere, I think. The economy began to improve, but young people trickled away. After World War Two the trickle became a flood and Dad said the G.I. Bill, wonderful though it was, lured men from farming."

"I'm not strong on history."

"I'll make up for that." Margaret grinned.

"What a voice. Asa. Oh, now everyone's on it and good news, Crawford's hounds are right there. He's gone through huntsmen like potato chips; the pack has been one riot after another. Hired this lady last year and for whatever reason, he listens to her, and to his wife. Miracles do happen."

Yvonne, window open, listened. The sound of hoofbeats was now deafening. Blended with two packs of hounds on full throttle she felt the hair on the back of her neck stand up. She would join them someday, whatever it took. This must have been what a cavalry charge sounded like.

Slowly driving toward them from the opposite direction was a young man, broad beard trimmed, baseball cap squarely on his head. The old Rangler, large spots with paint rubbed off, had seen better days, but it was running. The bed was filled with fence boards. He smiled and waved as he approached, then slowed.

"They're on fire. Thought I'd better get out of the way."

Margaret smiled. "Sounds great, Hank."

He passed, and she continued slowly. She knew some of the workers and he was gentlemanly, knew hunting, and worked very hard.

The combined packs hooked toward Chapel Cross, the intersection now three miles east, and a mile after that the railroad tracks, Tattenhall Station.

Hounds poured over the fence onto the road, called, obviously, Chapel Road.

Skiff took the sturdy black painted coop first, landing in the grass strip along the road. Shaker followed. Hounds sped across the tertiary road and blew through Binky DuCharme's Gulf station, the sign from the 1950s still hanging and intact. With no fences to impede them, hounds picked up speed, churning onto the front lawn of the chapel where they stopped.

"Try the graveyard," Reuben, one of the Dumfrieshire hounds, suggested.

The field clattered up, halted. Tricolor Jefferson Hounds and black and tan Dumfrieshire hounds worked together through the graveyard.

Diana knew this territory from her youth. She sat to study the terrain. No mud puddles offered quick kills to scent. The ditch by the road, when wet, also gave a fox the chance to slip away, baffle the pursuit.

Noses down, hounds diligently worked the immaculately kept graveyard. A whine here and there testified to their frustration. The two huntsmen, on the edge of the graveyard, where many markers were two centuries old or more, kept still and quiet. Let the hounds work it out. They could pack them up and move off soon enough.

Parker, young, came up to Diana. *"How does the fox do that?"*

She replied, *"I think I know. Follow me."*

Dutifully following his idol, Parker returned to the graveyard, walked past it to a filled wheelbarrow at the edge. The sexton, Adolfo Vega, upon hearing the hounds, had left his chore, returning to his house to wait it out. While he liked the hounds fine he didn't want to be in the middle of them, or even worse, the riders.

Diana backtracked to the road where they lost the scent. Asphalt or packed dirt holds scent so long as there's moisture in the air and it's coolish, but the temperature was now in the mid 50s. Not impossible but not great.

"He walked down the road, turned to the chapel. Put your nose down. Faint and fading," Diana ordered.

Wanting to make a show, Parker opened his mouth.

"Don't you dare," she reprimanded him.

"But he's been here. He turned here."

"Use your head, Parker. If you open everyone will rush here, and then what? This is a smart, smart fox. Just follow me." She walked to the wheelbarrow. *"We don't want everyone fouling what little scent there is."*

The other hounds hadn't given up, but they had checked every inch in that graveyard.

From the wheelbarrow, Diana took one stride to the first tombstone. Then the next. Parker watched, astonished.

"On top of the tombstones," she sang out as she stood on her hind legs.

In a flash every hound there ran to a tombstone. They opened one by one.

Diana, in the lead, reached the easternmost boundary of the graveyard. Woods marked the end of the chapel property and the beginning of Orchard Hill.

The fox didn't use the woods. Instead, Diana still working intensely, he jumped from tombstone to tombstone at the graveyard's edge, then with a mighty leap hit the ground, ran straight to the road, and there again scent became difficult.

Betty Franklin, now on the southern side of the intersection, didn't move. Hounds slowly walked toward her, working the grassy edge. Diana, in the lead, Parker fighting for his place next to her, moved deliberately.

"He had to get off this road sometime," she advised the youngster.

Ardent, right behind, working in tandem with Reuben, agreed. *"He didn't go to Tattenhall Station. Dragon and Dreamboat ran over there to check. That s.o.b. is using the road."*

Sister turned Lafayette's head toward the west. Crawford followed suit as did the field, still waiting patiently. The sight of hounds on their hind legs, literally walking with the scent, excited the people about as much as a terrific run.

People who don't hunt don't give foxes credit. Clearly, they've never read Aesop or writers from thousands of years ago. Throughout history, people have remarked on the intelligence of foxes. Even if they had read such materials, modern readers would assume this was all in the name of a good story.

Seeing is believing. Those people who hunted September 30, including those in the cars, would remember this day for the rest of their lives.

Tom was so overcome he couldn't speak.

Diana reached the intersection, lifted her nose for a moment, took her bearings. Picking up a trot she returned to the big coop they'd jumped out of Old Paradise.

"Over!" She scrambled over, immediately followed by Parker.

The two packs rushed for the jump; other hounds wriggled under the board fencing. And yes, they found fresh scent. Running, stretched to the fullest, the extraordinary grace of a flying hound mesmerized the people even as they kept their legs on their horses, hands forward. If anyone feared a hard gallop they got over it.

Betty kept up on the right shoulder of the pack. Tootie, farther in the pasture, hung on the left. Sam Lorillard, the only whipper-in Skiff had, moved about a football field behind Tootie. An experienced whipper-in, Sam knew that should the pack reverse, he had to be there and he'd be up front. The burden would fall on him to protect them from the road.

Sister turned for a second. So far the field kept up, no stragglers, no one hit the ground. Farther behind, Bobby Franklin kept everyone together.

The music was deafening. Both Shaker and Skiff blew "All on" in unison. This meant all the hounds were on the line. Then they blew "Gone Away," and a prettier sound was rarely heard.

Everyone's blood was up. Another jump at the end of the pasture, three logs tied together, challenged them onto a cleared path in thick woods. The fox, having a sense of humor, ran them through an illegal still destroyed a few years back. Riders circumvented the debris, heading up. They were literally at the foot of the Blue Ridge Mountains. Then he turned. Well ahead and with time to think, he came back down and, stretched to the max, he launched into a hard-running creek, water coursing down between crevices in the eastern face of the mountains.

The otters, merry fellows, hearing the commotion, quickly disappeared into their dens.

A red-shouldered hawk, high up, watched everything, knowing mice would scamper everywhere once the horses had passed.

Hounds reached the creek. Dragon jumped in, swimming to the far bank. He began searching for scent. Others joined him. Diana walked along the creek side. Yes, the fox had leapt in where

Dragon followed, but she knew he wouldn't emerge directly opposite. Also, he could just as easily double back if he swam downstream.

She walked and walked but whatever he'd done, he'd skunked them.

Flanks heaved; people slipped a hand in a coat pocket retrieving a handkerchief to wipe their brows. As this was a well-trained field of people as well as a well-trained pack of hounds no one spoke. But the sounds of heavy breathing, riders petting the necks of their horses, horses blowing out their nostrils, kept the otters securely in their dens.

If only the people would leave, then they could play some more.

Shaker and Skiff conferred.

"Let's head back to the open fields. I don't want to climb the mountains, do you?" the attractive huntsman asked.

Shaker nodded. "Good call. It's early in the season. Not everyone is quite hunting fit."

Skiff peered at the field, turned her horse toward the path leading to the westernmost field. Took them twenty minutes to reach the field.

Shaker hopped down, opened a gate. No jump welcomed them in this fence line, nasty barbed wire. If they picked up another fox there'd be jumping enough, farther along. Save the horse.

He swung back into the saddle with enviable ease, calling over his shoulder, "Gate, please."

Now the people chattered, as hounds weren't working.

Ronnie Haslip, the treasurer, dapper, eyes wide, swore to his old grade-school friend Xavier, "My God, what a run."

"The graveyard. How many years have we hunted with Sister? I have never seen anything like that."

These two men, in their forties now, had been best friends with RayRay, Sister's son. When the fourteen-year-old boy was killed in the farm accident in 1974, it hit the boys hard. They vowed to watch over Sister as RayRay would, if alive. They kept their vow, remembering to bring her gifts on special days, dropping by. She loved them beyond words.

Hounds moved within sight of the stable, trotting toward the southeast where Little Dalby and Beveridge Hundred lay. Had they continued east they would have been back at Chapel Cross but Tinsel stopped, her stern starting to move. Roger, one of Crawford's hounds from his R litter, joined her. They opened, heading directly southeast. Now the pack was all on again, moving fast but not at blinding speed for scent proved tricky. All wound up at the rock outcropping where Sarge, Earl's son, rested. He'd gone out early in the morning to a cutover cornfield on Old Paradise. His father, Earl, had stayed in the stable. Earl's den, a disguised burrow, led under the tack room. He had another den in a stall. Life was good. This morning Sarge drew close, then saw the horse trailers so headed back to his new den in the boulders. He'd made improvements. No marauder could touch him.

"He's in there," Roger bellowed.

"He'll stay in there, too," Pookah grumbled.

Folks, hunting hard for two and a half hours, finally turned back to the trailers. Had the day been cool, say a February day, everyone hunting fit, maybe they'd have kept casting but hounds performed beautifully. Stop while you're ahead.

Sister and Crawford rode side by side, reliving the hunt as was everyone behind them.

Ahead, Shaker and Skiff's horses walked in step, reflecting the harmony between the two huntsmen. Although they had hunted hard, hounds, heads up, stepped with a lively spring. They, too, recounted the day.

A bit of scent pushed them into a trot, but it was over before it began.

Back at the trailers, before dismounting, the two huntsmen blew in unison "Going Home," a long drawn-out melody, a touch mournful for it means the hunt is over.

In the distance, "Going Home" came back to them, deeper in tone.

Tootie, now on foot, helping Shaker load hounds, said, "That happened last time we were out here. What a strange echo."

Sister listened. Most people heard it.

Tom Tipton, getting out of Sara's car, remarked, "Sounds like a cowhorn. Who's doing a cowhorn?"

Sara shrugged. "Probably a bounceback from the mountains. Shaker and Skiff blew quite a little toodle."

Tom didn't argue with her. He just added, "Hardly anyone knows how to blow a cowhorn anymore. Weevil was good at it." He paused, smiled. "I used to think if a huntsman used the brass horn he was a Yankee."

Sara teased him. "You would."

Misty-eyed, he just tilted his head. "It's all gone now. All so far away."

Tables filled the center aisle of the main barn. Fried chicken, ham biscuits, sandwiches, sliced raw vegetables, and a variety of dips, and Crawford had a caterer slicing hot roast beef, which delighted everyone. Cooked carrots, tiny potatoes, asparagus, whatever you wanted, it was there. Most riders, having wiped down their horses, watered them, and put on a sweat sheet, zoomed straight for the bar.

A tub at the door of the stable was filled with raw carrots for the horses.

Tedi whispered in Sister's ear, "A big success. That echo was odd, wasn't it?"

"It's the second time we've heard it out here." Sister squared her shoulders. "We need to build on this success. Slowly, we've got to get Crawford to register with the MFHA as a farmer pack. That will solve a lot of problems."

Tedi sipped a perfect old-fashioned, which her husband had the bartender make for her. Crawford had hired a professional bartender as well as the caterer.

Ed came alongside. "What a hunt, and wasn't the hound work at the chapel spectacular?"

"Was." Both women agreed.

Sister made her way to Tom Tipton and Aunt Daniella, seated side by side in front of the mahogany-paneled tack room, which gave off a faint whiff of fox. Gray, on duty, fetched the drinks. Sara, juggling plates, brought their food.

"Oh, how I wish I had ridden today." Tom glowed.

"Next best thing, riding with Sara." Sister smiled.

"Who is the hound that found the scent on the tombstones? Sara thought it was one of your Ds but we were a bit behind."

"Diana."

"Extraordinary." He reached up to squeeze her hand.

"Gray has been keeping all this from me." Daniella lifted her chin. "I must come out more often." She turned to Tom. "Seeing you has lifted my spirits."

Shaker and Skiff talked hounds, enlivened by what they loved.

"You know, if you want to walk your hounds with ours it will be fine. Sister would like it. Well, you know the history. We need to get Crawford on board. No more potshots," Shaker suggested.

Chewing, as delicately as she could, a piece of divine roast beef, she swallowed. "Today ought to go a long way toward that."

Just then Crawford tapped a glass. Eventually silence prevailed.

"Allow me to show you what I'm doing at the big house."

With him leading the way, they trooped, drinks in hand, well fed, over to the four majestic in-line columns, with the long marble pediment on top. Having backfilled the foundation, the workmen now refitted any cut slabs for the basement floor, while another group checked the blueprints.

Men carried lumber, sawhorses, and tools to begin reconstruction of the house. At its prime the exterior had been a thin smooth whitish marble over the timber frame. It was supposed to resemble the mansions outside of Venice, those designed by Palladio.

As Crawford explained everything, the workmen stopped from time to time to listen.

Alfred DuCharme, Margaret's father, drove up, got out to join them.

Seeing Tom Tipton, he hurried over to greet

him. "Tom, how good to see you. My mother thought the world of you. She'd say 'Watch Tom. He's a good whipper-in.' Those were happy days, weren't they?"

The workmen stopped as Crawford nattered on. Also, Yvonne was certainly not lost on the men, but they were workers so they couldn't flirt. When Tootie came and stood next to her mother, the resemblance was astonishing. Sister noticed the men looking from one woman to the other.

Earl prayed for the people to leave. So much food had been dropped in the center aisle he would have his own feast.

Much as people admired the plans, what had already been achieved with the stables and outbuildings, they wanted to return to the food and the well-stocked bar. Alfred especially wanted to visit the bar.

Tom, transfixed, stared up at the top of the Corinthian columns.

"Come on, Huntsman. Bourbon calls." Sara followed his gaze upward. "Do you think anyone knows how to build like this anymore?"

"Yes." He took a deep breath. "But this kind of beauty isn't valued now. You go on, Sara. I'll be there in a minute. I just want to"—he paused—"remember. I was so young. It seems like yesterday."

"Okay." Sara left him as the workers started back to it.

Alone, looking out from the top of the forty-feet-long footsteps, Tom leaned on a corner column. The faces of the departed came to him, as did the feel of his favorite Thoroughbred, General Ike. How he loved that dark bay. He could almost hear Andrew, a sensational hound, along with Dietrich, a superb girl. Tears came.

"You were a good whipper-in," a familiar voice praised him.

Tom grabbed the huge column for support even though he barely could get his arms around it. He was afraid to look behind him.

"We'll never see days like that again. Fewer people, fewer roads, fewer cars. People understood hunting, even those in cities. Remember?"

Forcing himself to turn, Tom faced his huntsman. "I do. Weevil, you're dead."

Devilish smile on his handsome face, Weevil laughed low. "Maybe. But I'm here."

"How?" Tom felt his heart race.

"There are so many dimensions in life. We don't see them. The animals do. But we deny what we can't prove. I'm here. I needed to come back to Jefferson Hunt one more time. Maybe I came back to find the Old Paradise treasure. But I'm here."

Shaking, voice low, Tom managed to get out, "You won't hurt me, will you?"

Head back, laughing, Weevil answered, "If I was going to hurt you I would have done it when the trains still stopped at Tattenhall Station."

Scared or not, Tom shot back, "That wasn't my fault."

"It's always the whipper-in's fault." Weevil, smiling, pointed a finger at him. "Luckily, the whole pack made it across. Tom, you're white as a ghost."

"I'm talking to a ghost." Tom hadn't lost his wits.

"One question. Who is still alive? Who is still alive who remembers?"

"Daniella Laprade. Most everyone else is gone on. Their children, many of them, are gone, too, but there's still a lot in their sixties. Christ, we're getting old."

"Happens." Weevil paused. "When I disappeared, Brenden DuCharme accused me of stealing his wife's jewelry. I did not." Then Weevil turned, walking toward the old hay barns, all the old restored equipment sheds that lined the farm road past the stone stables.

Tom, still holding the column, breathed deep breaths. Sweat rolled down his forehead. He couldn't walk. His legs were jelly.

Below him, at the stables, the breakfast continued.

Sara, plotting with Sister about adding fixtures, hunt territory, changed the subject.

"I left Tom at the big house. He should be back

here by now. A trip down memory lane can't take that long."

"I'll go out with you. Maybe all this commotion pooped him out."

The two Masters, one active, one retired, left the stables by the enormous open wooden doors, leaded glass on top of the heavy, heavy oak.

"Uh-oh." Sara started to trot, followed by Sister.

Running up the steps like teenagers, they reached Tom, grasping the columns.

Sara put her arm around his waist. "I've got you. Sister's here. Where do you hurt?"

He shook his head but he did let go. "I saw Weevil. He spoke to me here. Right here." He took a ragged breath. "He hasn't aged."

CHAPTER 15

Sara, let's walk him to the trailers. We can sit in the cab of your car. Too many people." Sister inclined her head toward the stable.

Once in Sara's roomy vehicle, Tom loudly declaimed, "I am not crazy. I saw a dead man."

"Dead man walking." Sara repeated the common phrase.

Sister, voice quiet, reassured the shaken man. "We don't think you are crazy. Here."

Pulling out her cellphone from the inside of her tweed jacket, she played the video.

"God" was all he could say.

Sister explained how she and Marion found the video. "We don't know what to make of it."

"You feel okay?" Sara then added, "I can go fetch you a drink."

"No. Sober. I need to stay sober." He folded his hands, age spots on them, in his lap. "He looks exactly as I remember him. His voice, maybe a little scratchier, but same height, build, hair, eyes, and cocky as always."

"What did he talk about?" Sister inquired.

"Old times. He wanted to know who was still alive."

"What did you say?" Sister gently pressed.

"All gone except for Daniella Laprade. He

200

knew he'd been accused of stealing Margaret's jewelry. He said he didn't."

Sister's shoulders squared. "That's the first time I've heard that."

Tom explained, "Alfred and Binky, young men then, asked me if I knew anything. They pledged me to silence so as not to embarrass their mother. I think they knew."

"Did you see where he went?" Sara took up the questioning.

"No. I was so scared I was holding on to that column. After I saw him go behind the hay barns I shut my eyes. I couldn't walk. Could barely stand up."

"Any of us would have been frightened." Sister put her hand over his folded ones. "Did you notice what he wore?"

"Yeah, I did, kinda. He wore ratcatcher. No dust on him though."

Sister blinked, thought again. "Did he smell of horse?"

"No. At least I didn't smell that. My sniffer is still good. He gave off a bit of scent, same scent I remember." He smiled a little.

"When you and Sara followed the hunt you had the windows down?"

"Sure." He looked at Sister.

"And when Shaker and Skiff blew 'Going Home,' did you hear anything?"

"An echo." He swallowed. "It wasn't an echo.

Now I know that Weevil blew his cowhorn."

"Tom, this is an odd question, but—considering the circumstances—can you think why he has come back? Why he took his cowhorn out of the case?"

"He guarded that cowhorn. Loved it. Wouldn't let any of us blow it or touch it. Carved the hunt scene on it. Beautiful tone. Some huntsmen are techy about their horns."

"That they are." Sara started to recount just such a tale, then stopped, realizing Sister was super-focused.

Sister repeated herself. "Can you think why Weevil would come back?"

"I—Revenge? Curiosity? To see who was left?"

"So you believe he was killed? He didn't run to Paris or who knows?" Sister prodded.

"Hell, yes, I believe he was killed. If he had run away, even across the ocean, we'd eventually know. Man couldn't keep his dick in his pants." Then, realizing what he had said, he begged forgiveness. "Excuse me. I don't know what came over me."

Sara laughed. "Tom, so few men act like gentlemen around ladies these days, we are not offended."

"We are charmed." Sister grinned at her.

"You know, that was the thing about Weevil. Came from a poor family in The Plains. Started as a third whipper-in to Dickie Bywaters, the great huntsman. Made second whipper-in within a year. The boy was talented and he had good manners. But everyone did then. Didn't matter if you were rich or poor, black or white, man or woman, you had manners."

"True." Sister nodded.

"In those years I whipped-in to Weevil, I never heard him make an improper comment to a woman or give her the once-over look that some men would do. They kept their mouths shut, but their eyes were rude."

"Yeah, we know." Sara made a face.

"He was polite, proper, and just had a way about him. He could charm anybody, even the men whose wives he had, uh, *really* charmed."

"I expect one of those husbands proved immune," Sara said.

"That's what people thought at the time," Tom replied.

"What do you think? You knew him well. Whippers-in know their huntsmen inside and out. What do you think?" Sister's alto voice soothed even as she pressed some more.

Tom remained silent for some minutes, then with an inspiring breath, he said, "I was shocked. Worried. I liked him. Sure, he fooled around, but there was no meanness in him. He taught me so much about hounds and hunting. To be taught by a man who served under Dickie Bywaters was worth something."

"Indeed." Sister and Sara agreed.

"When I felt in my heart that he was really dead, I reviewed why he was murdered. I believe he was murdered. A jealous husband? An infuriated lover? A fearful father? There were candidates. Somehow I couldn't land on any of them. Couldn't put a man with the murder. Couldn't put a woman either. Sex might have been part of the reaction but, girls,"—he called them girls, as they were to him—"there was something more. I felt it then. I feel it now. I felt no hate from Weevil when I saw him. He was the same happy-go-lucky Weevil." A deep breath shook him. "Except he was dead."

CHAPTER 16

R abbit. Rabbit." Sister filed the treasurer's reports from the 1950s that she had given to Sara, who returned them. She figured Sister could always use the extra copies.

"You always say that the first day of any month." Shaker, at his desk, smiled at her.

"Yes. If you say it then it will be a good month. It's like eating black-eyed peas the minute the clock strikes the twelfth bell New Year's Eve. Good luck."

"Well, what about bad luck? The number thirteen? A black cat walking in front of you? You walking under a ladder?" His rust-colored eyebrows rose slightly in amusement.

She waved her hand dismissively. *"Pfiffle."*

"You surely believe in bad luck or you wouldn't be ensuring good luck."

"Shaker, don't be logical. I forbid it."

They both laughed.

He folded his hands together on top of his desk. "I've been thinking—"

"I'm already scared." She smiled at him, so happy in his company. "Go on. I've girded my loins."

"How about if we have a joint hound walk once a week with Skiff? She only has Sam to help her, and he's primarily working in the barn. The pack is much improved, but could use a little tightening up. With us, she'd have Betty and Tootie."

"If Crawford agrees to it, fine. As a courtesy we should take hounds there every other week; she hauls hers to us on the odd week. Say she comes here the first and third day, like Wednesday. We go there the second and fourth in the month. Remember, we're dealing with Crawford. If everything is mapped out, explained, quantified, he'll rest easy."

"Right. Hey, Sara gave you back the old treasurer's reports. Anything?"

"No. We have no bills or receipts from 1947 to 1954, but Sara's husband, Dale, said everything looked in order. He even checked back through other hunt club records and prices were in line. He's a whiz at the computer."

"Glad somebody is."

"You do the bloodline research on the computer. I still use the old studbooks. I can find information faster the old way than the new way. Why throw out decades of what works, for me, anyway?" She leaned back in her chair. "Yesterday's hunt was one of the best I've ever been on. You did a fantastic job and so did Skiff. You both kept those hounds together—and Diana, what a show. I know I've blabbed all this before."

"Was something."

"And Freddie Thomas missed it. You know half the club has called her to tell her." Sister smiled.

"Any hunt you miss is always a barn burner." Shaker smiled back.

She asked, "What do you make of it, the cowhorn echo—if it is an echo?"

"I don't know. If someone wanted to screw up the hunt, they'd blow while hounds worked. They'd try to get them off a line or onto a new one. It does sound like an echo, but deep, clear. Why would anyone blow the horn? Why would Tom say he saw a ghost?"

"I don't know," Sister said. She'd told him about Tom's encounter once back at the kennels after yesterday's hunt.

Shaker pushed his baseball cap back on his head. "Tom's pretty old. Seems sharp as a tack but maybe some gears slipped."

"I don't know. He seemed completely reasonable."

"Boss, you don't think it's a ghost, do you?"

"Well—no, and yet think about Hangman's Ridge, where I never go willingly. I feel something."

"It is creepy." Shaker exhaled so loudly that Raleigh, asleep, lifted his head.

Rooster was knocked out cold.

"Bear with me. If it is a ghost, it is beyond our powers to understand. If it is a live human being, there's something we don't know. This is too unusual. I have never heard of anything like this in any century vis-à-vis other hunts. You read about furious landowners, dukes in a snit, someone chasing hounds with a broom, that sort of thing. But a horn call following a hunting call, distant, mellow—beautiful, really. Never. A dead person appearing. Never."

"Here's my prediction: We'll be back at Chapel Cross in about two weeks. By mid-October, you usually go a bit farther for the fixtures. Beveridge Hundred, that's close to Old Paradise. If we hunt there and we hear the cowhorn again, then I'd say we have a true mystery," he confidently said.

"Good point."

While Master and huntsman exchanged views in the kennel office, Yvonne sat down at her computer. She'd rearranged some furniture at the dependency, created a small office overlooking the garden in the back. Mums, zinnias popped with color on the first day of October.

Before hitting "send," she thought a moment about yesterday. When she and Vic used to come for Parents' Day at Custis Hall, they'd only attended one hunt. Tootie asked them to do so. Vic complained the whole time. Their other visits involved the usual meetings, entertainments, campus strolls for parents. Yvonne was beginning to realize why Tootie loved what she did.

Vic threatened her through his lawyers to her lawyers that he would willingly go to court to prove she was in no way instrumental to the success of his now many business interests. He'd put her name on the documents to please her. Really, she deserved perhaps two million. He felt that was generous.

She didn't raise her voice; she listened to her lawyers present the offer, as they were legally bound to do. She had been critical to his success, and she knew it. This wasn't just ego, or a woman trying to prove she was as good as a man. She had been there every step of the way. Those steps added up to triple-digit millions, real power in the state of Illinois as well as a national platform, thanks to the magazine and cable stations.

Yvonne, as the younger woman, watched Oprah Winfrey and Sheila Johnson rise. She admired them, learned from them, kept her nose clean, literally—no cocaine, and the modeling world was full of it. Not terribly social, she watched everyone and everything. Coming from a solid middle-class family, she had acquired a good education at Northwestern University. But it was her looks that put her on the map. She was smart enough to use them.

When Vic came courting, he was one of many. Over time she warmed to him because of his drive, his commitment to economic parity and opportunity for African Americans, and his energy. Also, he allowed her, while dating, to advise him on the fashion section of his new magazine. Her advice was golden. She began to love him.

Not anymore. She hit "send."

"You reap what you sow." She half smiled, then repeated herself. "You reap what you sow, Victor."

Tomorrow, starting with the morning news, her prophecy would be devastatingly apparent.

Back at Roughneck Farm, Sunday night, Gray listened as Sister once again ran through her thoughts concerning Weevil. Gray was patient, a little curious.

She concluded with, "I don't know what the game is, but if Weevil or whatever is out there wanted to scare people, don't you think he'd be jumping out saying, 'Boo!'?"

"Let me fix you a drink." He kissed her cheek, walked to the bar, dropped two oversized ice cubes into a glass, made her an old-fashioned. "Here. Sit down and sip."

She took the glass. "This will drive me bats, absolutely bats."

Gray, Scotch in hand, joined her on the sofa. "It is driving you bats." He changed the subject. "I'm glad we bought that ice machine. Such big ice cubes." He rattled his glass. "Almost orchestral."

She smiled at him. Gray could always make her feel better, calmer, more focused. She returned to her obsession. "Any ideas?"

"One." He leaned toward her. "I'll ask Aunt Daniella to tell me more. I know she's holding back. She loves to be wheedled. Maybe she does know more."

"If anyone knows more, she will." Sister smiled. "I said I would do this, but I hadn't gotten around to it. I'll see if Ben Sidell will let me go through the old files on Weevil's disappearance. And I'll see if Marion has come up with something."

"She'd have called you."

"You're right, but I know she's out there digging."

"Digging. 1954. Where is the body?" Gray took a long sip.

"Maybe the ghost will show us."

"You know, you made a good point about whoever or whatever this is not being interested in frightening people. From what I gather, the man—or the apparition—didn't threaten Tom?"

"No. Just asked a few questions." She stared out the window. "And he knew we were having a joint meet."

"Can't be that hard to find out. He was a huntsman. He understands cubbing. He knows the territory." Gray put down his drink. "I'm not saying he's a ghost, but whoever he is, he knows something about hunting."

She looked into the night, stars now visible. Golly, stretched to the max on the coffee table, snored, a little tiny snore. The dogs slept on the rug.

"Gray, a man disappeared in 1954. He appears to have returned. Why did he disappear? Lots of theories, but no facts. All assume he was murdered. If Weevil is a ghost, he can take revenge if he so chooses. But the time is probably past. Whoever killed him surely is dead—or at death's door, being two years older than God. Which reminds me, Tom said Weevil recalled some hunt details from his time carrying the horn. Said he teased Tom about whipping-in."

This made Gray shake his head. "You know, it's crazy. Flat-out crazy."

Sister agreed, then said, "If it's not about revenge, all being dead, what's left?"

He blinked. "Love?"

"Wouldn't his love or lovers be dead?"

"What if she had his child? What if the child, who would now be in his or her seventies, was alive? What if there are now grandchildren? Curiosity? Love?" He then thought a bit more. "Money. Some sum that never materialized for Weevil, but was promised. Or maybe he did have the money, or whatever it was of great value, and managed to hide it before he was killed."

"A premonition?"

"Considering what we've learned about Weevil,

just the little bit, it wouldn't take much to have a premonition. Sounds like a lot of men were after his hide."

"What about a woman?"

" 'Hell hath no fury like a woman scorned.' " He nodded.

"Given any of those possibilities, what happens if one of us gets in the way?"

Gray, voice low, remarked, " 'Gone to Ground.' Perhaps, we, too, will be gone to ground."

"With one exception. When the fox goes to ground, he's safe. I don't think we would be safe."

"I don't think we would be either."

CHAPTER 17

"Thin gruel." Sister sighed at the papers she had organized on the table.

Betty, nose to a typed page, agreed. "We hardly ever see truly typed pages anymore. All this stuff was done before correcting tape. Whoever typed these reports was good."

"H-m-m." Sister returned to the papers. "The photographs, well, beauties all."

"Right. Wish there were more photos. I can't imagine that the women suspected of having affairs with Weevil willingly had their pictures taken."

"No. The officer on this case did his homework. Look." She pushed a photograph to Betty. "The illegal still site at Old Paradise. Ha. They knew it was operating. A suspected burial ground. Nothing, of course."

"Wonder why they didn't arrest whoever was operating it, then?" Betty's eyebrows knitted together.

"Paid off, or maybe it was easier to turn a blind eye. Excessive rectitude in law enforcement usually produces contrary results."

Ben Sidell walked into the small room, unadorned by certificates, photographs, anything on the walls. The county sheriff's offices were utilitarian and spartan. No one would accuse the department of squandering funds, what little they were allotted.

"Well?" He pulled out a chair to sit with them for a moment.

"Nothing much. The DeSotos and toothy huge Buicks bring back memories. The few photographs of Main Street do, too. But, Ben, whatever happened to Weevil, not a clue, really. The pictures of the women he was said to have wooed, some of them photos from the society page—no proof. The questioning certainly took into account the class of the woman being questioned. Obviously, no one admitted to anything other than hunting behind him."

Ben, who had seen the video on Sister's phone, pulled a photograph of Weevil toward him. "Eerie. The video. The spitting image. And you say Weevil—or whoever—talked to Tom Tipton?"

"Yes. Tom's words were 'Weevil to the teeth.' "

"Too bad Tom didn't ask him what happened to him." Ben smiled a little. "As no one is injured or in apparent danger, there's not much I can do to help you, but this is highly unusual."

"Thank you for finding the old file." Sister folded the papers back together.

"For my Master, anything. Actually, the county records are quite good. Then again, I have to remember that records have been kept since before the Revolutionary War. I flipped through this. Of course, the women are terrifically good-looking. The men, when questioned, tight-lipped. I'm sure each man realized he was a suspect. Since no body was ever found, everything faded away. It is still very difficult to get any kind of conviction without a corpse."

"I guess that's why in murder mysteries so much time is spent on disposing of the corpse," Sister added.

"If a body is just left out or tossed somewhere, does that mean the crime was not premeditated?" Betty asked Ben.

"Not always. Given the terrain here and the rivers, a body can go unnoticed for years. If an unburied corpse is found, it's usually by a hiker or a dog. I expect central Virginia hides many bones."

"It has certainly hidden Weevil's." Sister tapped the tabletop with her forefinger.

"You don't believe this is a ghost?" Betty inquired. "Just asking."

"No. Deep down, no. But then again, Tom truly knew him. He believes it was Weevil," she answered.

"Why would a man blow 'Gone to Ground,' then blow it again at the hunt where we ran the young fox into the rock outcroppings? Then again blow 'Going Home' at Old Paradise?" Betty wondered.

"You discount echo?" Ben was becoming fascinated.

"I do. What we heard was a cowhorn. Whoever had it knew how to use it, knows the calls," Sister replied.

"Weevil," Betty simply said.

"Some kind of weevil, that's for sure," Sister responded. "The other thing is I called Marion. She's asked questions. The most helpful person was Randy Rouse, Master of Loudoun Hunt. Ben, Randy is a hundred years old, and how shall I say, undimmed. He'd hunted behind Weevil a few times, but Randy was tied down by his own hunting obligations as well as his business ones. He told Marion so many people thought Weevil's disappearance had something to do with the rumor that he slept with the Falconers, both mother and daughter."

Ben shrugged. "That was a brave man, if he did it."

"Randy didn't indicate that he knew anything more than the gossip, but Marion played the video for him and he was shocked."

"Weevil?" Ben inquired.

Sister nodded. "Well, who is to say, but Randy swore he sure looked like the Weevil he remembered. And he, too, wondered why would he take the cowhorn. He recalled the scrimshaw on the horn. Said he remembered that from hunting, thought it was lovely."

"Isn't his wife thirty-eight years younger than he is?" Betty wondered.

"Is. A real looker and a fabulous rider. The two of them are well suited for each other," Sister replied. "You know, there are so many good marriages in foxhunting. I have often wondered, is it because we share danger?"

"Oh, honey, I don't know. I think marriage is danger enough." Betty laughed.

Ben put a hand on some of the untidied pages, for Sister had the rest in a neat pile. "I assume the Falconers are gone?"

"Yes. Both. And sad to say, the daughter Madeline—'Madge'—died of the same type of cancer that took her mother. They were Northern Virginia people but we all knew one another from hunting. Of course, I knew Madge and Christine only socially and from hunting. Makes me wonder if cancer is inherited. Ah, well." Sister thought a moment. "I keep coming back to that. Love or money."

Vic Harris, exposed and humiliated, knew in his gut Yvonne would kill him if she could, for love and money. Well, soured love. She did the next best thing. The decision was whether to just cave and tell the press they had settled out of court, or to fight back even harder just to make the bitch miserable.

Yvonne had instructed her lawyers at Hart,

Hanckle and Himmel to release to all the social media footage she had, thanks to the most expensive private investigation firm in Chicago: footage of her husband cavorting with his two blonde mistresses. The elect, the one receiving twenty thousand dollars a month, performed many a service, but what would knock back people of his generation was how Mistress Number One was only too happy to work over the close-to-sixty-year-old man with Mistress Number Two. He kept up, literally.

So there he was, a self-proclaimed leader of the black community, for decades extolling the necessity to praise and focus on African American women. He, of course, criticized Justice Thomas for marrying a white woman. Any man of color who married a white woman came in for a blast in his magazine, on his cable network. He even blasted Hispanic men who slept with white women.

The overground media reported this fall from grace. They showed head shots of the two knockout blondes, but could not show the home-style porn. The social media showed everything.

Unfortunately, this meant that Tootie beheld her father in action when a so-called friend sent it on to her. Unfair as her father had been to her, she didn't want to see this. She didn't want to know what a complete hypocrite he was.

She didn't bother to text her mother. She drove

over to Beveridge Hundred once her chores were completed. Shaker had not seen the trash, and Sister was at the sheriff's office. Tootie would have gone to Sister first, but confronting Yvonne would happen sooner or later.

"Mother!" Tootie opened the door to the cottage.

"In the back."

Within a minute, Tootie stood in the back garden on this perfect October day.

"I saw everything."

"Ah."

"Mother, why did you do it?"

"I didn't do it. That's the point." Yvonne dropped into a wooden red Adirondack chair as Tootie followed suit, in a blue one.

"I know, but"—she groped for words—"that was awful. Everyone we know will have seen Dad. I am so humiliated."

"You didn't do it. You have nothing to be humiliated about. He has acted without regard for his wife or daughter. If anything, people should be sympathetic to us."

"I don't know." Tootie's voice trailed off.

"I built that business. I worked every day for years to build that business. I made calls. I organized dinners. I talked to complete assholes and pretended they were brilliant. He thinks because I'm a woman he can cut me out, buy me off cheap. He's been married to me for thirty-one years and he thought he could back me down? He may be able to continue running the business without me—I expect he'll hire a regiment of ass-kissers—but he will no longer be an admired person. I wonder what the wives of our friends will do? Maybe nothing. Maybe cut him dead. What I expect is my half of the funds—quite soon, actually."

"You don't want to stay in the business? You liked working."

"I did. Most of the time. I didn't always like the people especially, but I liked building something and I liked working with him. I loved him once. I gave him everything I had. And what you saw was my reward."

"Mom, he wasn't always like that."

"No. This priapic behavior"—Yvonne was careful in her choice of words—"arrived with his fiftieth birthday. He panicked. People thought I would panic when my turn came four years later. Lots of speculation about how much plastic surgery I'd have, stuff like that. I was fine. I am fine, and sixty is getting closer, not too close yet but closer. I don't give a damn, but I do give a damn about respect."

Tootie sat there, wiggled her toes in her boots. "I don't ever want to see him again."

"He is your father. I can't interfere in your relationship or lack of one."

"You never fought for me when I tried to

explain to him why I didn't want to go to law school or med school. He called me a nuevo field hand!"

"Tootie, at first, I somewhat agreed with him. I did and I'm sorry. I thought your desire to hunt, to literally clean shit, was beneath us. We had risen so far in the world. Like most people of my generation I couldn't understand why any of our people would want to work in agriculture or with animals. We don't see it as a career. As time went by, I accepted that this is your life. When you said later you wanted to be a veterinarian, I thought, okay, she will be using her brain. But now that I have actually seen you out there, like at Old Paradise, I understand you are using your brain. In time I did stand up for you, but not when he was hot. There is no talking to your father when he's lost his temper."

"I hate him. I really do." Tootie clamped her lips shut. "I will never fall in love with any-one."

A wave of guilt, sorrow, and anger lapped at Yvonne all at once. "I have been an inadequate mother. Not bad, but not so good. I wish I could take back those years when you needed me and I wasn't there. I am so sorry." Tears rolled down her cheeks. "Tootie, don't say you won't love anyone. It can be the most wonderful thing in the world. Much as I loathe that son of a bitch now, when I was young, when we were working together, when you were born, I loved him. I didn't change; he did." She paused. "Well, I did change. I got older."

"Mom, I'm sorry." Tootie was able to look past her own feelings of the moment.

"Do you forgive me?"

Tootie lifted her shoulders. "You're my mother. I love you."

Yvonne rose from the chair, knelt before her daughter, tears streaming now, and took her hand. "I love you, too, honey. I think it has taken me a long time to grow up. In so many ways you are ahead of me." She stood now, leaned down and kissed Tootie on the cheek. "I pray someday you will find love. You will feel all the excitement and happiness I once felt, and your love will come to a better conclusion. Men"—she thought about this for a bit—"change."

"Don't we?"

"We do, but it's different. Men fear age in a different way." Noting Tootie's facial expression. "It's nothing to worry about now, and not everyone fears age."

"Do you?"

Sitting now on the flat arm of Tootie's Adirondack chair, Yvonne, voice lower, said, "When I hit forty I determined to fight it, and then one day, when someone said to me, 'Yvonne, still so beautiful,' I knew I couldn't fight time. No one ever uses the word 'still' when you are young. No, I don't fear age, but I fear not being able to do the things I like to do. I fear illness, some of the things that come with age."

"Still beautiful. I would know you anywhere, in any century." Daniella, stunned, listened to Weevil as he took her elbow.

Daniella enjoyed her early morning walk, and her sunset walk, as she thought of it. She missed her late son, Mercer, who would usually walk with her, but Gray and Sam, individually or sometimes together, would parade with her at least once a week.

The first Monday in October, temperatures in the high 60s, color at the top of the deciduous trees, filled her with delight. At six o'clock she grabbed her ebony cane with the ivory hound's head, flicked it in front of her, and started her sunset walk. West Leigh, a good neighborhood west of Charlottesville proper, pretty houses, always provided something for her to look at. If a neighbor, and the yards were large, worked in the yard, she'd swing up her cane as a hello, or stop and chat. Usually she kept walking, laughing at herself and saying if she stopped it would be hard to start the motor again. She hadn't been out for ten minutes when she heard a footfall, felt a strong hand on her elbow.

Keeping complete composure, she replied, "Weevil, you say that to all the girls."

He chuckled. "But you were the best one. We did have fun, didn't we?"

Brain whirring, she smiled. "While it lasted, yes. So tell me, Weevil, how is death? I'd like to know as I draw ever closer."

"You exist in another dimension. No hunger, thirst, work. You can see people here. You can visit them if you want to, obviously. But most of us realize it is too upsetting. I knew you wouldn't mind."

"You stole your horn from the museum."

"Did. Missed it. There's a little story on the scrimshaw. I wanted to see it again. Hold it. Blow it. Daniella, I can't escort you for very long. I don't think anyone around these parts knows who I am, but I can't take the chance, you know? I have two questions."

"Ask them."

"Who is still alive? Tom Tipton, you. Is there anyone else?"

"Randall Farley. His mind is gone, gone. He's in assisted living. But many of our generation's children are still living."

The long rays of the setting sun turned his golden hair to red as he inclined it toward her.

"Did anyone ever find Sophie Marquet's fortune?"

"The founder of Old Paradise? It must have all been spent. The DuCharmes finally sold the place to Crawford Howard. He's a rich, pushy white man."

"People have secrets. Evangelista Bancroft did." Weevil smiled, teeth straight.

Daniella, surprised, asked, "Edward's late sister?"

"H-m-m. She was three, maybe four years older than Edward. Always liked him. Liked the woman he married. Loved Evangelista. But Evangelista had her ways. I was not her first."

Daniella absorbed this. "I'm afraid I am of no help to you. I knew everyone, of course, but how could I run in the same social circles as Evangelista? I thought she was a dreadful snob."

Weevil squeezed her elbow, then lifted up her hand and kissed her palm. "Just speaking with you has been a help."

He dropped her hand, loped behind one of the houses, and disappeared.

Daniella, head up, breathing deeply, reached her house, closed the door, picked up her phone. "Gray!"

As she usually called with a request, Gray pretended he was glad to hear her voice. "Aunt Daniella, you sound chipper."

"I have just had a walk with Wesley Carruthers."

CHAPTER 18

W est Indian, George Trumper," Aunt
Daniella, perfectly calm, told Sister and
Gray. "It's an old men's cologne, established in
1875. Favored by rich men, as is Creed. One of
those things where if you know, you know. If you
don't, you're farther down on the ladder. Edward
Bancroft would know of it. Weevil imitated
the rich when he could. Cologne is afford-
able."

Sister and Gray had driven over immediately
after her call.

"No one else mentioned it. Tom Tipton vaguely
recalled a scent."

Aunt Daniella thought about this. "Tom might
recognize the fragrance but not know what it
was. Also, from your report, it sounds as though
Tom was terrified."

"Unlike you." Sister smiled at the nonagenarian.

"I am very close to the red exit light. Nothing
scares me."

"Nothing ever did." Gray complimented her.
"Mother used to say of all of the family, you were
the strongest."

"Ah" was all Aunt Daniella said, her lips, dark
red lipstick, parted slightly.

"He wanted to know who was alive?"

"Just as I told you. Tom Tipton. Randall Farley in assisted living."

"According to Marion, who has canvassed the two Northern Virginia hunts where Weevil started out, of his contemporaries, all gone."

"H-m-m. How is Tom, by the way?"

"Still a little shaken, but recovering. I spoke to Sara Bateman, who is keeping tabs on him," Sister replied.

"Good fellow, Tom. I always thought he would rise higher than he did." She wondered. "Mercer would mention Tom from time to time, as he remembered him from his childhood. Said Tom had been kind to him."

Mercer, her son, was a good rider, as were all the Lorillards and Laprades.

"It's a funny thing, Aunt Daniella." Sister spoke to this. "Carrying the horn is very different from whipping-in. Some people find they can't do it. Some can do it but much prefer whipping-in. I actually think the whippers-in often see more. They certainly see more foxes."

"No doubt." The old woman nodded.

"Aunt D." Gray called her by her nickname. "Have you any idea why he is here? Why he has showed himself?"

"No."

"Did you think he was a ghost?" Sister inquired.

"He seemed as alive as the three of us. He

looked like Weevil, smelled like Weevil, spoke like Weevil. A flatterer, as always."

"And Weevil mentioned Evangelista Bancroft?" Sister questioned.

"He said he had loved her and that she, in his words, 'had her ways.' He also declared Evangelista had secrets." A long pause followed this. "Don't we all? Would you want to know anyone who didn't have secrets?" A sly smile followed this.

Gray, having fixed his aunt her double bourbon, himself a light Scotch, and a Perrier with lime for Sister, cleared his throat. "Speaking of secrets. Now don't fuss at me. Did you have an affair with Weevil?"

"Of course I did. If anyone else asks me I will lie, lie through my teeth, but to you and you,"— she inclined her head toward Sister—"I will tell the truth. It was one of those mad things. The kind of affair Cole Porter wrote songs about. We parted friends. I was in no way prepared to settle down, and neither was he."

"Aunt Daniella, you couldn't have married him back then. The miscegenation laws." Gray recalled the law forbidding whites and blacks to marry.

"I didn't say I would marry him. I said settle down. They couldn't arrest us for that, plus I can easily pass for white. However, everyone here knew I was not." She waved her hand dismissively. "When are people going to realize you can't control human behavior? Do you think for one instant Weevil and I were the only young, attractive people in the state of Virginia enjoying each other's bodies? Ha."

"Did you think he was a good man?" Sister drove to the heart of it.

"Yes. Weevil was the grasshopper. Remember the story about the ants and the grasshopper? The grasshopper fiddles, sings, and dances while the ants work, prepare for winter. Winter comes, the grasshopper will die, but the ants save him. That was Weevil, and I declare, someone would have saved him. If he were ninety-four as I am, some woman somewhere would be ministering to him. But he didn't have a mean bone in his body, and in his own way, he could be uncommonly sweet." She paused. "Almost feminine, really, his sensitivity to other people."

"Do you think he had a feeling he would be murdered? Do you think he felt it?" Sister continued.

"I don't know. By the time he disappeared our frolic had ended. Oh, I would see him, but time had passed and in its way, passed us by."

"And what did you think of Evangelista?" Gray jumped in.

"Gorgeous. Impossibly rich. A creature of her time and place. A snob. It's interesting that her brother isn't. Edward is an open fellow."

"You didn't tell Weevil that Edward was alive," Gray remarked.

"Edward was at Dartmouth back then. He wasn't really our contemporary. His father, as I'm sure you heard, broke up the relationship and packed Evangelista off to Europe. Paris, London, Moscow. God knows where she traveled once there. She did marry upon her return, but I can tell you, she didn't love him. He was well-bred and rich. She did what she was raised to do, except she never had children." Aunt Daniella held up her glass, which Gray promptly refilled, giving her the tiniest twist of orange.

"What's this?"

"A little twist just for you. You have lemons, oranges, and limes sitting at the bar."

"For show." She grinned. "Love the color."

"Back to Evangelista. How had she changed?" Sister plucked the lime out of her Perrier and sucked on it for a moment.

"How can you do that?" Aunt Daniella asked before returning to the question. "Too tart for me. Ah, yes, Evangelista. Well, she never had children, as I said. Swore she wanted them. Said she and her husband tried. I actually think she didn't want children. It was as though some of her colors had faded, like a salmon taken out of the stream. She performed all the duties of a woman of her class. She delighted in Tedi and Edward's two girls, but after her return I never once saw her laugh spontaneously—or do anything spontaneous, really. It was clear she tolerated her father and vice versa."

"Aunt D, do you think Evangelista's father could have killed Weevil? Or Edward, for that matter?"

She looked at her handsome nephew. "No. If old man Bancroft was going to kill him, or have him killed, I think he would have done it during the affair. Same with Edward, but he was up in New England. I really don't think Edward could kill anyone, unless defending his family."

"I don't either," Sister agreed. "And he asked about Sophie Marquet's fortune?"

"I said I thought it was a story and nothing more. Those two worthless brothers lost everything. If there had been treasure and they found it they'd have fought about that, too, and blown it. I told him Old Paradise had been sold. I did not describe Crawford as new money. He would figure that out anyway. Ah yes." A slightly malicious smile crossed her lips. "Money talks. Crawford intends to tell us all. The vulgarity of that man, that awful new mansion. Does he think we can't tell the difference?"

"I think, Aunt Daniella, that's why he bought Old Paradise."

"Gray, really? How extraordinary. As to Sophie's fortune, Virginia bubbles over with stories of buried treasure, lost fortunes, entire estates vanishing amidst wine, women, and song. Maybe he likes the drama of it."

"Tell me more about the gossip about Weevil and Alfred and Binky's mother?" Sister urged.

"She was married. I can't swear to anything. If they did carry on, they were discreet. Weevil actually could cover his tracks, usually by engaging in a flamboyant affair to divert people's gaze."

"One wonders what Margaret DuCharme thought of it." Sister couldn't suppress a smile.

"When you have as much at stake as Margaret, I guess you put up with it. I heard that was how Weevil managed to sleep with the Falconer women. He actually trotted out a fan dancer. You know, a Sally Rand type. However, people did get wind of it because the mother, not the daughter, had a nervous breakdown." She took a long drink. "Oh, there's no gossip like old gossip. I feel quite giddy."

They all laughed.

Gray, who did love his aunt even when she was at her despotic worst, inquired, "Do you think Weevil could kill?"

"No. Not the Weevil I knew. If he became angry, it was over as quickly as it began."

"Did he care about money? It seems all the women he bedded except for the fan dancer were rich," Sister asked.

"I wasn't rich. Not then." She nestled in her

chair. "There's a lot to be said for marrying a man for money. Well, my dear, you married well."

"I did. Ray was a good provider. Your nephew certainly has made his way in the world."

"Thank God one of them did."

"Sam isn't going to make money, Aunt D, but he's doing okay and he's clean, clean as a whistle. He's giving riding lessons, well, one so far, to Yvonne Harris."

"I see." Daniella tapped the edge of the side table. "Your brother could have done anything. Be rich as Croesus. Well, did he waste much of his life? He did. But you know, a thirst for alcohol runs in the family. I can drink. I watch it, but I can drink. Your mother hated the taste. Who is to say that, had I been a man, subject to a man's pressures, I might not have turned into a drunk? But sometimes I look at Sam and he breaks my heart. All that talent."

"True, but, Aunt Daniella,"—Sister's voice was warm—"you can be proud of him. He works hard, takes horses that untalented people can't ride, turns them into babysitters, and he loves the horses. He has such a big heart. You know he goes down to the train station, goes under the bridges, and talks to his old homeless buddies. He encourages them to get help. He brings them food. You can be proud."

Aunt Daniella looked at Gray. "Does he?"

"He does."

"Well, why didn't anyone tell me?"

"He wanted to keep it to himself—and really, Aunt Daniella, you had your hands full with Mercer. When he had clients, you often had to entertain," Gray reminded her.

Mercer had been a bloodstock agent. He'd died about two years before.

"Aunt Daniella, I know I asked this but let me ask it again. Did you think you talked to a ghost?"

"As I said, Weevil was as alive as the three of us. But I don't understand how that can be. He was about thirty-two. Looked exactly as I remembered. I have no answers."

Driving home in Gray's big Land Cruiser, Sister stared out the window. "I look at the lights on in people's houses, the twinkling lights out on the land when we get out of town, and I always wonder, what are they doing? Are they happy?"

"Me, too."

"Honey, why is this man, or this ghost, here now? Why steal his cowhorn? Why blow it? And why is he now showing himself to his old comrades, so to speak?

"When all this first occurred, the video, we talked about holograms. I don't know who came up with that first, but I thought, well, maybe. Why, who knows? But a prank. Now, I don't think this has anything to do with technology. Weevil

235

is with us." She paused. "Gray, it can't be good."
She watched a light go on in an upstairs bedroom
as they passed Ramsay, an old spectacular estate.
  "I think you're right."

CHAPTER 19

Kettle House, a clapboard farmhouse built after the War of 1812, rested below the west side of Hangman's Ridge. Hounds carefully worked their way down, pastures beckoning below. This Tuesday, a light drizzle kept away many hunters. Then, too, the Tuesday and Thursday hunts didn't attract as many people as Saturday. People needed to work for a living, such a bother.

Shaker, up ahead, leaned back in the saddle. HoJo, a sure-footed fellow, proved perfect for a day like today. Betty whipped-in on the right, Tootie on the left. Sister, on Aztec, led a field of fifteen people.

Leaves, turning a bit more color, glistened in the drizzle. A hard rain made hunting difficult for all, scent washing away, but a drizzle could intensify scent if everything else was right. The temperature, low 50s, might have been cooler but it was cool enough.

"Target." Giorgio inhaled the familiar scent.

"What's he doing over here?" Zorro put his nose down.

"New owners. You know how curious he is." Cora also inhaled the familiar scent.

Hounds opened. Shaker blew them together

with three doubled notes. The riders, not yet concerned with footing for it wasn't yet slippery, kicked on, to keep up with the Master.

Once down on the pastures the pace increased. The club had paneled the country at Kettle House with jumps from fallen logs and the ubiquitous coop. As they had not yet had time to paint the coops, quite a few horses balked at the fresh wood. No one came off, though.

"Turn left. You'll overrun the line," Cora commanded Thimble; although not a puppy, the hound's enthusiasm could lead to mistakes.

Thimble hooked left, as did everyone.

Target, climbing back up the ridge, trotted. Far ahead, scent now blowing away from him, he would be in his den in all of fifteen minutes if he ran hard. Trotting, maybe twenty-five minutes. Just to be sure, he stopped, looked down below. The entire pack was swinging left near the white clapboard house with the dark green shutters. Just in case, he decided to move along a little faster.

Hounds raced across the pasture back over the coop in the fence line to start climbing upward. Huntsman and whippers-in, over easily, slowed for the climb. The field did also.

The grade, tricky, varied from an easy angle to forty-five degrees in spots. That angle could be tiring. Since hounds had not lost the scent, the wonderful mounts worked hard to trot upward.

The horses knew horn calls and hound work better than the humans.

Aztec, ears forward, watched hounds. He loved hunting. He could become a bit bored on a trail ride, but as long as he was outside, life was good.

Finally Target reached Hangman's Ridge, the long flat land with the hanging tree in the middle. He shot across it, reached the down path to Roughneck Farm.

Crows flew overhead. Looking upward, he saw his enemy, Saint Just, the huge raven. Crows could be terrible foes as they screamed and shouted at the fox, informing hounds where he was. But this flock had been disturbed by something else. They flew over him without a peep, even Saint Just, a born big-mouth.

Dasher, fast, reached the flattop of the ridge first. He raced over the buried criminals—no tombstones, a few flat markers. Some families retrieved bodies from the tree. Others left them there, angry at their besmirching the family name, or they didn't care anyway. Those were finally cut down and buried. Originally, the crown's counselor and then the county judge thought leaving the corpse exposed to the elements would deter further crime. But Hangman's Ridge was far from Charlottesville proper, even farther from Scottsville, the county seat. Very few people saw moldering remains swing in the wind. Even if they did, it's doubtful the grisly sight would have the desired instructive effect. Criminals don't think they will get caught. People have been stealing, raping, murdering for thousands of years.

Dasher ignored a murmur. None of the hounds nor horses liked being up on the ridge. They could see and hear what humans could not.

The rest of the pack, now well up with Dasher, cut right, headed down the path to Roughneck Farm.

The people followed. The rain picked up.

Target reached Tootie's house and ducked under the oldest part of the foundation, to the irritation of Comet. Comet had stashed a bunch of grapes there, which Tootie left out for him. Target devoured the fruit, all the fruit, while Comet bared his teeth. He couldn't throw out Target until hounds left.

"I hear you munching," Dasher called at the door, so to speak.

"I'd offer you some but you don't like fruit," the handsome red sassed.

The whole pack gathered at Tootie's house. The rain, steady now, slid down people's collars, down their backs.

Shaker blew "Gone to Ground," lifted hounds, walking them back to the kennels.

The people gratefully rode to their trailers, dismounted, untacked. Some threw a rain sheet over horses and tack. Horses were led into the trailers to happily munch on hay hung inside.

As the hounds were put up, Sister tended to Aztec in the stable. She called out to Freddie Thomas, who usually took off Tuesdays. "Freddie, just take food into the kitchen. I'll be there in a minute."

Shortly, the small band, happy to be inside, out of now wet coats, jabbered with one another. Sister, Shaker, Betty, and Tootie, all inside, made certain there were hot drinks, should anyone need a little warmth. Liquor was there, too, and Tedi Bancroft had brought her famous clam chowder. Ham biscuits, cornbread, the usual basic fare covered the kitchen table in abundance.

As Kasmir opened the mudroom door, Betty opened the kitchen door for him. In the distance they heard "Going Home" blown on the cowhorn.

"That's no echo." Kasmir removed his Barbour coat.

"Sister, did you hear it?" Betty called out.

"I did."

"We all did," Tedi replied, and others affirmed this.

"This will drive me right around the bend," Sister blurted out.

Shaker, to calm others, said, "It's a prank. When we find out the culprit, we'll tan his hide."

Again people agreed, some laughed.

After the small breakfast ended, people didn't linger, as no one wanted to drive in a hard rain.

The rain had ramped up from drizzle to steady, would probably pound down shortly. Sister and Tootie cleaned up the kitchen.

"Tootie, I'm sorry about the publicity."

Tootie dried plates. "Val texted me from Princeton. She told me not to worry. Just forget it. It doesn't have anything to do with me."

"She's right." Sister stretched to her full height to put away some of the cleaned glasses. She stopped a moment, looked out the window. "Coming down hard."

"My weather app said it would rain but not this hard."

"Good for the water table. Didn't Kettle House look inviting? All those years we couldn't hunt there, and now we can. It's such a pretty little place."

"We're lucky to have such good territory."

"We are. One of these days, you and I will have to fly to Red Rock, outside Reno, Nevada. High desert. Now, there is territory not made for hunting, but Lynn Lloyd and Angela Murry hunt it. You can see for miles. In some places, fifty miles."

"Guess they don't need cry like we do," Tootie sensibly stated.

"Well, they do need it if the pack goes on the other side of a ridge. A ridge out there can be three thousand feet high. Hangman's Ridge is about nine hundred feet, I think. The top of

Humpback Mountain is three thousand feet, give or take. All you smell is sagebrush at Red Rock. I don't know how hounds can pick up quarry scent but they do," Sister enthused.

"One of my goals, when I get to be your age,"— Tootie smiled mischievously—"is to have hunted wherever there is mounted hunting. So Australia, New Zealand, Great Britain, France, Canada, Uruguay, South Africa. Bet there's more."

"Bet you'll do it."

"There. All done." Tootie swept her hand outward to show the kitchen was clean, the flatware and plates washed, dried, put away.

"Amazing what one can accomplish if you just keep working. Come on and sit in the library with me for a minute. Golliwog hasn't had any opportunity to snuggle in your lap." Sister smiled.

The two women, accompanied by the dogs and Golly, repaired to the library. Each happily sank into a club chair. And Golly leapt onto Tootie's lap.

A distant rumble of thunder presaged no good. Both turned to look out the window as the sky grew darker. It was one in the afternoon.

"The horn call." Tootie spoke. "It sounds so mournful. Strange."

"That it is."

"Well, if a cowhorn was stolen from the Museum of Hounds and Hunting, hearing a cowhorn might mean something. Might be the same horn. Old stuff. Old sins." Tootie paused. "At least with my father we know it's new sins."

Sister laughed, glad Tootie could see some humor in all this. "You know what, I'm going to call Marion, right now. You've given me an idea."

Her landline phone rested on the handsome desk. She reached Marion at work.

"Marion, does the museum have any photographs of the entire cowhorn?"

"Yes. Every piece is photographed and catalogued before we put it in the cases."

"Weevil's horn was inscribed. Scrimshaw I think is the proper term. Can you get me pictures of the entire horn?"

After more discussion, Marion promised to do so, hopefully no later than the end of the week.

Sister and Tootie chatted, glad to be inside as the rain lashed at the windowpanes. They talked about hounds, who to breed to whom, the fixture for Thursday and Saturday. Yvonne's second riding lesson. The small details of everyday life, talked over, discussed, like tiny coral bodies floating onto one another; such details build the reefs of friendship.

The rain lightened briefly.

"I think I'd better make a run for it."

"Take an umbrella. You know where they are,"

Sister suggested as she walked Tootie to the mudroom.

The young woman selected a large maroon umbrella, opened the door, popped the umbrella open, and headed for her house. The rain waited until she reached the kennel and then it was a deluge. Sister didn't close her door until she was sure Tootie made it.

Closing the door, she listened to the pounding overhead, the rapping on the windows. Being inside in bad weather always made her feel safe. She did feel safe but she wondered about hearing the horn here. *Whoever this is is becoming a steady presence* she thought to herself. She wondered if she would see him. She kind of wanted to, and then again, she kind of didn't.

CHAPTER 20

A clear picture of Weevil's cowhorn appeared on the large screen of Gray's computer. Sister and Gray sat side by side.

"Marion did a good job." Gray again showed the photos of Weevil's cowhorn.

Every angle had been covered.

"It's lovely. The four columns of Old Paradise are beyond Chapel Cross. The little cross there, the tiny graveyard, Tattenhall Station. He was an artist."

Gray agreed. "Accurate, too. A bit of a mapmaker. Well, what do you think?"

"I like the fox peeping out from the stable door at Old Paradise. Tack room door, actually." She smiled. "A unique horn. It could only belong to someone who hunted Jefferson Hounds back then. Chapel Cross has always been fabulous hunt country. For us, more than a century. And there's a fox looking out from the fallen-down cabin, what is now Tootie's house. There is the arcade of the kennels. The bricks are drawn on. This one looks like it has a smudge, maybe an X."

"Weevil came on in 1947?" Gray glanced over at her.

"Right."

"The sixtieth year of the hunt. Did he make the drawings or someone had them made for him?"

"Gray, he did it himself. There was a mention of that in his framed photograph at the museum."

"Only a patient man could inscribe a cowhorn like this."

"Who is left who knew him well? Apart from Aunt Daniella." She pushed away silently from the desk. "I can see why the horn would mean a lot to Weevil. If this is Weevil. If it isn't, I can't fathom this."

"You said Dale Bateman found nothing in the old treasurer's reports."

"Nope."

"While I'm sitting here I can send out an email as to where we're hunting tomorrow."

She leaned back in the chair. "The problem is footing. Where can we park the trailers? I don't worry so much about the horses. I mean, horses have been dealing with mud for millennia."

He laughed. "Some people don't realize that."

She smiled. "There are fewer and fewer horsemen. In the old days, if one was a good horseman it was seen as an insight into character. Horses trusted him or her. Now—" She shrugged.

"I know you've thought of this, but we really only have two choices. Mill Ruins or After All. The parking is good there. Two days of steady rain, good in some ways, not in others. If it had been below freezing, imagine the mess."

"Wonder if we'll get a hard winter?"

"Snow," he replied. *Farmer's Almanac.*"

"Haven't looked that far ahead. Give me one minute. I'll call Walter on his cell."

She reached him, asked if they could hunt at Mill Ruins on Saturday. Of course. This Thursday looked like a wash. The Weather Channel predicted rain through Wednesday. As Gray listened he started tapping out the information.

"Push back the time to eight A.M. More light now," he said.

"You know I hate to do that," she replied.

"I do, but most people hate getting up early." He held up his hand. "I know there's only a half hour's difference but it's psychological, and it is now October."

"Okay," she said as he finished sending the email and requested, "Go back to the cowhorn."

They both studied it again.

"It really is distinctive." Gray admired the horn.

She slapped her hands on her thighs. "This is giving me a headache. I might as well get used to the cowhorn at the end of our hunts. I am nowhere near figuring this out, and no one has been murdered. So why worry?" She tried to convince herself.

"Honey, someone was murdered. In 1954."

Weevil stood in front of the receptionist's desk at Brightwood Assisted Living, an expensive place to park the old and incompetent, unloved as well as loved.

No one manned the desk or commanded it. He peered over the top, read the room assignments. The building near downtown Charlottesville on a well-kept side street was a formerly handsome large house converted into suites as well as individual rooms.

Randall Farley lived in room nine. A guide affixed to the wall provided a map of the rooms. Weevil walked down a short hallway, plush carpet, which struck him as odd for it's hard for people to roll wheelchairs on carpet. But perhaps the people on this hall could still walk unaided, or not walk at all.

Wearing thin goatskin gloves, he knocked on number nine. A TV played within, the sound dimmed. He knocked again.

"Who is it?"

"Your past." Weevil opened the door.

Randall's jaw dropped. He tried to rise from the easy chair before the TV; a large bed was visible in a small adjoining room. Weevil produced a bottle of stiff rye that he'd hidden in his inside coat pocket, just in case liquor wasn't allowed.

Like many whose minds slip, Randall remembered the past clearly.

Randall collapsed back in the chair. Eyes bulging, he jammered, "I didn't have anything to do with Lennox Bancroft knowing you were sleeping with Evangelista. As for Margaret, those two years later, maybe you did, maybe you didn't. I swear, I kept my mouth shut."

"So you say." Weevil handed Randall the bottle, which the old man opened and greedily gulped.

"You're dead."

"In a manner of speaking." Weevil smiled. "Lennox is dead, his wife is gone, Evangelista, Margaret, too—just about everybody. You made out all right."

"Just go."

"That's no way to treat an old buddy." Weevil grabbed the remote, cut the volume. "I think you ratted me out to Brenden DuCharme, too. You know, Randall, you were just too interested in where I parked my pecker. If you hadn't been so fat you might have gotten lucky, too."

Tears welled in Randall's eyes. "I had nothing to do with any of it."

"I think you did. You're dumb as a sack of hammers, Randall, and all of a sudden, after I was gone, you had investments, investments managed by my detractors, so to speak."

"I swear I had nothing to do with it, and I didn't know you were murdered. I thought you were but I didn't know." He sobbed. "Why are you here?"

"For the truth. You spread stories about my stealing Margaret's bracelets, necklaces, and rings. Many of them major jewels. Her husband believed it. Alfred and Binky believed it. Such an old, malicious gossip. I would have thought you had died of shame."

"Alfred and Binky"—Randall stopped himself, shifted the sentence—"are emotional and stupid. Someone stole a fortune in jewels."

"Why think it was me?" Weevil's face was close to Randall's.

"You had opportunity, if you did steal them." Randall hastily added, "I don't care if you did. Feeble and Meeble"—Randall used the nicknames for the brothers—"believed it."

"They spent money like water. How do you know they didn't steal their mother's jewels to pay their debts? If Brenden had known how bad it was, he would have killed them." Weevil took the bottle of rye from Randall.

Randall greedily grabbed it back. "Goddamned pansies in here. No liquor. No tobacco. No sex." He grimly smiled. "At least we can still enjoy the pleasure of a drink or a drag."

"What happened to Margaret after I disappeared?"

Randall shrugged. "Nothing."

"Nothing."

"No divorce. She traveled to Paris. Brenden bitched and moaned that she spent a fortune on clothes."

"Idiot."

"He realized he ignored her. I remember when she came back she was awfully thin. Lived out her life doing good works. One charity ball after another."

"Was she happy?"

Randall shot Weevil a withering look as he gulped another slug. "Who's happy?"

"Clearly you're not. I should kill you, Randall, for your evil mouth, but I'll spare your sorry ass, not because I'm forgiving you but because your future will just be more and more miserable. You hurt a lot of people."

Randall didn't reply. Weevil left the still unsupervised assisted living. If those people coughing up eight thousand bucks a month for starters only knew. Randall had no one to tell that he saw Weevil. And if he had, they wouldn't have cared.

At Beveridge Hundred, Yvonne listened to her lawyer, the head one, on the phone.

"He's thinking it over," Bart Hanckle reported.

"Bart, you might inform my soon-to-be ex-husband and business partner that what we showed him is a preview. I have more. Much more and it's far worse."

"I like a client who is prepared."

"Let him know I have such a fascinating play-by-play of him in Mistress Number One's highrise. She is sitting on his lap. He's naked. Never a good idea when you've hidden your six-pack behind a wall of fat, but there he is. They are on a very expensive sofa. Mistress Number Two is straddling his face and between his ministrations, when he comes up for air, he praises Jesus." She paused. "Such a religious man."

Bart chuckled. "I will be sure to tell him."

"And you might hint that I also have footage of him with sisters. He treats us far less kindly than he treats the white girls. I don't know whether if anyone had died her hair blonde it would have helped. This isn't to say that I like him sleeping with any woman, but there does seem to be some difference in how he handles them depending on race."

"Yes, ma'am." Bart knew, as did Yvonne, that whatever else she had would ruin Victor Harris forever.

No amount of money can buy your way out of some types of wrongdoing.

"It is Monday. I expect papers delivered to your office on Tuesday, clarifying that I will receive half of all future earnings of Harris and Harris. I expect half of all cash accounts and stocks and bonds by the end of Tuesday's business day, central time. In exchange I will give you all footage, and I will switch all my credit cards to my name alone after October 10. If he does not comply, we go to Round Two."

"It will be done."

She hung up, leaned back in the office chair. Two days of rain had not dampened her spirits. If anything, she felt fabulous.

She had returned from another riding lesson, held in Crawford's indoor arena due to all the mud. The arena, climate controlled, full of light, blended in with the other structures. The cost was $350,000 when he built it, but Crawford had the money. Marty, a garden designer, cared how things looked, hence the pleasing exterior and landscaping.

The only oddity that Yvonne noticed was a bit of sound bouncing around, for it was cavernous. Sam, on the ground, told her exactly what to do. She trotted for a few minutes.

After her lesson—she paid cash each time—she drove back to Beveridge Hundred filled with confidence.

The last two days, as she drove toward Chapel Cross, she could see men working despite the rain.

Today, coming back from Beasley Hall, they were still at it. She found herself drawn to the progress at Old Paradise, to this part of the county.

After her lesson and the invigorating phone call, she determined to find a used SUV, not horrible on gas, for Tootie, before that Toyota died a well-deserved death.

CHAPTER 21

In the distance, the *slap slap slap* of the huge waterwheel could be heard. Saturday, October 7, Sister did as Gray suggested, moved the cast time to eight A.M. Given that Thursday had been canceled due to the torrential rains of Tuesday and Wednesday, a large field assembled.

Wind after the rains helped dry out the soil just enough so the footing was springy, slick in spots. Rickyroo, Sister's Thoroughbred mount, at thirteen, loved the footing, loved foxhunting, loved Sister. What he didn't love was other horses pushing his behind. Wolsey, turned out with Rickyroo, actually didn't push him but unkind words were spoken. Irritated the hell out of the Master's horse. He was first, not even first among equals, but first. He didn't need any lip about his hindquarters.

Shaker's horse for the day, Kilowatt, would not have lowered himself to chat with a peon in the field. Betty Franklin's Outlaw, a friendly Quarter Horse, would flick his ears and swish his tail when he passed the field, but he usually had something pleasant to say. Kasmir Barbhaiya's Jujube, ridden by Tootie at the request for some seasoning, paid not the least bit of attention to the fifty-two horses and riders. All his senses focused on this new task at hand.

Kasmir on Nighthawk rode with Alida on Lucille Ball, so named for her flaming chestnut coat.

Many a horseman or houndsman would counsel newcomers to foxhunting not to name a horse something like Devil's Boy, nor a hound Viagra. The wisdom was that the animal would live up or down to his or her name. Hounds and horses understand language. This old wives' tale, as many newcomers thought of it, proved to be true more often than not. And thanks to studies at a Hungarian university, as well as at American ones, it was becoming evident to those needing scientific proof that yes, animals did understand language—at least higher vertebrates did. And they learned it like humans: left brain for logic, right brain for emotion and creativity.

Had anyone known that, witnessing Lucille Ball cut a caper would have made them laugh. Too late to change the redhead's name now. Once a run commenced, Lucille would settle down. Until then there was prancing, snorting, sideways trotting, casting her eye backward to let Alida know she saw everything, absolutely everything, including the fact that Alida carried her crop sideways so Lucille knew it was in her hands. Lucille could have cared less. She knew her 1200 pounds pitted against Alida's 135 meant she would win. Alida put up with it because Lucille could jump the moon, had gaits smooth as silk, and was bold, wondrously bold. You put her to anything, you were going over.

A guest, Marilyn Davidson, told Alida to take Lucille to the back of the field. Alida, too much of a lady, squelched the retort, which would have been, "Why don't you learn how to ride? Then you wouldn't mind my horse." All she did was turn her head to reply, "Once we're going she's an angel."

No sooner was this out of her mouth than *bam,* they were going.

Mill Ruins sat four miles north of Chapel Cross. The soil was not as rich as that at Chapel Cross; the lay of the land was similar, good flat pastures that, heading west, quickly turned into ravines with thick woods. Mill Ruins took advantage of the faster running waters of the feeder creek, wide, to the Tye River miles and miles away, which poured into the James at Buffalo Station. That fast-moving water provided the energy for the mill's waterwheel. The original settler back in 1752 knew what he was doing. The waterwheel still turned. A miller could grind grain, if one could be found.

Hounds struck to the right of Walter's house. Sister took a little feel of Rickyroo's reins, for the pastures were extensive and with a slight roll. They were perfect for galloping, as was the footing.

Staff smiled broadly because a youngster had found the line and had been honored by the pack for the first time. Audrey, nose to the ground, knew she'd joined the big kids. Her littermates, not quite two years old, Aero, Angle, and Ace, desperately wanted to prove themselves. Young, fast, they bunched up right behind their sister. Dasher flew by them. He was called Dasher for a reason. His littermate, Diana, joined him. Pride of place belonged to them and, in their prime, they had plenty of gas in the engine.

Pride of place in the hunt field belonged to the Bancrofts, in their eighties still riding First Flight. Gray fell back to allow them to move up behind Sister. An hour of hard running didn't faze them. By the second hour they would wind up in the middle of the field.

At this moment, no one was too concerned with their place in the field, because the entire pack shot across the newly mown pasture, jumped over a tiger-trap jump, and headed north into another pasture, large hay bales dotted about like shredded wheat.

Tinsel stopped a moment to check out a hay bale. Yes, the fox had been there but was now gone, so Tinsel needed to catch up.

After twenty minutes of sublime music, hard running, hounds threw up at the junction of Miller's Creek with Tidy's Corner. No one ever knew how Tidy received the name. Off of

Miller's Creek, the mill run ran like an arrow back to the mill. Tidy's creek's lesser force added to the sometimes turbulent Miller's Creek. The mill run smoothed out the water to the wheel, but baffles existed along its mile-long route, where water could be slowed if necessary. Too much force could harm the gears in the wheel. If the paddles broke, that was an easy fix. If the gears were damaged to the wheel or the grindstones, that caused big problems. Those former millers thought of everything.

So did the fox. He dabbled at the corner, zig-zagging between both creeks. Hounds found tidbits of scent but nothing held. Given that they were American hounds, their work ethic was sensational. The devotees of the three other types of foxhounds would praise their hounds, too: Crossbreds, English, Pennmarydel. But American hounds have ever been prized for their drive. What could be lacking sometimes was biddability, listening. That's why Sister, Shaker, Betty, and Tootie played with them once they were six weeks old, and walked hounds throughout the year for the rest of their lives. You want them to listen. Even more, you want them to want to listen.

They were listening now as Shaker encouraged them.

"Find your fox. He's here."

"Where?" Parker wailed.

"If you'd shut up and put your nose to ground, you big baby, you might find him," Cora reprimanded him.

Tatoo, steady, not a flashy hound, walked northward. A tingle. He walked a bit faster. More tingle.

"Think I've got him."

Cora loped over, putting her nose to ground. The two lovely animals walked shoulder to shoulder. Both made hounds, they didn't want to open if they weren't sure, or if the scent faded. Important to push a hot line in the direction in which the fox was moving. And no made hound wanted to run heel—which is to say backward—although they do it for a few moments to double-check their efforts, the intensity of scent.

Foxhounds, bred as we know them for over a thousand years—and more than that if one goes back to ancient Greece, where they might not be recognizable as our foxhounds but they were scent hounds—over all those centuries, the animal improved. A foxhound is born to hunt. That is what it lives to do.

Sister and some of those with her were also born to hunt, a drive unfathomable to many people in the so-called modern world. They couldn't realize that the human is a medium-sized predator. It's how we survive. It's what we are.

So those foxhunters, rapt attention, observed the ancient ritual.

Even Marilyn Davidson, unaccustomed to the pace, watched. As she hadn't parted company with her horse on that hard run, her own confidence soared.

Now Ardent joined Cora and Tatoo. Sterns waved slightly.

"A lot of back and forth," Ardent commented.

"New fox," Cora replied. *"We haven't picked him up before. He'll learn we don't give up."*

The fox, young, moved into the woods, ground falling away now. A vixen, Hortensia, who knew Mill Ruins well as pickings were good, called to the youngster.

"Come over here to me."

"Yes, ma'am."

"The pack will find your scent again. You've never run before. I've never seen you here. This place is overrun with those stupid hounds about once every three weeks."

"I came off the mountain. Too many coyote."

"Follow me. Step in my footsteps if you can. We will reach another fork in the creek. You jump into the creek and swim as far as you can. I'll lead them away."

"Aren't you scared?"

"What's your name, son?"

"Ewald." Noticing her raised eyebrows, he said, *"Mother named me."*

"Well, Ewald, the hound doesn't exist who is as smart as the fox. But you have to learn." A loud

song picked her head up; she listened. *"Okay. They've found your line and they're about seven minutes away. Jump in. Swim as long as you can and don't worry, they'll pick up my line. Climb out and if you swing back toward the mill, you'll find an old abandoned outbuilding. Good place for a den. I take it your father threw you out?"*

"Yes, ma'am."

"A little early for that. Usually you young fellows are sent on your way the end of October through November." She listened again, as the whole pack was singing now. *"Don't leave the building until you hear the big trailers pull out. Rumbling engines—you'll know. Make that your den. Been empty for years. Oh, one last thing. James is the big red fox who lives behind the mill. He's a pain in the ass. Don't fret. I'll fix it if he becomes troublesome. He wants to tell everyone what to do. Go. Go now."*

Ewald jumped into the creek, swam upstream. Hortensia watched, waited until she could identify Dasher's voice, then trotted due west, heard Cora, Ardent, Trooper, Tatoo, and broke into a flat-out run. This was going to be like taking candy from a baby.

Tootie, on the right of the creek, watched as Betty did from the left side of the creek. Dasher reached the spot where Ewald had leapt into the creek and Hortensia had turned right.

"Vixen! Hot, hot, hot!" he screamed.

The whole pack screamed behind him as the field turned right on a rutted farm road, the worse for the recent rain. After the rain the red clay was serviceable if slick. A few downed trees, trunks conveniently without limbs, provided impromptu jumps. Bobby Franklin had a devil of a time getting around a few of these.

On and on they ran as woods got thicker, the temperature slid downward.

Hortensia paused at an open meadow, then scorched the earth running to the other side, in which stood a two-acre crop of marijuana just ready to be harvested. She sped through plants as high as a horse's head, laughing as she ran. On the other side of this botanical treasure, she, being a gray, easily climbed a tree, walked out on a thick branch, and dropped onto the heavy branch of another tree, where she flatted herself to watch the show.

Four minutes later, the entire pack blasted into the marijuana. Tootie rode to the right of the crop. Given the density of it, she couldn't ride between rows so she rode at the edge. Betty, now on the other side of the creek, held up far down at the southern edge of the crop, in open pasture.

Sister held up as Shaker blew hounds to him.

"She's here. The scent burns!" Twist was beside himself.

Hounds, baying, continued to thrash through

263

the thick crop. Reaching the foot of the tree, no vixen.

Cora, wise, looked up. *"How do you do?"*

Hortensia grinned. *"Lovely day."*

The conversation abruptly ended as a scythe of rat shot whooshed through the tall swaying plants.

The owner of this illegal crop, hearing the commotion, had been following it in his truck, now parked about forty yards back on the farm road.

Tootie, startled, as was Jujube, called out to the hounds, "Go to him!"

"Go to hell." An irate, middle-aged man, cap pulled low over his head, cussed at her, then shot at the hounds again.

"Ow!" Tatoo screamed, blood now squirting from the rat shot in the hindquarters and leg.

The hounds melted into the marijuana to join Shaker.

Tootie dismounted and, reins in hand, walked to Tatoo, on the ground. "Good boy. Good hound."

"I'll kill that worthless cur!" The grower leveled the rifle at Tatoo's head.

"No, you won't." A handsome blond man appeared behind the grower, wrapped both hands around his neck. "I'll kill you first. Drop the goddamned rifle!"

The fellow did just that, choking for air.

"Hold hard, young lady. I'll help you with the hound." He then whispered in the grower's ear,

"If you ever harm a hound again or speak filth to a lady, I will kill you." He tightened his grasp and the grower's arms flailed. "Do you understand?"

All the man could do was try to nod his head.

Hortensia watched with great interest.

The handsome fellow pulled the man to the ground, picked up his rifle, and smashed the butt of it into his head as he, coughing, tried to crawl. Then he calmly wiped his fingerprints off the rifle, checked for a pulse, smiled at Tootie. "He'll live, unfortunately. You walk your horse. I'll carry the hound until we near the field. Are you all right?"

"Yes. Thank you." Tootie, dazzled by this fellow, noticed he wore ratcatcher; a cowhorn on a rawhide string hung on his back, out of harm's way.

Shaker sat still, worried, blowing hounds back. They hurried out of the field to him.

Sister, hearing the shots, held the field at a distance from the marijuana. Shaker couldn't go into the crop because hounds would go where he did. Sister, keeping the people calm, resolved to go in if hounds did not come out and if she didn't see Tootie. Hounds wouldn't follow her. They would stay with Shaker.

Betty covered her ears. The sound of gunfire never proved reassuring. Sweat trickled between her breasts. Outlaw, ears forward, stood like a rock.

One by one, Shaker counted hounds. No Tatoo. No Tootie. He blew again.

Tootie, moving at the edge of the heavy crop, called out, "We're okay."

Nearing the open pasture, the man stopped, lifted Tatoo over her saddle. "I think he'll stay. You'll need to pick out the rat shot and wash him, but nothing's broken." He paused, smiled at her. "You're a good whipper-in."

Tootie, overwhelmed, simply nodded her thanks.

"Are you all right? That was a nasty shock."

"I'm okay. I'm just worried about the hound."

He lifted off his cap, faded, hard used, and kissed her on the cheek. "The hound always comes first. Go on now."

Jujube, tractable now, slowly walked toward the pasture.

When she turned to look back, the man was gone.

Seeing her reach the corner, Sister began to dismount.

Gray rode up. "A master's feet should never touch the ground. With your permission."

She smiled. He rode off and she thought, *Now there's a foxhunter.* She also thought to herself what a divine man Gray was: calm, collected, in control, and hers, all hers.

"Hold hard, Tootie." Gray rode up, swung his leg over, and lifted Tatoo, who whined, off the saddle.

Tootie, ashen, breathed deeply. "There's a crazy man in there. He shot at the pack. I'm lucky he didn't shoot me."

Gray put his arm around her shoulder. "All's well. Let's get Tatoo back."

Shaker, on sight of Tootie, rode up, dismounting. The pack followed. Gray put down Tatoo, Shaker knelt, examining the rat shot.

Tootie filled them in. She said she had help but she didn't know who it was. Someone well turned out.

Neither man paid too much attention to this. "Ronnie!" Shaker bellowed.

Ronnie Haslip left the field, hurrying up to Shaker, Tootie, and Gray.

"Ride back to the trailers, will you? The key to the party wagon is in the truck. We'll get out to the road. Bring it up, will you?"

"Of course." The trusted fellow nodded and turned, riding off.

"Let's not broadcast too much. Sister will know how to handle this. If it were up to me, I'd find the bastard and throttle him," Shaker said as Gray lifted Tatoo in his arms again.

"The fellow who helped me choked him, threw him on the ground, then hit him in the head with the butt of his rifle. He took his pulse—he's not dead."

"If I find him, he will be." Shaker on foot, leading Kilowatt, walked, the pack with him, while Gray continued to carry Tatoo. Tootie led his horse and her own.

Gray, to the other two, quietly said, "We can tell Sister what occurred once hounds are on the trailer. Or Tootie, you can tell her, and Betty and Shaker can get hounds back. The less people know of details, the better. God only knows what will be on Facebook."

"Jesus Christ." Shaker spat. "People have no sense."

"You just figured that out, did you?" Gray lightly said.

Reaching the road, Gray gratefully put down Tatoo, who stood up, wobbly. Blood trickled out of a few rat shot holes.

"Digging out the rat shot will sting. Some of this will have to fester out." Shaker again examined the sweet hound. "Goddammit. Goddammit it to hell!"

They waited as Sister took the field back in. Betty joined the pack just in case someone took a notion, plus there was no reason to stand at the far end of the marijuana patch now.

Tootie filled her in.

"Think we should call 911?" Betty asked.

"Hell no. Let him suffer." Shaker smiled, then added, "And I bet you fifty smackers that marijuana crop will be burning soon. Someone will call Ben Sidell from back at the trailers."

"Ah." Betty blinked.

"That's where Sister is different. She'd find the fellow, speak to him about foxhunting, and pay him off. Woman would have made a great old-time politician," Gray commented.

"What's the phrase, 'Better to have them inside the tent pissing out than outside the tent pissing in'?" Betty remembered it correctly.

"Now everyone is morally pure." Shaker laughed.

"Right." Gray laughed also.

They chatted, petting hounds, loving on Tatoo. Famous Amos, Ronnie's horse, regaled Outlaw and Wolsey with tales of Ronnie trying to tie his stock tie in the trailer.

Kilowatt listened. *"Why doesn't he do it at home? Shaker does. Mirror's better."*

"Because my human is always late. He needs a wife."

"Famous, Ronnie's gay." Outlaw giggled.

"You think I don't know that? I said he needed a wife; I didn't say that poor soul had to be a woman. She should hear Xavier"—he mentioned a childhood friend who had been out of town for two weeks on business—*"who says to him to go online and look for a date. It gets worse."*

"Can you imagine if we could go online?" Kilowatt wondered.

"You're cracked." Jujube finally said something.

"That Lucille Ball is a babe. What a beautiful mare." Outlaw half closed his eyes

"Redhead. She'll run you crazy. Push you away from your feed bucket on the fence line. Squeal if you even brush by her. Too much work," Kilowatt sensibly spoke.

The conversation didn't finish because Ronnie drove right up.

"Quick work." Shaker, leading Kilowatt, loaded hounds.

Betty and Tootie, on foot, also helped.

Gray laid Tatoo on the passenger seat in the truck.

"I can sit with him on my lap," Tootie offered.

"He'll be fine. They'll be glad to get to the kennels. You all go in to the breakfast." He slid into the driver's seat, drove off.

Tootie, Betty, Gray, and Ronnie, on the ground, reins in hand, looked toward the mill, which seemed so far away.

"Anyone need a leg up?" Gray offered.

"Not yet," Ronnie replied.

Once in the saddle, they walked back, talked about Audrey hitting the line, older hounds honoring, what a good day it had been until hitting the weed.

"How much marijuana do you think is out there?" Gray asked.

"Government flies over in helicopters," Betty replied. "Infrared photography, right?"

"Waste of time and money." Gray's legs lightly hung on Wolsey, a fine horse, very kind. "They get a photo, cops are on the ground. They rush over to destroy the crop. Someone else goes to who owns the land, and half the time the owner is absentee. Big deal. Here's the way it works. Why is one form of relaxation—or self-destruction, if you feel that way—legal and another is not?"

"Got me there." Ronnie nodded.

"Because some people think smoking a joint is a gateway drug. Next come heroin and cocaine." Betty provided the usual argument.

Tootie, patting Jujube's glossy neck, said, "No, what comes next is an opioid crisis. It's got nothing to do with marijuana."

"A fine mess, isn't it?" Ronnie felt tired, although they hadn't hunted more than an hour and a half. The half was standing in the pasture.

"Sometimes I think our entire country is just one big contradiction." Gray liked things to make sense.

"You know, it probably always was. Now we have news, non-news, and fake news twenty-four hours a day. The contradictions jump right out at you." Ronnie half laughed.

"The trailers." Gray, jubilant, headed for Sister's rig, as did Tootie and Betty.

Ronnie and Famous Amos walked onto Ronnie's trailer, not far from Sister's.

Horses tended to, the four finally made it to

the breakfast. Walter pressed a drink in Sister's and Betty's hands. Ronnie grabbed an ice cold beer, one of the craft brews from Route 151, remembered his manners, and brought Tootie, in the middle of a group questioning her, an iced tea.

Sister broke up the group, put her arm around Tootie's shoulder. "Let's sit for a minute. We can go into Walter's tiny reading room."

She pointed to the reading room. Walter nodded and they walked in, Sister closing the door.

The room, about the size of a big stall, ten feet by twelve, was tiny but perfect. A chintz sofa with green pillows to match the leaves from the print invited them. The walls—bookshelves, top to bottom—testified to Walter's abiding interest in medical history as well as regular history, especially medieval England. The walls were painted hunter green; a fireplace with a mahogany surround took up one wall, with a glorious Heather St. Clair Davis painting over it. The two women fell onto the sofa.

Tootie tried to remember everything.

"I should know who owns that land, but I don't." Sister finally tasted her drink, a gin rickey.

A gin rickey is a summer drink, but it tasted perfect at that moment.

"I didn't recognize the guy with the gun. Maybe he's not from this county. The weed growers cover a lot of ground. Then again, he could be a Washington lawyer out for an extra buck." Tootie raised her shoulders.

"Walter told me one marijuana plant sells for twelve hundred dollars right now. A lot of money back there. Tell me again about the man who helped you. I want to make sure I've heard things correctly."

"He walked up behind the guy, the farmer, and he put his hands around his throat. He must have been strong because the man dropped his rifle, threw it down, really, which he was told to do. He choked. He tried to get away. My savior"— she smiled—"was strong. He told me he'd help me with the hound. He said to the farmer if he ever hurt a hound he would kill him and if he was ugly to me, he'd kill him. Then he threw him on the ground. The farmer had had his own hands on his throat, and he was coughing. The blond man picked up the rifle and smashed the butt into his head. Then he picked up Tatoo and walked with me until we got near the field."

"Tell me again what he was wearing."

"He had to have been in the field, although I didn't notice him. He wore ratcatcher—a bluish tweed, beige britches, old brown hunt cap, tails down, which was odd because tails down is only for staff. And the cowhorn was odd. He had it slid behind his back. Oh, his tie was, I don't know, one of those regimental ties."

"And he was blond?"

"Blond. Six feet, at least. Gorgeous. Sister, he was one of the most gorgeous men I have ever seen. You think I would have noticed him in the hunt field but I pay attention to the hounds. I don't know how he got behind that farmer but I'm sure glad he did. The farmer said he'd shoot the pack and shoot me. I said that before, didn't I?"

"You did. When something like this happens, details come back bit by bit, I think. And this man, how old?"

"I'm not good with age. He wasn't middle-aged. Young, but not as young as I am. Sister, he was gorgeous. Didn't you see him?"

"No. He wasn't in the field."

"He was in hunt kit."

"I believe you. It's just he wasn't in the field. I think you encountered the man who is blowing his cowhorn after our hunts." She paused, took another drink, thought a moment. "You liked him?"

"I did. He was a real foxhunter. I could tell that just by how he handled Tatoo."

"Yes."

"But why would he follow the hunt and blow his cowhorn? I've heard it."

"I don't know."

"Thank God he was there, Sister. I don't know if that guy would have killed me, but I think he would have killed Tatoo. The blond man really did save me, and he was so kind, kind eyes." She blushed a moment. "He said I was a good whipper-in."

"He would know."

"Who is he? You know him? I want to meet him, thank him properly. I should do something after what he did for me and for Tatoo."

"He is—or was—a huntsman. I believe you saw Wesley Carruthers. Weevil." She took a long, deep breath. "He's been missing since 1954."

CHAPTER 22

Hounds and horses were washed, wiped down, put up by Betty and Tootie. Sister and Shaker cleaned out Tatoo's rat shot wounds.

"What a good boy." Sister praised him as she used the long narrow tweezers to pick out a bit of lead.

"Ow," he murmured, but stood still as Shaker held him.

The poor fellow, riddled with the tiny pellets, would get a breather, cookies given to him. After one hour, they wiped him down with bluecoat, literally a blue coating that staved off infection. The colors of antiseptics ranged from silver to orange to blue. As Sister sprayed this on it did sting a little.

"All done." She beamed. "Shaker, when that marijuana patch is burned, we should celebrate. This sweet fellow didn't deserve to be peppered."

"Sooner or later we'll figure out who is growing the stuff." Shaker lifted up the tractable animal, carrying him back to the special room with its own stall walkout.

Sister followed, opening the chain-link door.

Zane, goldbricking about his claw, immediately put on his sorrowful look. *"A cookie would help me so much."*

Sister laughed at Zane. "You've been in here long enough for heart surgery."

He took a few steps with a pronounced limp.

Tatoo, made of sterner stuff, chided the youngster, *"Will you stop?"*

"I am seriously injured. We're making sure my paw doesn't become infected. See?" He held up a healed paw, the claw clipped very short but no swelling anymore around it.

"I need to sleep. You can shut up at any time." Tatoo shot Zane a sharp look.

"Well, we can walk out Zane tomorrow and put him back with his group." Sister observed the young hound, who curled up next to Tatoo.

Tatoo didn't growl, but he did ignore him. Zane smacked the raised bed box, nicely stuffed with soft blankets. That tail was going.

"Zane, go to sleep if you're going to be next to me."

"I will. I've been in here for days all alone. Oh, I have suffered. I need a friend."

"Dear God." Tatoo lifted his head, looked at the young dramatist, then flopped his head back down. He was asleep before Zane could think of another play for attention. So the youngster decided to sleep as well.

As Sister and Shaker walked back to the office, she remarked, "Isn't it something how there is such a variation in one litter? Zorro and Zandy are not little mimosas. Zane will just close up

277

with a touch." She smiled. "His grandmother was like that. Ever notice how certain qualities jump a generation? You see it in horses, hounds, and humans. Ace is a dead ringer for grandpa Asa."

"You and I have talked about this before. I've talked about it with other huntsmen. Just something we learn. I'm sure there's science behind it and someone will prove the generational jump, probably about humans first."

"H-m-m. Makes me wonder about Genghis Khan's grandchildren." She picked up her gear, which she'd laid on her desk.

"Only you would think about Genghis Khan."

"I was thinking about him because if we breed Giorgio to a G girl at another kennel, different bloodline, we will have a G line. We can name a hound Genghis Khan."

He shook his head. "I don't know if that's fair to the hound."

"Kind of like naming a son Adolf. Italians can name a son Adolfo, but English-speaking people don't name a son Adolf. Odd."

Tootie popped in. "Done."

"None of us got anything to eat because of the uproar. Come on up to the house. I made chicken corn soup last night. It's always better the next day. Shaker, what about you?"

"Thank you, no. I'm going over to Beasley Hall to walk through Skiff's kennels. She bribed me with food."

"Is that so?" Sister's eyebrows raised slightly.

He smiled as Betty Franklin joined them.

"What a damned mess. How's Tatoo?"

"He'll be fine. Once we could examine him I figured we could do the work here, as he is such a good guy even if something hurts. Will save a trip to the vet and the bill, too."

"He is a good boy," Betty agreed. "We missed all the gossip. I'll bet you one hundred dollars someone in our club knows who is growing weed." She continued. "Do I care? No. But I sure care when a man blasts our hound and threatens Tootie. Even if he doesn't get caught, he will lose thousands and thousands of dollars."

"I—" Tootie didn't finish her sentence.

Sister placed her hand on Tootie's shoulder and squeezed.

"Betty, I made chicken corn soup. Would you like some?"

"I'd love it, but I have a husband at home who is waiting for his steak. In his defense he cleans up the grill and the kitchen."

Tootie asked, "I thought men liked to grill. Were competitive about it."

"Not Bobby, bless his heart." Betty smiled. "That's all right. He does other things." She glanced at the old wall clock. "Let me get going here. Maybe he picked up some news at the breakfast."

She walked outside to her ancient but cool

yellow Bronco, fired up that old motor, and rumbled off.

Sister and Tootie walked up to the house. Gray often spent a Saturday with Sam and Aunt Daniella so it was just the two of them.

Once in the kitchen, pot on the stove, Sister sat at the table, which Tootie had set. She'd even put out a nice bowl on a plate for Golly, who was looking her best.

A timer sat by the stove. Sister had learned to trust the timer rather than herself.

"How do you feel?" she asked the young woman.

"I'm okay."

"We couldn't really talk about it because we had to get hounds back. It's a miracle that only Tatoo was hit."

"If it hadn't been for that hunting fellow, he would have shot again."

"Let me show you something."

"What I want to know is what do you mean— we got interrupted—he's been missing since 1954?"

"That's what I want to show you." Sister picked up her cellphone lying on the counter. "Look at this."

Tootie studied the video. "That's him!"

"Wesley Carruthers. Weevil. He hunted the hounds here from 1947 to 1954, when he disappeared."

"That can't be true. This is the man who saved me." She looked at the image, gratitude and curiosity flooding over her. "There's no way this man could be . . . however old he would be. But it is the same blond man, same smile. I have to find him."

The timer rang out. Sister rose to ladle out two big bowls of soup. Tootie, knowing Golly, opened the large drawer, pulled out some treats, and put them in the bowl. She also picked up two Milk-Bones for Raleigh and Rooster, each of whom thanked her.

As they ate their soup, Sister told Tootie everything she knew about Weevil.

"Sister, he was no ghost."

"Well, it certainly makes me wonder. Is there anything you can add to what you told me?"

"He knew hounds. He wore ratcatcher. He had the cowhorn on a rawhide string, pushed on his back. He was strong. Wide shoulders, really fit, strong and handsome. He had a kind of light scent. We walked side by side so I could pick it up. Sister, he had such kind eyes. I don't know what would have happened to me if he hadn't appeared like that."

"I'm glad he did show up. I hunted behind Weevil once as a child. Mother took me around. He was good, forward with hounds, and handsome as you said. At that age, it didn't exactly register but he was handsome. I recall his voice, which was deep."

"This man had a deep voice and an accent. Light. Maybe Canadian. I don't think anyone here would notice it because the Tidewater accent is like a Canadian one. Think of how people pronounce 'out and about.' "

"Interesting. Canada has eleven hunts, I think." She paused. "Wherever there are English-speaking people there are horses and hounds. New Zealand, Australia—there used to be hunting in India under the Raj. Don't know if there still is. We do excel at chasing things on horseback with hounds. You know, Tootie, some things are so deep in a culture it's harmful to fool with it. Know what I mean?"

"Like music for African Americans? Think of what we brought to the New World. Just the rhythms alone. Dad would talk about how we gave jazz to America. The problem is, I don't much like jazz but I like the old music from the 1940s, you know, like Ella Fitzgerald." She thought a moment. "If Weevil is a ghost, that would be his time, wouldn't it?"

"He was born in 1922. More soup?"

"No. I should be hungry, but I'm not very." Tootie's cellphone went off. Looking down, she made an apologetic face. "Hello."

Her father's voice, loud and clear, perked up Golly's ears as well as Sister's. "If you will testify against your mother in court I will reinstate you in my will."

Without a second's hesitation, she fired back. "And how long before you cut me out again? Dad, I'm not stupid."

A pause followed this. Vic didn't really underestimate his daughter but he was a businessman and if he could short you, he would.

"One hundred thousand dollars. Now. And I will sign a contract promising not to cut you out of the will in future."

"No. I don't want any part of this. I saw the video, Dad."

An even longer pause followed that. "I'll fire up the jet and come to you." He mentioned his Gulfstream G150. "I wasn't thinking clearly."

"Well, I am. I will never testify against Mom."

"Triple-digit millions probably before you're fifty. Money is power. Why stand by your mother? She didn't really stand by you."

"No."

"Those Virginia snobs have turned you." His voice took an edge.

"They aren't snobs. They're my friends. They've done more for me than you have." She nearly spat that out.

"The hell! I sent you to the best schools. I paid for your riding lessons. I bought you whatever you wanted including Iota. I paid for your coming out and that cost a half a million. I outdid and outspent all those goddamned clabberfaces."

He used the old country word for white people although he was a city boy.

Calm now, Tootie acidly replied, "I didn't ask for any of it except for Iota. You used me to reflect your power. I didn't want to be a debutante. You don't own me, Dad. You never will. You know what's really sick? You believe white people are your oppressors. You hate them. Some were and some are. I know our history.

"I know my opportunities came from you and from all our people before me. I know how lucky I am. But Dad, you are defined by your oppressor.

"No one defines me but me. I will never testify against Mom. I never want to see you again." Tootie threw her phone on the floor. "I hate him."

Sister, bending over, picked it up, and dropped it in Tootie's hand. "Still works. These things are tough."

"I was stupid to throw it down. I'm sorry." She looked to see if it had dented the random width pine floor.

Had, a tiny bit.

"You're upset. You have good reason to be upset." Sister put her arm around Tootie's shoulders. "I'm no psychologist but I figure he's fighting for the only thing he knows: money and power. A lot of people are like that. They're empty."

Tootie searched Sister's cobalt eyes. "You know what scares me? What if I turn out like

Dad or even Mom? She's trying but I wasn't the daughter she wanted. She wanted a carbon copy of herself. . . ."

Sister kissed Tootie on the cheek. "As she learns to really know you, she'll be proud that you're not a carbon copy. You are exactly yourself."

Tootie nodded, wanting to believe that, then said, "People must look at me and think of my father naked, not a pretty sight, with those two women. Gross. It is so gross."

"I'm sorry."

"You and Gray mean more to me than Mom and Dad."

"Tootie, for all their faults, they gave you life. One can only hope he will grow up, see the error of his ways, and make amends. And let's give your mother credit; she is turning over a new leaf."

Silent, Tootie got up, put on the tea kettle, sat back down, then got up, more treats for Golly, Raleigh, and Rooster.

"You spoil them," Sister said.

"Learned it from you. It's you who says, 'What's the point of loving someone or something if you don't spoil them a little?'"

"Well, I guess I do. This day has been overwhelming. I thank the good Lord no one was really hurt. You never know about these people with illegal crops, although I know what drives them to it."

"Money?"

"Yes, but so many people in Virginia and Kentucky, they've been wiped out by the war on tobacco, the war on coal. They only know but so much. They aren't going to be computer coders. As for tobacco, it takes years and years to learn how to successfully grow that crop, the varieties—and then curing it, that's a real art. Is smoking bad for you? You bet, but does anyone hold a gun to your head and say, 'You will smoke this cigarette'?"

"No, but someone just about held a gun to my head." Tootie was bouncing back. "And smoking is vile."

"It is, but this is where our generations possibly diverge. I believe in people. I believe they should make their own decisions, even if those decisions are not always the best. I have no right to tell someone else how to live. If you started smoking, I would be horrified, but it isn't hurting me."

"I could blow smoke in your face." Tootie laughed, spirits restoring.

"You would, too." Sister laughed with her. "While I'm thinking about it, let me show you Weevil's horn. Maybe you will have an idea about it, something that Marion and I missed. She was able to send me the complete pictures of it, since the museum catalogues everything. In case you noticed the carvings."

Tootie clicked through all the images. "Look, here's my cottage, what was left of it. Comet's ancestor is underneath."

"I saw that. By the time Ray and I inherited Roughneck Farm, it was teetering, but good chestnut logs, I might add, and we've used them. Used to be chestnut everywhere. Same with elm."

Tootie clicked through again. She peered. "My cottage fox, he's looking at the kennels."

"Smart."

"The chase scrimshaw sort of goes from Roughneck Farm to Chapel Cross, the four Corinthian columns. The stables and the fox at the tack room door."

"Does."

Tootie returned to Weevil himself. "I must find him. I will find him."

"Just a minute, now. Whether Weevil is a ghost or has found the fountain of youth, he's back, but no one knows why. He's secretive and, remember, this started with a theft."

"A cowhorn!"

"He broke into the case at the Huntsman Hall of Fame. That's a theft." Sister said so with feeling.

"Sister, if you had a pencil in that case used by Dickie Bywaters,"—Tootie named the great huntsman from the first half of the twentieth century—"you would think it valuable."

Sister laughed. "You're right, but still." She

breathed in. "Sometimes, Tootie, I think you are older than I am."

"Past lives," Tootie replied.

Under the circumstances, that was a mouthful.

CHAPTER 23

Sugar maples flashed red on the top leaves, oaks blushed with a bit of yellow or orange on top. High color, about ten days away, perhaps a few more, electrified everyone; humans, horses, hounds, foxes, and all the birds who didn't fly south became extra busy. Dens, nests, and roofs were repaired. Chimneys, if they hadn't been cleaned, were cleaned now. Windows were caulked, firewood stacked. Neither man nor beast could afford to be lazy during fall, all the more so since you never really knew when winter would arrive.

This Monday, hounds had a day to relax, recharge after Saturday's memorable hunt. Skiff trailered over Crawford's hounds, which blended in with Jefferson Hounds as they walked out.

The air sparkled so Sister, Shaker, Betty, Tootie, Sam, and Yvonne walked across the footpath of the wildflower field, crawled over the hog's-back jump into the now cut cornfield at After All. Black-eyed Susans, deep purple flowers as well as tiny white ones enlivened the long walk to the covered bridge. There hounds stopped, dashed into strong-running Broad Creek, drank, played a bit, then packed in as both huntsmen called them.

Roger, shiny and mostly black, walked shoulder to shoulder with young Angle.

Lifting his head, Roger noted, *"Deer."*

"After All is full of them," Angle replied. *"A lot of fox, too. We hardly ever have a blank day here."*

"Good. Blank days mean hard work for nothing. Well, getting out of the kennels is good, but I want to run foxes," Roger declared.

As hounds chattered so did the people.

"Ben Sidell had the marijuana burned. Yesterday," Shaker informed them, a big smile on his face. "Wish I'd known. I'd have gone over for the spectacle."

"Wonder if we'll ever know who the planter was, or is," Betty mused. "He couldn't have been that bright. You don't pass a rifle over someone's head when dozens of people sit on the other side of your crop. He heard the horn. He saw the pack of hounds. Pretty stupid. As for burning crops, I think burnings aren't made public. People would descend upon them to inhale." She laughed.

"Hundreds of stoned people." Yvonne kept her eyes on Pickens, who would turn his head to look at her. "You know, this dog is flirting with me." She pointed to Pickens.

"Mom, he's still young and he wants to be friends. The P litter is so sweet."

"And I'm not," Dragon sassed.

"What you are is an arrogant cur," Cora

pronounced with finality, making the other hounds laugh, that little intake of air they do.

"I guess protecting his crop blinded the man's judgment," Shaker said.

"If you point a rifle at someone or shoot their hound, you think that person isn't going to retaliate?" Skiff found the episode unsettling.

"Years ago, Binky DuCharme's son Arthur kept a still farther back from Old Paradise. There's always been a still back there. Water's so good. Of course, hounds got on a blazing run and smashed through it. All I could hear was tinkling glass." Shaker laughed. "And the miracle was, not one hound with cut pads. We didn't tell the sheriff's department because Arthur is the son of one of our two non-speaking landowners. What a mess. Poor Arthur." Shaker shrugged. "Binky had higher hopes for his son."

"And his cousin, Margaret, is whip smart. So much for breeding," Betty remarked.

"Brenden DuCharme, father of Alfred and Binky, wasn't intellectual but he worked hard, was smart about business things," Sister remembered; Brenden and his wife were alive, just barely, when she moved here.

"Margaret died your first year here. Now there was the paragon of fashion," Betty recalled.

"She was kind to children. She patted my pony, said some good words when Mom brought me here," Sister said. "Had to be 1953. I was old enough so I wasn't a pain when we traveled. Remember those two-lane highways? You'd crawl through every town."

"Funny how things pass, isn't it? We see it with horses and hounds. The DuCharmes, a mixed bag." Betty returned to intelligence being inherited. She mentioned her late father-in-law. "Mr. Franklin said Margaret died of a broken heart. She never complained. She put her energy into her sons, but there was a sadness there. At least, that's what he said."

"Don't you think some people are just born sad?" Yvonne piped up.

"Depression, but that's beyond sadness. Most drunks are depressives." Sam surprised them. "I was not. I liked the taste. That's the best explanation I can give."

"You fought it off." Sister complimented him.

"Thank you, but I am an alcoholic. I don't drink but I will always be an alcoholic. I'm on guard," he said.

"Your aunt Daniella can drink us all under the table." Sister laughed.

Sam, laughing as well, agreed. "Woman's got a hollow leg but you know, she's not an alcoholic. A heavy drinker, yes, but not an alcoholic. Gray and I take her to church every Sunday, as you know. She's a walking history book in search of a double bourbon."

"It's a genetic trick. Like a good nose in a

hound, a genetic program. People aren't any different. I think a lot of things run in families. I swear cancer does." Skiff patted Reagan's head as he slipped next to her.

"I believe that." Yvonne nodded. "But maybe we all have cancer and something trips the wire. Know what I mean?"

"Well, something's going on." Shaker slid over the hog's back. "I'm forty-four. Already lost three high school buddies to it. A couple of my friends have wives battling breast cancer. Scares me. Scares me because I don't understand it."

"Shaker, I think even doctors don't understand it, but going back to bloodlines, you and I were talking the other day about how a quality often skips a generation. Our A line. Ardent, son of Asa, is a good hound and somewhat resembles his sire, but Aces and Angle, the grandsons of Asa, dead ringers. It's uncanny. Same deep voices, same drive."

"Tootie looks more like my mother than I do," Yvonne noted.

"Maybe, but everyone knows I'm yours." Tootie found it difficult to think she looked like her maternal grandmother, who was getting old.

Mentally, Tootie knew she would get old. Emotionally, she didn't believe it.

Back at Roughneck Farm, Skiff and Sam loaded their hounds on the party wagon, a two-level

293

trailer so hounds could choose where to ride. Half of them were asleep once they found their berth.

Sister, Shaker, Betty, and Tootie called each hound by name.

"Pansy." Tootie motioned to the pretty girl.

"I liked the walk." Pansy slid by Tootie to go into the girls' side of the kennel.

Each hound waited until his or her name was called then stepped forward to go either right or left. Yvonne stood back to watch, surprised at how obedient the hounds were. They were happy creatures.

Once everyone was in their respective places, Sister offered drinks. They trooped up to the house, gratefully drank iced tea or soda, chatted.

Then Sister walked everyone back to the kennels.

"Skiff, before you go, let me show you something. Won't take long. Yvonne, Sam, you all can come inside, too."

She walked them all back to the record room. Betty pulled down a green leather volume from 1972. She opened it on the desk inside that room.

"You can see our records go back to 1887. We are so fortunate to have them."

Betty pointed to a 1972 staff photo. "This was the year before Sister was elected Master. She's a whipper-in."

"Betty, they don't want to see that."

"Yes, we do." Skiff and Yvonne studied the photo.

"You look exactly the same." Yvonne smiled as Tootie looked at Sister.

"What a fib." Sister laughed. "But here. This is the biggest help." She flipped through the hound photos, each accompanied by a pedigree. "I can follow a bloodline for one hundred and thirty years."

"Astonishing." Skiff was impressed.

"I was seventeen. Last year of high school and hunting with Jefferson." Sam looked back. "Then off to Harvard, where I hunted with Myopia."

"There are hounds in Boston?" Yvonne was surprised.

"Outside the city. Myopia was founded in 1882. Of course, when they found out I hunted in Virginia, they actually invited me to hunt with them. What a surprise when I turned out to be black plus, forgive me, I could ride." He laughed.

"Bet it made them competitive." Sister knew the story.

Sam smiled, which made him even more attractive. The man, in his early sixties, didn't have an extra ounce on his frame, and neither did Gray, his older brother.

"Sam, tell them." Sister prodded him.

"Well, second hunt, they knew I was black, so those that could stand it did. Those that were horrified said not a word to me, but one of the whippers-in didn't show. I volunteered and did just fine. Anytime you are from Virginia, other hunts do get competitive, but the truth was I was young, fearless, and could ride anything. And I did. Those white folks who were offended to have me in the midst couldn't keep up, so it was a moot point."

"I can certainly understand that. The first time I walked down the runway you could hear the intake of all that breath." Yvonne relayed her beginning. "But I sold clothing. The stuff I wore brought in the money. Before too long other young women of color, as we used to say, were walking the boards."

"It's hard to believe things were that way, and I grew up in the South." Betty was sincere.

"Betty, it's still that way for some people." Yvonne looked at her sport Swatch. "When it's twelve-fifteen here it's 1930 in Mississippi."

"You know, I actually think in some ways Mississippi is ahead of say, Iowa." Sam defended the often attacked state.

"You're probably right—and if I'm correct, I have a riding lesson." Yvonne looked at Sam.

"You do. Get in that big-ass car of yours and follow us to Beasley Hall. I'm going to put you up on Don Juan."

Skiff exclaimed, "What a sweetheart. He's called Don Juan because you'll fall in love with him."

After everyone left, Sister returned to the record room, pulling down the books from 1947 to 1954. Tootie happily played with puppies in the puppy palace. She'd attack her other chores later.

Sister studied every single pedigree in those seven years. Slapping shut 1954, she leaned back in the seat, exhaled. "I'll be damned."

She hurried back to the house. The landline proved clearer than her cellphone.

"Marion."

"What did you find out? You have that tone," Marion replied, not at all surprised.

"Weevil had an odd way of naming hounds. If a mother's first initial started with B, he might name some of the girls Birdie, Betty, etc. But then he would, out of the blue, name a girl Christine. Never did this with the boys."

"Yes." Marion waited.

"The nonconforming names were those of women he was rumored to have had affairs with, like Christine Falconer. Two years later, Christine bred, had her puppies properly named except for Madge, Christine's—the human's—daughter, in real life. He used every name you gave me plus the ones down here."

"That devil."

"And he called his bitch pack his 'Fast Ladies.' That's brazen if ever anything was."

"Well, I don't know if we're any closer to

finding out what's going on but we're certainly getting a sharper picture of Weevil."

Sister had informed Marion of the Weevil sighting, plus his protecting Tootie.

"This is what drives me crazy, Marion. I feel like I'm so close, like it's right under my nose and I don't see it."

"Want a wild guess?"

"From you? Always." Sister trusted Marion, as did most people who had the good fortune to know her or work with her.

"Tootie is beautiful, heavenly, a beautiful rider. She's so intelligent. If Weevil is Weevil and he has seen her, I predict he will . . . maybe not make a pass, but he will try to make a connection. Do ghosts make passes?"

"Well, there's *The Ghost and Mrs. Muir.*" Sister cited a wonderful movie from the forties.

"A ghost in love," Marion mused.

"The longer this goes on, the more I think this is a flesh-and-blood man. Why be Weevil, I don't know. He knows hunting. He asks questions about the past. He blows the cowhorn. Is it a signature or is it a warning?"

"You'll find out."

"You might be right about Weevil contacting Tootie again. She has no interest in men or women, as much as I can gather."

"Sister, a drop-dead gorgeous man protects and defends you. I know drop-dead gorgeous is a play on words, but there you have it. Any woman, even if she were gay, would be drawn to this knight in shining armor. Wouldn't you?"

"Of course, but then I always displayed a weakness for good-looking men, as have you, my sweet."

"But when?"

"When what?"

"When did you discover men?"

"I can't think that far back."

"Yes, you can. Don't be coy."

"Really, my first little whiff of lust? I guess I was sixteen. I didn't really get it until I was twenty."

"I rest my case."

CHAPTER 24

Margaret walked with her cousin Arthur on the Charlottesville Mall. He'd driven down to pick up a tiny Bokhara rug from a store on the Fourth Street side street. Margaret met him for an unusual lunch. She rarely had time for lunch, but given that both their fathers proved difficult they carved out time.

"Martha Jefferson," Arthur cited the old hospital at a new site east of town, "how can you find your way around it?"

"Compass," she replied, slipping her arm through his.

"I guess when Mom and Dad's time comes, that's where they'll go."

"Not soon, I hope."

Arthur, a decent fellow with no ambition, murmured, "I thought selling Old Paradise would solve problems. Money problems, sure. But the constant back and forth between my dad and yours. If one said 'A,' the other would say 'B,' and then you and I would spend hours, months, working it out. I can understand fighting over our grandmother's jewelry, what's left of it, but fighting over the manure spreader? There were six manure spreaders at the farm."

"Yeah, but only one worked." She stifled a laugh.

A smile crept onto his face. "How hard would it be to install new chains in an old one?"

"Not hard, just costs money. Those chains, for lack of a better word, are flat metal. Metal always costs, and both of our fathers are so damned cheap."

"They have millions now and Dad still keeps the Gulf station open, repairs a few cars. I tell him, close it down, spend time with Mom in your new house. I'll keep the station running if he doesn't want to shut it down. You don't have to work. Travel. Nope. Change terrifies him."

"What about your mother?"

"She'd love to go to Hawaii."

"Arthur, they're comfortable in their hostility, their misery, their pinched little lives. I blame some of this on our grandfather. When the boys were young there was still money. Old Paradise meant something. Binky and Alfred were at the top of the social pile. Went to their heads, I think."

Arthur nodded, quiet for a few steps. "I love my mother. Without her I don't know if I could stand Dad. But much as I love her, was losing her worth decades of anger and silence? Your father went ballistic."

"He did. Now he's retreated into a kind of coldness. He loves me, he has a few social friends, but Dad's in the deep freeze."

"Margaret, ever wonder if there's more to it?" Arthur turned his head to look at her directly.

"Funny you should ask. I was thinking that myself. Have off and on for years. It's just so— extreme." She paused. "Has your mother ever talked about when she dated Alfred?"

"Only that she and Alfred liked a lot of the same things. I asked her why she ditched Alfred. She shrugged and said that Dad paid more attention to her."

"H-m-m. Ever wonder if neither of us got married because of their example? Actually, Dad and Mom got along pretty good, but she died so young. At least I think they got along," Margaret second-guessed herself.

"Mom says your mother just wanted the social prestige. Then she always adds in the next breath that that doesn't mean she wanted her to die of lung cancer." Arthur put his hand over Margaret's. "I don't get this latest flare-up."

"Can't stand seeing Old Paradise come back to life without them. That's all I can figure." Margaret, like Arthur, was sick of their behavior. "You'd think they'd enjoy it. You'd think my dad would like his new easy-to-take-care-of house in Crozet. That dependency had electric wire wrapped in silk. Nothing had been done since the 1930s. I swear. He complains about the fireplace in his new house. He misses his stone fireplace. He asked me would I ask Crawford if he could remove the old one? I flatly refused. Crawford is touchy."

"You can be so diplomatic, cuz." He praised her.

"I get along with him but I don't have much to do with him. We had a joint meet, which you know about. Actually was a fabulous hunt. Crawford rode right up there with Sister and all went well."

"That's a miracle."

"The strangest thing happened, though. Both Shaker and Skiff blew 'Going Home.'" Sounded beautiful, and then it was followed by an echo that lingered. Deep. Mournful."

"Sometimes the mountains will do that."

"Yeah." She squeezed his arm. "So what do we do?"

"About Grandmother's earrings?" He shook his head. "Hell, when Mom dies, I don't want them. I'm not a drag queen."

"Oh, Arthur, there's still time."

He burst out laughing. "Can I wear a dress with a beard?"

Arthur, a touch vain, sported a trimmed well-kept beard. He almost looked like a rich Spanish grandee from the sixteenth century.

"I don't see why not. You'll have to borrow falsies. I do not recommend breast surgery and while I'm on that subject, be glad you don't have to carry them around."

"I don't mind holding them." He laughed.

"Worthless. If you like holding them, why don't you get married? Haven't found the right size? D? C? I am shocked."

A wry smile crossed his lips. "Much as I worship the female body, I am not always happy with the female mind."

Margaret was not one to scream sexist. "You can't stand that we're smarter than you?" Then she paused. "You know, Arthur, I actually know what you mean. There are some women, like some men, who exemplify the worst of their gender. For instance, what I have found working with other doctors and the nurses is if I have a disagreement with a man, we fight it out. Might get hot but when it's settled, that's it. Might settle a disagreement with a woman—but she will never forget it. Never. Sooner or later it will reappear. I just can't stand that. So I'm a pig."

"No, you're honest. Obviously not all women are like that, just like not all men are arrogant and not very insightful, but there are enough to make you wonder how the human race ever survived. Back to marriage. If I found a woman I could talk to, honestly talk to her and vice versa, I'd give it a shot. I see Mom wrap Dad around her little finger. I don't ever want a woman to try that with me."

"I understand. But, Arthur, you aren't going to find the right woman with your head under the body of a car. Exhaust pipes don't make for fascinating conversation. Who do you meet? Get out."

"Ah, Margaret. I never know what to say."

"You talk to me just fine."

"We grew up together. You're really my sister."

"Then talk to a woman as though you were talking to me. You're a good athlete. Take up golf or tennis or kayaking. You'll meet interesting people. I golf, as you know. I'd be happy to set you up with a good pro. Won't take you long— well, golf is a bitch, but you'll learn more quickly than others."

"I'll think about it."

"Consider this. I buried myself in my work. I met lots of young male doctors. They were okay but the spark wasn't there. I think we were all too focused on what we had to learn, and our career path. You don't meet too many doctors who don't want to make money and be set by our forties. Then I started foxhunting. Walter Lungrun sandbagged me into it. I met Ben. Chemistry." She grinned.

"Mom says no DuCharme should be dating a sheriff. Beneath us. You should be with another doctor, or preferably a senator."

"Interesting coming from a woman who married a garage mechanic." Margaret couldn't resist.

"But a DuCharme?"

"Do you give a shit?"

"About the name? Hell, no. But I am kind of proud of being descended from Sophie Marquet."

"Me, too. She must have been something. If they'd caught her they could have executed her. Probably not. But she'd have been imprisoned or sent to England. So we know we're descended from someone smart and tough, who loved our country."

"Yeah."

"Okay. Back to the damned earrings. Let's make a deal: You just tell your mother and father that when they leave this earth, you do want the Schlumberger Tiffany earrings. Worth a fortune, I might add, and they are stunning. If you marry, they go to your wife. If you don't marry, they go to me, unless you change your mind about being a drag queen. You'd be the only drag queen in America with real Schlumberger earrings."

"That's motivation. Will you help me dress?"

"Sure. You need to start practicing walking in high heels now."

"That means I have to shave my legs. If I keep my beard why can't I keep the fur on my legs?"

Margaret shook her head. "Not the same. You're handsome with your beard. You might get away with it, and the earrings would really set off your beard. Legs, never."

He pressed closer on her as they walked. Arthur loved Margaret. He felt she was the only person who actually understood him. Who wanted to do so. She accepted him for himself. She never once, never, chided him for being a car mechanic.

"I'll think about it."

They walked in silent companionship to the rug store, where Margaret stopped. She needed to get back to the hospital.

"Arthur, are you worried about your mom and dad?"

He looked straight into her eyes. "He's getting frail. As long as Dad and Uncle Alfred had Old Paradise, even though they couldn't repair one fence board, they felt important, you know? People would come to stare at the columns, the stables. They'd drive by Alfred's house all the way to the other side of the thousands of acres to see our house, an exact replica. People would tell newcomers the story of Old Paradise, of the brothers who hated each other because of a woman. They were somebody. Now Dad bitches that he has pots of money and lives on one acre."

"My dad's going down, too." She inhaled deeply. "They made this life. They can damn well deal with it. I'm not going to be in the middle anymore. When there was no money, and I was starting to climb in my profession, I tried to make peace. You did, too. Arthur, the hell with it."

"I think they never grew up. But I'm with you. I'm not taking messages from one to the other.

And before I forget, your solution to the earrings is good. I agree."

She kissed him on the cheek, turned, then turned back. "Remember, shave your legs."

Milly DuCharme closed up the front of the Gulf station, stuck her head in the garage. "Binky, I'm going home. Try to get there by six, will you? I don't want to warm up lamb chops."

Red bandanna hanging out of a grease-stained pair of pants, Binky called back, "I promise."

She hopped in her Mazda 6, which she loved. Being married to a car mechanic she knew better than to buy one of the fancy brands. She loved her Mazda, loved to drive it, and loved the gas mileage. Nothing went wrong and she'd owned it for a year now, bought with the money from the sale of Old Paradise. She could have bought a Rolls-Royce dealership if she'd wanted. She thought it all silly. She lived in a wonderful new house where everything worked. She could afford a cleaning company to come in once a week. The place sparkled. They even did windows. Thrilled, just thrilled to no longer be chained to Old Paradise, she tuned in the forties radio station on Sirius, and sang along with Duke Ellington's band.

As she drove off, Binky rapped the rear axle with a heavy wrench. He used sound to guide him. Fortunately, the axle on the heavy Silverado truck wasn't bent, but something had secreted itself into the wheel well.

He didn't hear the door open and close, nor the footfall. On his back on the roller, he started to roll out to grab another tool when he saw a pair of cowboy boots.

"I'll be right with you. Didn't hear you come in." He pushed off, rolled out from under the truck, stopped.

"How time flies," Weevil said.

Binky, flat on his back, moved his mouth but nothing came out.

Weevil put his right foot onto Binky's chest. Not hard, but Binky stayed put.

Eyes wide, Binky said loudly but to himself, "I did not have a drink. I am sober."

"You are. I dropped by to tell you, Binky, you were always an asshole." Weevil lifted his foot and walked out, boots crunching on the concrete floor as he left, closing the door.

Binky, shaking, swung his legs over, sat upright. "I've got to call Alfred."

He stopped, held his right wrist with his left hand to stop the right hand from shaking. "The hell I will. Nothing will ever make me speak to Alfred. Nothing."

CHAPTER 25

"Take your feet out of the stirrups," Sam, in the middle of Crawford's enclosed arena, ordered.

Yvonne, one eyebrow raised, lifted her chin, did as she was told. "Bet you thought I'd make an excuse."

"No. You're tougher than that," he complimented her. "Now, relax, shoulders relax, wiggle your toes. There you go. Toes up. Toes down. Feet level. Okay. Now take your stirrups and cross them over the front of the saddle. Now I want you to walk with energy. Squeeze."

Squire, a kind gelding, moved out a bit. Yvonne, in synch, moved along.

"Hands down, Yvonne. Now ask him to stop. There you go."

"Can I put my feet in the stirrups now?"

"No. You are going to trot without stirrups along one side of this ring. When you reach the end, stop, and remember, downward transitions take more thought than upward. Ready?"

"You think I'm going to bounce off. I will not," she declared.

Those first few steps without the stirrups woke Yvonne up. She wasn't lurching, but she used muscles trotting she never knew she had.

"Whoa," she softly said as she pulled back, not hard, and the angel glided to a stop.

Hands on hips, Sam called out, "Now, walk up to me. When you reach me, stop and dismount."

Turning Squire's head to the center, Yvonne, still no stirrups, walked up to Sam. "May I drop my stirrups now?"

"No. I want you to dismount without pushing off your right foot. You'll slide a bit but you can do it."

She did slide off, knees bent a moment, then she stood up straight. "What's the purpose of that?"

"Just in case you lose a stirrup, you need to function without. Most of us push off when we dismount and swing our leg over. But what if you've lost that stirrup? I want you to be comfortable, confident, no matter what. When you can trot for twenty minutes without stirrups, you'll have your leg."

"Is that what Tootie calls an 'educated leg'?" She pulled the reins over Squire's head and held them, following Sam out of the arena and to the stable.

"No. An educated leg covers a lot of ground. For instance, when you foxhunt, your leg might be on the girth. If ground becomes difficult or you take a downhill jump, you'll move your leg forward, the amount determined by the challenge. Then there's turning your horse around your leg.

311

It goes on, but my task is to make you a strong rider, a survival rider. Hunting is about surviving. You encounter obstacles, tricky conditions, sometimes just dumb stuff you would never face in the arena. Like what if you're going into a jump and the horse in front of you falls, slides right into the jump? Do you pull up going at a canter or do you jump both horse and rider, and the jump, yelling for the rider to stay down? You have to think fast out there, and you have to trust your horse and yourself."

"Seeing a few hunts, I'm beginning to understand that. Of course, I want to jump. I know it will take time."

"You'll get there. A jump is an interruption in your flatwork." He smiled. "Anyway, lots to do. Next lesson: your first canter. It's easier than the trot. At least, I think it is."

"Whatever you say." She untacked Squire as they were now in the center aisle of the stable.

"How's everything going?"

"Good. Funny, I'm in my early fifties and I have never lived alone. I quite like it."

He nodded. "Beveridge Hundred is beautiful."

"You live alone, right?" she inquired.

"I live on the old home place. It's behind After All. Gray and I have been fixing it up over the years. He usually spends three days with me and four with Sister or vice versa." He paused. "I owe my brother everything. He saved my life."

Brushing down Squire, she looked over his dappled gray back. "How so?"

"I lived down at the train station. Not so bad when the weather was good, but when it rained or snowed, we'd live under the bridge there. If we started a fire, the police would pick us up or chase us off. No one wanted to go to the Salvation Army because of the Bible readings and stuff. I was a drunken bum. I couldn't stop." He inhaled. "People must have told you. Everyone knows everything around here."

She smiled, giving Squire another brush. "Nobody knows everything but, yes, I've heard of your fall from grace. Met your aunt at the Old Paradise hunt. Formidable."

He grinned. "Diplomatic. How very diplomatic. Anyway, Gray picked me up, drove me down to Greensboro, put me in a thirty-day program. I couldn't get out, couldn't call, had to face myself. He paid for everything, came and picked me up. I have no one to blame but myself for my fall from grace, as you put it."

"Doesn't that apply to us all? My soon-to-be ex-husband—I do like saying that—had every-thing. Thought he was above the rules, thought he could lie. It's the same thing. We don't face ourselves. I finally had to. No, I'm not a drinker, but I had to face that I was living a lie." She walked around and kissed Squire on the nose. "Why does it take so long?"

"Beats me. These horses in the barn are smarter than we are. They live in the moment, have no illusions, and trust their hearts. Horses are emotional and sensitive."

"That means he likes my kisses." Yvonne laughed.

"Well, yes, but he'd like you even more if you gave him a Mrs. Pastures cookie." He pointed to the feed room where a bucket hung on the wall overflowing with the expensive cookies.

Naturally, horses, like cats and dogs, like the costliest food best. For people, it's Louis Roederer Cristal.

She fetched a few cookies—what a happy horse, as she led him to his stall. "Do you want me to turn him out?"

"No, we just switched to our winter schedule. Inside at night. Outside during the day."

Yvonne slid the stall door closed. The top of it was bars so horses couldn't reach out and nip you, but lots of air and light flowed in. The nipping is often a pay-attention-to-me move. However, if it's directed at another horse, harsh words can be spoken.

She slid her hand in her britches pocket, pulled out a fifty-dollar bill, handed it to Sam.

"Yvonne, that's too much. I only charge twenty-five dollars."

"Oh, I had a good time, but I can feel my inner thighs."

He laughed. "Yes, you will. Tell you what, this means you've paid for two lessons."

She started to argue but Sam spoke again. "How about after your first hunt, we'll go celebrate? A twenty-five-dollar lunch."

"Will I make it before the end of the season?"

"Easy." He smiled.

"What about the clothes? I don't want to embarrass my daughter."

"Let's cross that bridge when we come to it. If you're willing, I'll drive you up to Horse Country in Warrenton."

Having seen his car, she smiled. "Deal, but you can drive my car."

He laughed. "Deal."

Sam swept out the aisles. Yvonne had told him she'd gotten what she wanted from Vic Harris. He could only imagine the sum but Sam didn't much care. He liked her. She was game.

He hung the broom up on the wall in the small implement closet, brushed hay off himself, hopped in his aging truck, and drove to Aunt Daniella's.

She was out the door before he could knock on it. She pointed to Mercer's car, hers now, a BMW 5 Series. Sam climbed in, fired her up, and off they drove to Harris Teeter, the high-end supermarket.

He rolled the cart while she tossed stuff in, including a few items for him.

The shelves, crammed with foodstuffs, forced decisions. Actually, Sam liked the Food Lion in Lovingston better. The produce was so fresh and the lighting so good. The produce at Harris Teeter was fresh, too. Food Lion, a little less expensive, irritated Aunt Daniella. She remembered when it was mostly for poor whites and poor African Americans. She was not going in. So Harris Teeter it was, with stops along the way as she visited with everyone. Given her age, she knew everyone.

A jar of sweet gherkins in her hand, she looked down the length of the aisle.

In a stage whisper she said, "Alfred and Margaret. Let's roll right on over."

Sam did as he was told.

"Why, Margaret, how lovely you look." Aunt Daniella complimented her as she nodded in recognition of Alfred.

"It was so good to see you at Old Paradise. I hope you come out more often. Tom Tipton was so happy to see you." Margaret held a jar of Jif peanut butter in her hands, which Alfred took from her, placing it in the cart.

"Tom Tipton can talk a tin ear on you." Alfred laughed.

"Can, but he was a good man in his day. You were in your very early twenties as I recall, Alfred. You rode with Jefferson Hunt."

"Did."

"You'll be surprised to know I spoke with Wesley Carruthers." She beamed, a hint of malice in her voice.

He looked at her as though she was crazy, then replied, "I see."

"Perhaps he will call on you." She smiled, then rolled away.

"Dad, who's Wesley Carruthers?" Margaret knew nothing.

"Old foxhunter." Alfred clamped his mouth shut.

Of course, Daniella was losing it, but why Weevil? What was going on in her brain? Puzzled, Alfred pushed the cart.

In the next aisle, Sam, who had heard a bit about the museum video from Gray, cocked his head. "Aunt Dan, what are you up to?"

"Revenge. Revenge for myself and for Weevil. Alfred told tales about Weevil. He's what, twelve years younger than I am? As I recall, when I was in my middle thirties, Alfred was just busting twenty and so arrogant. A DuCharme, you know. He figured that as I was a lady of color—the description in those days—I would be eager to sleep with an FFV, First Family of Virginia. I was not and would not. Course, now he probably can't even get it up. Revenge." She smiled broadly.

"Aunt Daniella," Sam spoke in wonder.

"Oh, Sam, I may forgive, but I never forget."

CHAPTER 26

Sister peered at her phone as she listened to hounds merrily eating in the large feed room. Not that she could hear them chewing; what she heard was the enthusiastic pushing of the long metal feeders.

She was smiling, for they'd worked well at Close Shave this morning, pushing out one fox, one coyote, and a huge herd of deer. They ignored the deer, ran the coyote until he zipped out of the territory. On the long walk back to the trailers, they hopped another fox. This particular fellow headed for Foxglove Farm, but they lost him in the woods between Foxglove and Close Shave.

Sister had hunted in her mother's womb. She toddled after hounds as soon as she could walk. In the early part of her seventh decade she still had no idea how a fox can vanish. As near as she could tell, neither did anyone else throughout the centuries.

One could always tell a bullshitter in fox-hunting, an individual who answered all the mysteries. How she would love to inflict the shade of Squire Osbaldeston, an extraordinary Master in nineteenth-century England, upon said know-it-all. Osbaldeston wrote an autobiography about his hunting life, which she would reread for fortification. He obviously couldn't write an autobiography about the rest of his life—too many ladies of quality would have been compromised, as well as ladies kept by a gentleman for pleasure. Thinking about the squire, a small, well-built man, a true natural athlete, she returned to Weevil. Medium height, also well built, it would seem that the gorgeous man had much in common with the rather handsome squire, with the exception that he lacked a great fortune. A fortune the squire and his family squandered. He rather unchivalrously blamed his mother for extravagant tastes.

Peering at the close-ups and complete views of Weevil's cowhorn she wondered if the legendary squire's horn was in someone's hands. All those great huntsmen from the late-seventeenth century to today—what had become of their crops, horns, hats, coats?

Nose to the phone, she flipped through the views. Rising, she placed the phone on her desk and walked to the feed room.

"They earned it," she said to Shaker and Tootie. "Aces, what a good puppy."

The sleek youngster, still a bit skinny, lifted his head, softened kibble falling out of his jaws. *"Thank you."*

"I ran ahead of him!" Aero bragged.

Sister listened to Aces's littermate, remarking

to Shaker, "He's so keen, Aero, but he did overrun the line today. Aces has an old head on a young body. A careful boy."

"Is." Shaker beamed at his charges. "The young entry will settle though, even Aero. It's the magic of the A line."

"Tootie, I need your young eyes. Come into the office when you're done."

Shaker said, "She can come now. We're done here."

"Well, that was a fast power wash." Sister was impressed.

"Since the hounds spent most of the night outside in their condos, not much to do. Building those condos was one of the smartest things we ever did. They love them."

"Has turned out. I figure part of it is lounging on the decks in the sun. There are enough condos that they can be with friends. Really they're no different from us. Some get along and some don't. Which reminds me: Saturday's hunt starts at After All. I expect a large field. All to the good, of course, until we get in tight territory or jammed at Pattypan Forge. You know we'll have to reverse field. I dread it."

Shaker laughed. "You're the field master, cuss 'em out."

"Right. They're nervous enough as it is, trying to back their horses into the bush. I'm amazed none of us has ever been kicked in there."

"There's always a first," Shaker replied as he opened the door to the boys' room.

The girls stood over the feed troughs. First, they were obedient. Second, they could still lick the troughs with less competition.

"What a reassuring thought," she called over her shoulder.

Tootie, in tow, took a last moment to pat Cora.

Once in the office, she pulled up a chair, for Sister motioned for her to do so. Wedged next to the tall woman, she watched the tiny screen.

Sister stopped on one angle. "Look at this."

"The fox under the then fallen-down cottage. He's looking at the kennels."

"I wonder about that, too. This scrimshaw is delightful, but a bit crude in spots. Keep looking."

"The kennels, the arcades."

"And?"

Tootie squinted, held the phone up to her face. "Kind of looks like a mark on a brick."

"Like an X?"

More scrutiny. "Yes."

"Let's go find it."

Out they walked, the sun bright, the sky now sparkling blue, for it had been cloudy. The possible mark was on the arcade leading to the girls' big indoor room.

Both women looked up at the arcades.

"Shaker."

Answering her raised voice he hollered back. "Yo."

"Bring the little light hammer."

"Why?"

"Just bring the damned hammer and while you're at it, the stepladder."

They could hear his grumbling—good-natured grumbling, that of a man taking orders from his beloved Master. He soon appeared, the stepladder over his shoulder, the hammer in his belt. "Madam."

"I love it when you listen." She teased him. "Right here, under the third arch, but next to the pillar."

He unfolded the six-foot ladder, sturdy.

"I think this ladder is as old as you are. They don't make them like this anymore." He teased right back.

"It's older than I am. Was here when Ray inherited the property. And you're right, they don't make them like that anymore, nor people like me either." She folded her arms across her chest. "Tootie, up you go. Next to the top step."

Sister then slipped the hammer from behind Shaker's belt and handed it up to Tootie. "You saw the X. Tap those bricks."

Tootie leaned over, tapping the pillar, not the arch. They all listened.

Sister checked her phone again. "Try the bricks

next to the edge and near where the arch stands."

"Okay. Hard to tell from that drawing."

"It is," Sister replied.

Tap. Tap. Tap. Ting.

"Do that again."

Ting.

"See if it's loose." Sister stood on her tiptoes.

Tootie handed down the hammer, wiggled with both hands. "It's a little loose but I can't move it out."

Shaker, now as curious as the two women, offered, "Let me do it."

Tootie stepped down. Shaker climbed up as Sister held the ladder.

He pressed the brick with his fingertips. Then he slid it side to side.

"A little movement." He began to sweat. "This isn't a full brick. What's that expression, 'one brick shy of a load'? This isn't shy, but it's been altered in some way."

For almost ten minutes he worked and worked.

"What if I get a putty knife? You can slide it underneath," Sister offered.

"Good idea." He took a break as Sister trotted to the toolroom and opened the drawer of the old bureau, containing everything from Gorilla Tape to a hand sander and a power drill. Those tools reposed in the extra-large bottom drawer.

Spying a larger putty knife, Sister grabbed it, hurried back, handed it up to Shaker.

"Got it!" He removed the brick, which was a façade with sides to hold it in place.

Reaching in, he delicately removed a black box that fit perfectly in the space. Stepping down, he handed it to Sister.

Sister realized this wasn't a black box. "It's silver. Tarnished."

She opened it; the hinges were a bit stiff. Inside rested a velvet drawstring bag. Underneath that lay a heavy paper envelope, with exquisite handwriting in blue-black ink.

It read, "My Love."

"Come on." Sister led them back to the desks, where she gently removed the contents of the box.

"God," Shaker exclaimed.

Tootie, wordless, picked up a stunning diamond-and-emerald necklace. The center emerald had to be seven carats. Each emerald to the sides of this, as they went up toward the clasp, was a reduction of about a half carat each, until close to the clasp, where two small emeralds surrounded by small diamonds flanked the clasp. The diamonds also diminished by a half carat each until this point.

A bracelet matched the necklace. A bounty of rings, with large stones of the precious and semiprecious varieties, rested on the desktop, along with a man's Patek Philippe watch, paper thin, an alligator band, now cracked and dry, attached.

The three, mesmerized, were speechless.

Finally, Sister broke the silence. "I believe this is the first time these treasures have seen daylight in sixty-three years."

Then she carefully lifted the envelope, the crème-colored paper still crisp, proving its highest quality.

They almost held their breath, then Sister flipped up the back of the envelope, which had been opened, removing the paper.

CHAPTER 27

Dear Wesley,

Fate threw us together. Fate tears us apart.

The happiest days of my life have been with you. The sound of your voice, the grace of your walk, your poetry on a horse, your devilish sense of humor, your kindness. I regarded being with a man as a duty. You showed it can be a joy.

Brenden would never give me a divorce. He values me as much as he values a new tractor, cherishes my old Virginia blood, which now flows through his sons. Of course, I have told him nothing. He barely notices me anyway, but I have been exhausted, sad. I've told him I need a bit of time away from Old Paradise. I will set sail to London, then Paris, wherever my fancy takes me. I will return to Toronto before coming home.

I will have the baby in Toronto. My college roommate, Ceil, has offered shelter and a home for the child. She and her husband, a wonderful man, a doctor, are unable to have children. She says I am the answer to her prayers. In a sense she is the answer to ours. Our child will be loved, will want for nothing.

You will be in my heart wherever I may be. Not a day will pass when I don't long for you, want to hear your laugh, see the light in your eyes.

You gave me your hunting diaries when I told you I was going to have your child. You said, "Give them to our baby. He or she will know me a little." I will take them with me. Read every word and then leave them with Ceil.

You, dear, are an extravagantly gifted huntsman. However, it is not a line of work that offers much remuneration. To your credit, you are not a spendthrift, but then what do you have to spend? You could be injured, unable to work. I pray that will never happen, for you were born to hunt hounds, to be outside, to be free of the petty, consuming drive for profit that twists so many men. But I wonder, if and when the day comes when you must retire, if you will have enough to buy a house, a bit of land?

You will not want to take anything from me. Take it. These are my grandmother's and my mother's jewels. Nothing here is from Brenden. It is all from my family and in truth, it is worth a fortune. Like our child, you will never want for anything. These jewels will provide for generations of Carruthers. I hope you have children. You will be a good father.

As I am already on my way to New York, to board the ship, you can't return these anyway. And when I am back in Virginia, returning them will be difficult. We really can't be seen alone. I will see you only in the hunt field. I suppose it is some consolation.

I would gladly give up everything for you: the money, Old Paradise, the empty status. But I cannot give up my sons, even though they are young men and no longer need a mother as once they did. Should I leave Brenden, he would turn my boys against me, find a way to keep them at Old Paradise. He's not so much a bad man as a small one.

Fate is cruel.

My memories will be my own paradise and I will love you until the day I die.

Margaret
18 February 1954

"That poor woman." Sister's eyes misted.
"A different time." Shaker felt sorrow for Margaret as well. "They would have been ruined. He would have lost his job as a huntsman. No

other hunt would have hired him. A man has to have work, no matter how much he loves a woman. Fate was cruel."

Tootie traced Margaret's feminine signature with her forefinger. "She came back to find out Weevil had disappeared. Another blow."

"A pity we can't talk to her. She loved him so. Surely, she had a feeling, a sense of what truly happened to him." Sister folded the paper, sliding it back in the envelope. "Love changes you."

"Life changes you," Shaker said.

Placing the jewelry back in the silver box, Sister couldn't help winding the watch; she was rewarded with a ticking. "This is why you pay a fortune for these things."

"Well, you get what you pay for," Shaker remarked.

"This cost a bundle when it was new. It's worth six figures today." Sister kept up with values in jewelry, art, antique furniture, and horses, ever horses.

She liked knowing what things were worth—as Ray used to say, "What the market will bear."

"Do we give this to the DuCharmes?" Shaker wondered.

"Never!" came the swift reply. "Never."

Shaker, not arguing, asked, "Explain this to me."

"This jewelry never belonged to the DuCharmes. Margaret was a Bradford, hence the old blood, 1607 blood. The jewelry belonged to her mother, her grandmother, and I suspect she bought the watch just for him. Brenden had nothing to do with any of it, and if she had intended it for Alfred and Binky she would have willed it to them. She gave them the jewelry that Brenden had bought her. I saw those jewels on her at the hunt functions. Brenden had good taste, I'll give him that. Margaret was still alive when Ray and I inherited Roughneck Farm. A woman of peculiar elegance and quietness. Now I know why. She never got over Weevil." Sister felt the weight of the silver box. "Shaker, get back up on that ladder and put this where we found it. You can get the façade brick to stay put. It was reliable for sixty-three years; it will be reliable now."

Back they walked, ladder in place. He climbed up and she handed him the box, which he slid into the space, then jiggled and tapped the brick front into place.

"Thank you," Sister said as he climbed down.

"So this is why Weevil stole his horn? For the map." Shaker folded the ladder, leaning it against the brick pillar.

The day, perfect October weather, felt wonderful.

"But Weevil knows where the jewelry is. He drew the map." Tootie looked up at the brick; you really couldn't tell.

"Then why doesn't he reclaim it?" Shaker asked a reasonable question. "I mean, if he has the horn, which he does."

Thinking, Tootie wisely noted, "How can he? If he comes here with a ladder, if he gets anywhere near the kennel, the hounds will blow up. We'll all know. He'll be caught red-handed."

Sister thought. "Except he's not red-handed. The jewelry and watch are his."

"He doesn't know we know." Shaker added this.

"You're right there." Sister appreciated his thoughts.

"Why did he make that damned video? Why does he blow the horn at our hunts, at the end? He's my echo." Shaker shook his head in puzzlement.

"Maybe that deep, mellow call is meant for someone else." She inhaled deeply. "If we knew that, I think we'd have this solved. Weevil hasn't hurt anyone. He might have frightened them, but he hasn't laid a hand on anyone, other than the marijuana farmer, who had it coming. Margaret is gone. I would think he would want what she left for him. It was a big love."

Tootie placed the ladder on Shaker's shoulder as they walked toward the main office. "How can he be here for revenge? They're all dead. Maybe he's here for vindication."

Shaker kept walking and said, "She has a point.

331

The DuCharmes accused Weevil of stealing jewelry. They never said it was her own jewelry, but he was marked as a thief. But she's right, too. They're all dead."

"Including him," Sister added. "Perhaps."

"The man who saved me was as alive as we are." Tootie spoke with firmness. "He was forceful. He was looking out for me. I don't know how he knew to be there—or maybe he was back there all along—but he was a good man. I can understand why Margaret, even though married, fell in love with him."

Sister stopped as Shaker placed the ladder in the broom closet. "Right. We can assume he wants her gift but there's something else. Something painful."

"Isn't this painful enough?" Tootie wondered.

Sister's alto voice carried emotion. "Rips your heart out but there is something else. I feel it. I can't find it but I truly feel there is more."

Shaker closed the closet door. "Boss, what I feel is that we will find out. How, I don't know."

She nodded. "Obviously, we keep this to ourselves—for now, anyway. Like you, Shaker, I believe we will find out the whole story, and I think it will be devastating."

CHAPTER 28

The clatter of hooves in the covered bridge at After All reverberated. Sister thought each time they rode through the red painted bridge that this is what their ancestors heard, the sounds common in the past. Now few covered bridges remained, although some people did build them on their estates. Romance lingers in a covered bridge.

A good fifty-two or -three people, in their best ratcatcher, as it was Saturday, October 14, walked through. Hounds on the east side of the bridge, the house side, already began working Broad Creek moving north.

Tootie remained on the left bank of the creek while Betty Franklin covered the right.

Dew glittered on the deep green grass, on the few leaves that had already fallen. The temperature would lift in twenty minutes as the mercury was rising. A robin's-egg-blue sky, never helpful as it meant a high pressure system, filled with a few creamy cumulus clouds, added to the beauty. However, just because it was high pressure didn't mean hounds wouldn't find scent. The temperature, nudging just over 40°F, would help; drawing along the creek would also help. Often little wind tunnels blew over creeks, the moisture carrying scent.

The field, jammed with the regulars, added to the excitement of the day. Kasmir and Alida rode together. Tedi and Edward rode right behind Sister, as this was their property and they were the oldest riding members of the hunt. Bobby Franklin shepherded Second Flight. Cindy Chandler, Foxglove's owner, sat on Booper, who looked at everything. Booper wanted to hear hound music. Walter Lungrun, Ben Sidell, Freddie Thomas, visiting for the day, Monica Greenberg—sidesaddle, as always—and Amy Burke—also sidesaddle—dazzled everyone.

Yvonne and Aunt Daniella rode in Gray's Land Cruiser. Each time Yvonne beheld the smartness of cubbing hunting kit, she became more determined to ride. Cubbing allowed more individual expression in attire. She couldn't wait to put her list together. She knew it would take years before she earned her colors but her clothing, formal or informal, would be bespoke, her boots made just for her, and she would wear a derby, perhaps with a veil rolled up on the ribbon. She'd tapped the inside of a derby and found out it was hard, as hard as a hunt cap. Tootie told her it depended on the derby, just as it depended on the hunt cap. She also inflamed her mother's desire by telling her that when she earned her colors she would be entitled to wear a shadbelly: tails. That did it. Tails and a top hat. And perhaps just the lightest touch of lipstick, for a lady should not be made up in the hunt field. This did not prevent "the girls" from their mascara and a hint of blusher. Hairnets contained long hair and some ladies, in a derby, wore an elegant bun just outside the hat.

The men pretended not to be too aware of fashion, but every single one riding this October morning wore a tweed or light tan jacket, cut to perfection, drawing the eye to those broad shoulders. Their britches were also tan; a few rode in brick britches. The true hard-to-find mustard britches were usually saved for formal hunting, and at that time if he had his colors he wore white britches. Each man wore his butcher boots, no tan tops. The coats carried the subtle colors of the tweed or windowpane stripes. The boot color was in synch with the coat colors. Dark brown, peanut brittle, plain black, or an elegant oxblood/maroon, boots reflected a brown tweed, a blue tweed, or a jacket with a burgundy windowpane. A man's shirt might be pink, white, light blue, or an egg crème, with a tie that echoed something in his tweed coat. His cap would be brown if the boots were brown, black if the boots were black or oxblood. And, of course, he was nonchalant about it. Getting the harmony between cap, boots, and jacket took concentration. Over the years it became second nature.

Even if a woman was wildly in love with the man in her life, she couldn't help but breathe deeply upon observing the smartly turned-out men.

Sometimes Sister thought the entire point of men foxhunting was to weaken women. She and Betty would giggle about it, and they supposed a lady riding sidesaddle weakened the men. The point was foxhunting was extravagantly heterosexual regardless of one's sexual pro-clivities. It was one of the few venues where straight men competed with gay men for who was the best dressed.

Hounds checked a large tree log alongside the creek. Sister turned to examine The Jefferson Hunt field. How splendid they looked, how shiny their horses. She was not a bragging woman, but she was extremely proud of the field and the condition of the foxhounds. Coats gleaming, fluid movement off the shoulder, bright eyes, and such happiness she loved being part of them. She greeted most of them when they left their mothers' wombs. What is it about watching an animal or human grow, mature, fulfill its destiny?

Once in a discussion years ago with Ray, he said, "Destiny is slavery." Without rancor, that discussion continued for years.

The last of the field left the bridge. No more *clop clop.*

Noses down, hounds worked that log. Someone had walked over it hours ago.

Giorgio swore, *"Aunt Netty. Has to be the biggest crab in Virginia."*

Angle, only his second time at After All, as young entry, wondered, *"Who is Aunt Netty?"*

Dreamboat laughed. *"We'd be here all day but I can tell you, old as she is that girl can run."*

Zandy added, *"She also ran off her husband, Uncle Yancy. She's a neat freak."*

"Uncle Yancy had a relaxed attitude about order." Diana kept pushing.

Dreamboat joined her. *"Heating up a little."*

"Let's be sure before we open. Scent will be tricky today. Good low. Will vanish high as the temperature rises and this is Aunt Netty's signature. She knows everything," Diana counseled.

"Here!" Dragon had run ahead.

"That ass!" Diana spat, ran up to check the spot.

Now all the hounds, sterns waving, walked in a line as the line literally heated up. Soon they trotted and finally they opened, but they weren't running hard, working but not running flat-out.

The territory, expensive and manicured near the house, was easy going, but soon the line slipped into the woods, tidy near the house but the farther away they moved, the rougher it became.

"She'll head for the forge," Pickens predicted.

"Unless she goes to the Lorillard place for extra treats." Taz knew his quarry.

Aunt Netty's den, very impressive and very neat, was in Pattypan Forge. Uncle Yancy had two outside dens at the Lorillard place as well as his special nest on a wide plank above the mudroom door. Aunt Netty tried and tried again to horn in on it all. She said she'd clean for him. A big fib. She'd nag him to clean. So Uncle Yancy would buy her off with doughnut pieces, or yesterday's T-bone, to take back to the forge. After wheedling, she would scoop up her bounty and head back, often eating it all before she arrived home. Then she'd fall asleep in her den. The old girl ate a lot but didn't put on weight. She refused to reveal her secret.

Hounds stopped, for Aunt Netty had stopped. A conversation with a bobcat must have taken place. The two predators parted. Aunt Netty turned toward Pattypan Forge, across the creek, water flowing southward, a mile and a half away. The path narrowed.

The club cleaned up the trails just before cubbing. In the nineteenth century the road to the forge, wide enough for horse-drawn carts, had closed in after World War I, when the forge closed. But half a road remained open, thanks to the hard work of the club members and Walter Lungrun's small Caterpillar bulldozer.

"Hotter," Dragon, out front, called.

They opened, running hard on the solid dirt road. Goldfinches in bushes complained and flew up, which meant Aunt Netty had not passed by in the last fifteen minutes. On they ran, the footing good, the grade slightly downhill.

The forge appeared, wrapped in vines. Hounds sailed through the long windows, glass long gone on most of them.

They gathered around one of Aunt Netty's entrances and exits. She prudently had a few. In the rafters, Athena observed the commotion below, blinking from time to time.

"Aunt Netty," Giorgio called her.

Nothing.

"We know you're in there." Pickens stuck his nose in the den.

Not a peep.

Asa, deep voice, said, *"Oh, come on out and show us your bottle-brush tail."*

A hiss floated up from the depths of the den. *"You'll pay for that, Asa. I used to have a full tail until I got that skin problem."*

"Why didn't your fur grow back?" Zandy, in all innocence asked.

"How the hell should I know?" the red fox growled.

Asa, older, replied, *"Netty, Sister put out sardines in an open can with medicine. You ate everything. She did this once a week. So you were cured. I think you shave your tail."* He baited her.

Shaker, off Gunpowder, walked into the forge. "Well done."

"What's so well done about it? They have noses, don't they?" Aunt Netty bitched from her den.

Shaker, hearing the barking, couldn't help but laugh. He blew "Gone to Ground," then praised everyone as he led them out of the forge.

Athena laughed, too. *"Hoo. Hoo. Hoo."*

As the hounds moved off—people, too—Aunt Netty emerged, looking up at the huge owl. *"How can you laugh? They were so rude."*

Athena spread her tail feathers. *"Tails are important."*

"Feathers don't count. Whose side are you on, anyway?"

"Yours, of course, darling, but the young hound didn't mean any harm."

"He needs to learn his manners. This younger generation." Aunt Netty turned up her nose and repaired to her den, where she had leftover pie crusts, such a delicacy.

Shaker headed toward the Lorillard place. Usually a bit of scent was there. His hope was he'd pick up scent, run for a good ten or fifteen minutes, then retrace his steps to see if Aunt Netty had gotten sloppy. He doubted she would, for he knew her, too. Everyone knew Aunt Netty, but hounds might pick up visiting fox, since the food supply drew them in. After All enticed foxes, bobcats, even bears, as there was a lot to eat. The berries ripened. Many were already stripped off the bushes and vines, but enough remained to bring in anyone who liked fruit. Foxes love grapes, berries, sweet treats. Bears do, too. The harvested cornfields delighted all but the obligate carnivores.

On the left side, Tootie faced fallen trees, thick woods. She picked her way through, as she had only a deer path for guidance. Sooner or later she'd come out near the old toolshed at the Lorillard place.

Betty, on the cleared roadside, had a much easier time. But if hounds turned west, Tootie had to be there.

All she heard was the crack of twigs, an occasional *boo-hoo,* but hounds didn't open. If they did, she'd need to wiggle her way through all this.

She heard more twigs crack behind her, then slow hoofbeats.

Turning around she saw Weevil on Clipper, one of the Bancroft Thoroughbreds.

He squeezed alongside of her, tipped his hat. "Miss Harris."

"How do you know my name?"

He pulled a fixture card from his tweed pocket.

"Do the Bancrofts know you're on Clipper?"

"No. No one in the stables. I can tack up a horse in two minutes. I'll take him back shortly. He's a splendid fellow but then, they can afford the best." He paused. "Still have to ride them, though—which they do."

"Thank you for what you did for me. I've been trying to find out who you are and—" Now it was her turn to pause. "Sister showed me a video of you at the Museum of Hounds and Hunting. That was you, wasn't it?"

"Yes." He trained his deep brown eyes on her.

Brown eyes and blond hair, a warm combination, which was not lost on Tootie, who found herself simply staring at him. Then she managed to say, "People say you disappeared in 1954. You're a ghost."

He heard the horn. "Follow me. I can show you a better way through this and you'll wind up behind the house instead of the old shed."

"You know this country."

"I do, but anyone with good topographical maps can figure it out."

"You're not a ghost, are you?" Tootie smiled.

Weevil smiled back, clearly taken with her. "Give me a little time. I will tell you everything once I have matters settled."

"Revenge?"

"Justice." His voice was even. "Simple justice and honor. Come along. If they hit, we'll be thrown out."

He picked up a trot, ahead of her now, and she followed. They reached some large rotting fallen tree trunks, and jumped them, then Weevil stopped. He pointed to the earth off the path.

"See the old stone pile? It was once a marker, fallen down. In colonial times, here and in Canada, people piled stones at crossroads, or put up numbered squares. So go left—which seems wrong, as you are going away from the shed. Pick up a stronger trot. We have more ground to cover."

She followed his lead and within seven minutes, at the edge of the woods she saw the back of the Lorillard house. She also saw Uncle Yancy sitting on the back porch. As hounds sounded louder, he circled the house, laying down fresh scent. Then he walked to the family graveyard, jumped on the stone wall, left more scent. Ran across the graveyard, jumped back up, retraced his steps exactly, and ducked under the large front porch, to one of his outside dens.

"Tallyho," Tootie whispered, and laughed.

"Miss Harris, I need to get back, untack, and turn out. But I wanted to see you and I hope I haven't frightened you. I can't very well call upon you until I get this thing settled."

"Well, you can call me Tootie."

"Weevil." He grilled a rakish grin. "But I promise you will know everything."

"You aren't going to kill anyone, are you? This is so peculiar, unnerving."

"Well, that's the point—and I will draw out the game. Not much longer. You have no reason to do so, but trust me."

She looked into his eyes. "I do trust you. I owe you, and if I can help you, I will."

"You don't owe me anything and I truly pray you don't have to help me. You said you trust me and that lifts my heart." He grinned again. "Good hunting."

He melted back into the path, asking for a trot. He was the most relaxed, fluid man on a horse she had ever seen.

Then hounds rushed up the road, now out of the woods, right on Uncle Yancy's line. Tootie drew near the graveyard; she stayed well away from it, but where she was pleased Shaker. Sure enough, hounds ran the circle around the house, ran to the graveyard, leapt up the wall, leapt down, moved through the graveyard and back out again, and then were stymied.

She smiled. How smart of the fox to draw them out, then retrace his steps. She heard Weevil's voice in her head: *I will draw out the game.*

When? Where? How? And what was the game?

CHAPTER 29

Crawling along in the Continental, Yvonne driving, the two women listened intently.

"Heading toward the old home place."

"Yours?" Yvonne inquired.

"Um-hum. The Lorillards were free blacks, and way back in 1790, the men all became blacksmiths, much in demand. After All wasn't much at the time. We worked in Pattypan Forge as well as traveled to stables. A skilled metalworker commanded good money and respect."

"Can you imagine life without cars, airplanes, trains? Not much noise. Well, birds and stuff."

Aunt Daniella smiled. "And a blacksmith's hammer. Things were different down here from Chicago. We—the Lorillards, the Laprades, the Davises whom you haven't met—descend from families older than most of the white people's. They might have seen us as beneath the salt but we certainly didn't feel that way."

"Do you think we will ever know our history? The true history of our country?"

Aunt Daniella, ear tuned to the outside, murmured, "No. History is twisted by whoever is in power or wants power. That's why it's important to know your family, your people, your neighbors."

Yvonne considered this. "Yes. Even in a huge city like Chicago, once the second largest city in America, you have your family." She sat up straighter. "Who is that? Someone leaving early?"

Aunt Daniella recognized Weevil, although she didn't recognize Clipper. "Heading back to the stables. Maybe the horse threw a shoe. Happens. He's an old friend."

Yvonne smiled. "He looks like a young friend."

Aunt Daniella folded her hands in her lap. "Honey, it's a long story for a snowy night. Move on a bit, they're going to swing out from Pattypan Forge, and you'll see my childhood home. Has a charm to it."

Yvonne rolled along in second gear as Aunt Daniella turned and watched Weevil stop at the stables, dismount, and whip the tack off Clipper in the blink of an eye.

What's he up to? she wondered, then spoke: "Stop. They'll pop out in front of you. There's a little trail."

Yvonne stopped. Sure enough out came hounds, moving briskly. She saw Betty out of the corner of her eye, moving on a trail to the right in the woods. Then those woods ended, and Betty took a coop into a well-kept pasture, a few big hay rolls dotting the green.

"How old is she?"

"Betty? Fifties. Early fifties. A low-key rider.

346

Draws no attention to herself, but she gets the job done." Aunt Daniella said this with praise. "Here comes Shaker."

All business, Shaker reached the road and turned left, moving at a collected canter. Hounds were speaking but not screaming. The line, good, wasn't red hot.

"Where's Tootie?"

"She should be on our left. She might have moved on, since it's best to clear the woods on the left. Someday, get your daughter to take you back to Pattypan Forge. Quite interesting, and the heavy enormous furnace from 1792 is still there, along with some old tools hung on the walls."

"I'd like to see it. I must say being here I'm not always sure what century I'm in."

Aunt Daniella laughed, then ordered, "Okay, last of the field has passed us. You can creep forward."

The blue car inched forward, the Lorillard house came into view, and the hounds circled the house, hopped on the graveyard wall—did exactly what Uncle Yancy planned for them to do. Tootie sat quietly on the other side of the graveyard.

"What a lovely house." Yvonne admired the white clapboard home, old slate roof intact, front door painted marine blue, as were the shutters.

"Memories." Aunt Daniella smiled. "All of us rest in that graveyard. Mother. Father. My sister

Graziella and my son Mercer. I expect soon it will be my turn."

"I hope not" came the swift reply.

"Do you believe in ghosts?" Aunt Daniella asked as hounds leapt back out of the graveyard.

"People have spoken of them for thousands of years in every culture. There must be something to it. I've never seen one."

Having just seen Weevil ride out of the woods, Aunt Daniella smiled. "Not that you know. Here's what I think—oh, look at young Pickens. Head under the front porch, butt in the air."

"You know the hounds? How can you remember them?"

"I know some of them, thanks to Gray or Sam occasionally driving me along a hunt. Where was I? Ghosts. Yvonne, there is so much we don't know, but we're a nervous lot. We want answers. We want things tied in a bow, so whoever comes up with a convincing answer pacifies the rest, even if it's false."

"God help anyone who disturbs the status quo." Yvonne enjoyed watching Shaker dismount, speak to his hounds, and convince Pickens to leave the front porch. "Think of Galileo."

"Well, here's the thing. Galileo. Copernicus. Men who shook up the status quo. Yes, the earth moves around the sun. Big deal. We can plant, plan, live just as well thinking the sun revolves around the earth."

"Can't do space travel that way," Yvonne answered.

"Honey, firing men up in rockets seems an expensive way to get rid of them." Aunt Daniella's eyes twinkled.

Yvonne laughed, happy to be in irreverent company.

Then the old lady remarked, "Gray and Sam have repainted the house, done quite a lot of work inside. Speaking of men, they are good men, but I'm prejudiced."

"Good men and good-looking." Yvonne smiled.

"Never hurts, does it?"

"That fellow riding back to the barn. Good-looking."

"Oh, Yvonne, that he is." She took a deep breath. "Now Shaker has to figure out what to do next. Temperature is rising. The fox is in his den. What next?"

Shaker drew back along the road but scent proved spotty. Really the day was done, but he stayed out another hour, hunting and pecking, then finally rode back to the trailers.

Clipper, in his pasture, wished he could have finished the hunt. His coat, a rich dark bay, shone in the sunlight. Weevil had wiped him down, picked out his hooves, and turned him out.

And, as usual, Weevil vanished, but not before blowing "Going Home."

Tootie and Betty loaded hounds on the party

wagon with Shaker. Sister, being Master, fielded chat, inquiries from members, as did Walter.

Rickyroo, happy to be free of the tack, was wiped down as he munched on hay in a string bag. Most of the horses stood, tied to the sides of the trailer, happy to eat. They were always happy to eat. And most had a light cotton sweat sheet over them.

Sister adjusted his sheet, patted the wonderful fellow, fished a baked cookie with apple bits in it out of a bucket in the tack room, and fed it to him.

Alida, trailer next to Sister's, called out, "You spoil that horse."

"And you don't spoil Mumtaz?" She named one of Kasmir's Thoroughbreds, which Alida often rode, and rode well.

Kasmir sounded off from the other side of his horse, Nighthawk. "She spoils me."

They all laughed, then Sister asked, "How's Lucille Ball coming along?"

"Wonderfully well." Kasmir filled her in. "Sam tunes her up once a week." He paused a moment. "That was a good idea to have a joint meet with Crawford."

"Thank you. Well, are you ready for that famous Bancroft hospitality?"

Given the loveliness of the day, the Bancrofts hosted the breakfast outside. Fall color, nearing its peak, added to the beauty of the day.

Long tables in a row held the food, and smaller round tables, complete with table settings, covered the immaculate formal backyard, the gardens just beyond.

Aunt Daniella, given a good seat so she could see everyone, had her bourbon in hand, thanks to Gray. Yvonne sat with her, a good idea since everyone knew Aunt Daniella. Anyone she hadn't met, Yvonne did today.

Betty plopped down at a table, her husband with her. "Can you believe we are about three weeks from Opening Hunt?"

"Three weeks to the day," he replied.

Alfred DuCharme joined them. "Good day?"

"Given conditions, pretty good." Betty leaned forward. "Drove by Old Paradise yesterday. Crawford is starting to frame it up. It's coming back to life."

"I'm as curious to see it as you-all. The house was burned down by the time I was born."

Binky, on the other side of the gathering, chatted with Edward. The two brothers did not acknowledge each other. Given that The Jefferson Hunt was one of the hubs of the county, people came to watch the hounds, to partake of the breakfast. Technically, the DuCharmes were no longer landowners. Didn't matter. Anyone was welcome, and over the years they had been a big part of the hunt.

Edward, standing, glass in hand, waved to

people, turned to Binky. "Glad you could make it."

"You know, I haven't been on After All for most of a year. I don't know where the time goes."

"Who does?" He nodded as Tedi came up by his elbow, kissed Binky on the cheek.

"Where's Milly?" she asked.

"Hanging curtains." Binky grimaced, then changed the subject. "Why anyone ever wants to move is beyond me. But I picked up a pile of books last night and noticed a family scrapbook. Sat down and studied every picture. There was one in there of you and Evangelista. Thanksgiving Hunt. You looked like you were still in college, or just graduated. Hard to believe we were that young."

"I feel young. Look old." Ed knocked back his drink, rattled the cubes in his glass.

"I thought your sister was a knockout. She was my idea of a movie star." He grinned. "But I was just busting twenty. Way beneath her."

"Funny, how we remember our early crushes. For me it was the actress Irene Dunne." He smiled. "Then I met a real star." He squeezed his wife.

"Edward, you are so sweet." She glowed.

"My sister could have run the business. She was whip smart, but women didn't do that then. I did okay. But I really think Evie would have done better."

"She took over the Warrenton Horse Show. Did

a splendid job for decades." Tedi mentioned one of Virginia's premier outdoor horse shows, held over Labor Day.

The Warrenton Horse Show signals the end of the show season—outdoor, anyway—and the beginning of cubbing.

"Loved it. She just loved it." Edward chewed an ice cube. "Now we have women CEOs of major corporations. It's good, I think. Opens us up. New ideas."

"I often wonder if Mom would have been happy with a career," Binky replied.

"Another really smart woman." Tedi nodded.

"Mom never really found her way." Binky shrugged. "And I took to fixing cars." He paused. "Haunting, that horn echo."

Tedi nodded again. "Happens almost every hunt now. Very odd."

The people at the gathering nattered on. A lively discussion erupted concerning red cords for gentlemen's top hats. "One can't find them unless you go online. Easier to find in England."

This provoked all manner of why isn't someone here doing it.

The subject of garter straps provoked opinions. A leather strap, slid through two slits in the back of one's boot to hold up the boot, is a garter strap. However, boots are no longer turned over as they were in the seventeenth century. As boots tightened in the eighteenth and nineteenth centuries, garter straps became no longer useful.

However, as they had been worn since the reign of Charles II, they were still considered absolute proper turnout.

Everyone had much to say. Sister settled it as she usually did by following protocol.

"I understand that thin leather can cut you at the back of the knee. I don't much like it but on the High Holy Days, I wear the damned garter strap. Four days out of a hunting season, how bad is that? Put a strip of moleskin under your britches at your knee. Saves the blisters."

Finally, the breakfast broke up.

Gray, now in Yvonne's Continental, carried Aunt Daniella home. Yvonne squeezed in with Sister and Betty, as Sister drove the hound trailer. She wanted to be with the girls and Gray was curious about her new car. Worked out. Tootie rode with Shaker in the party wagon.

The trip took maybe five minutes, but that was long enough to talk, laugh, plan Tuesday's hunt.

Back at the farm, Yvonne stood by while hounds walked into their quarters. Tootie and Betty washed the horses. Sister joined them once hounds were put up.

Yvonne, enjoying the company, dropped into a director's chair. She offered to help, but she didn't know enough to be really useful.

The horses loved their bath, being scraped down, and then more cookies before being turned out. Each horse was led to his or her pasture. Rickyroo was first. He turned around once in the pasture and faced Sister; she slipped off his halter. Every single time, he would stand there for one moment, then turn and run, run, run to the end of the large pasture. He'd twist around, he'd stand on his hind legs, he'd buck.

"Happiness." Sister grinned.

Each gelding, in turn, performed his own ritual.

Back in the stable, the center aisle was swept out while Betty, Sister, and Yvonne cleaned tack. Yvonne proved a good tack cleaner.

"Sam showed me how to do this."

Betty was impressed that a formerly famous model dipped her sponge in a bucket and got to work.

Yvonne regaled them with Aunt Daniella's comments. "She is ninety-four going on twenty-two."

"True." Sister and Betty agreed.

"We're sitting in the car and this divine-looking young man rides by and Aunt Daniella says she's known him for years. I wonder what her definition of years is," Yvonne added.

Just as her mother told this story, Tootie walked into the room.

Sister and Betty continued cleaning but didn't say anything as Yvonne repeated the sighting for Tootie's benefit.

"Was he blond?" the young woman asked.

"Yes. Do you know him?"

"Mother, that was the man who saved me at the marijuana patch."

"Well, I hope he keeps hunting with Jefferson so I can thank him for saving my baby."

"Oh, Mom." Tootie rolled her eyes, then added, "He'll probably be out sooner or later."

"Think so?" Sister asked.

"I do."

CHAPTER 30

Y ou could text her," Tootie suggested. It was now Monday.

"Then I wouldn't hear her voice. If I hear her voice, I know she's in a good place—or not. People's voices are like hound voices; they tell you a lot."

Tootie closed the gate to the feed room as she and Sister left for the stables. "I never thought of that."

Sister smiled at her. "Of course not. You're twenty-one. Or is it twenty-two?"

Tootie teased back. "I'm going to take a lesson from you and Betty. A woman who will tell me her age will tell anything."

That made the older woman laugh. "I never said that."

"No, she did—but you agreed." Tootie teased some more.

"There may be some truth to it. I've wondered for years how many years Aunt Daniella has shaved off her age."

"She's ninety-four, five?" Tootie was shocked.

"Actually, I suspect she's closer to ninety-six or maybe even ninety-seven. But we all dutifully repeat that she's ninety-four."

"How can it matter?"

"Oh, honey, look at all those women whose hair is dyed change-of-life red. Naturally, out of kindness, I will not mention any lady in our hunt club."

Now Tootie's curiosity took over. "Do they really think we don't know?"

"Some do, but I think for most of us we only know what we looked like when we were young. We can't bear to look at this somewhat different face. Which brings me to face-lifts. You can always tell."

"I can't. I mean if they've just had it done and their face and eyes aren't quite settled, I can. You know, Sister, it's major surgery. I mean, it's dangerous."

"I do know. And any surgery can be dangerous. One never knows. I have seen some fabulous face-lifts. Like you said, the face has to settle and then it can look terrific for a couple of years."

Hearing that tone in Sister's voice, Tootie asked, "What next?"

"Well, gravity always wins. So sooner or later your face will fall a bit, and the wrinkles, if you've had your face lifted, never quite fall in the right place."

"Oh." Tootie happily walked to the closest pasture, leaned over a fence, and whistled.

Ears pricked up. Iota, Rickyroo, and Matador thundered up.

"Sweet crimped oats. I have a taste for them."

Iota gave her his softest most loving look.

Matador, a gentleman, waited as the gate opened. Sister put his halter on with his very own nameplate. Tootie did the same for Iota. Then they pushed the gate back open to walk to the barn.

Rickyroo, the oldest, followed along. He didn't need a halter or lead rope. He stuck right with his beloved Sister.

"Crimped oats. You are spoiled," Matador called to Iota as Tootie put him inside his stall to eat quietly at his feed bucket. Otherwise, each horse would bump another horse to eat out of that bucket. You had to make sure no one was getting better food than yourself.

Rickyroo walked into his stall, bucket filled. You could hear him eating, knocking his bucket a bit against the heavy stall side.

Raleigh and Rooster slept in the tack room. They'd walked hounds with the humans, listened to endless hound gossip, then worn themselves out when Rooster stole Sister's old ball cap. This ball cap could have been a museum exhibit. Raleigh did finally drop it in the tack room. Sister picked it up, wiped it off, slapped it on her silver hair.

In the rafters, Bitsy peered down. Oats, bran, even cracked corn proved no temptation. She wanted the ham from a ham sandwich, or any kind of meat. It was too early in the day for sandwiches. She paid close attention to when and where the humans ate. When they went inside the house her disappointment engulfed her for all of two minutes. It did mean, though, she would need to hunt.

Opening her little wings she glided down to sit on top of the wrought-iron railing between Rickyroo's stall and Aztec's stall.

"How can you eat that stuff?"

Rickyroo, who liked the little gossip, replied, *"It's so sweet. Now I like my hay, don't get me wrong, but there is something special about sweet feed in a bucket."*

"I'll take your word for it. Isn't this the best time? October, early November, and then mid-April and May. Just the best," Bitsy babbled.

"I like it because even though our schedule changes, when the weather is so good we're out most of the time. But spring means the end of hunt season. Makes me sad," Rickyroo stated, then changed the subject since he knew Bitsy redefined nosiness. *"Do you know who this young fellow is who comes around at night?"*

"The broad-shouldered blond fellow?" She lifted up her wings, then folded them down again. *"Don't. He parks an old work truck off the road in that little place in the woods where Sister has a feed box. Then he walks down here. He looks at everything, especially the cottage, then he walks back. Doesn't disturb the hounds."*

"He brings carrots, feeds us over the fence."

Rickyroo told her what she already knew, since Bitsy watched everything. *"He likes horses. I like him."*

"He knows where things are. He usually has a folded map in his back pocket. I can fly close but he can't hear me. He doesn't take anything. He just looks."

After the horses ate, Sister and Tootie turned them out again. They then headed for the kennels.

"You forgot to make your call," Tootie reminded her.

"I'll do it later. I want to pull out a few hounds, have a critical look. It's not too early to start thinking about hound shows."

"Giorgio," Tootie said.

"He is gorgeous. I want to look at Aero and Aces."

Once in the kennels, Sister asked Shaker to bring out the two littermates, as well as Asa, the grandfather.

He stood by Aero; she had a beautiful head.

"Well, she's still a little weedy," Sister remarked. "I don't know if she'll fill out in time for the shows." Then she looked at Aces. "On the other hand, he's right there, isn't he?"

"A good-looking hound." Shaker stood Asa next to him for comparison.

When younger, Asa had won a few shows.

Sister studied them, then stopped. "I am so stupid. I can't believe how stupid I am!"

She rarely raised her voice so both Tootie and Shaker stared at her.

Aero, young, said, *"Would a Milk-Bone make her feel better?"*

Asa replied, *"She's usually so calm. Maybe a wee drop of Scotch would help."*

Sister looked at the wonderful hounds, then at Shaker and Tootie. "My God, it's right in front of my face and it took me this long to see it."

"What?" Shaker had no idea what she was talking about, nor did Tootie.

"Look at Asa. Look at his grandchildren, especially Aces. Like as spit."

"That's why we're considering them for the shows. A lot of times, qualities skip a generation," he said.

"Weevil."

"What?" Tootie was now very interested.

"Weevil. He's not a ghost. I am willing to bet you just anything, Weevil is Weevil's grandson. Skipped a generation."

"Then what the hell is he doing here being a ghost?" Shaker handed each hound a cookie.

"I have no idea. Not one. I am getting in the car and driving to Aunt Daniella. If anyone would have an idea, she would."

Calling first, Sister appeared at the formidable lady's door within twenty minutes.

Hearing her theory, Aunt Daniella, in her wing chair, nodded. "Could be so."

"But Aunt Daniella, why? You knew Weevil. Do you know how he died?"

"No. When Weevil walked with me that sunset day, he unnerved me, as he truly looks, sounds, even moves like Weevil. But even though I believe there are spirits, people can conjure them down, but then can you conjure them back? He seemed so alive—and he is. I believe you're right."

"Then he must know something about how his grandfather disappeared."

"Maybe not. Maybe he just has an idea and he thinks he can scare it out of people."

"But Aunt Daniella, wouldn't the guilty parties be dead?"

"Sister, perhaps there is more. He needs proof, and being a ghost is a good way to weasel it out of people. Why now, who knows?"

"All we do know is that he's spoken to you and Tom Tipton."

"True. But he may have showed himself to other people who fear talking, and he may be relying on Tom and me to talk. I just don't know."

"Do you think he's dangerous?"

Aunt Daniella immediately responded, "Not to us."

"I see." Sister folded her hands together thinking. "Time. I need time to figure this out."

"Honey, in time, even an egg can walk."

CHAPTER 31

A thin blade of wind slid across Sister's face. Fall had truly arrived, for last night, Friday, a frost, not hard but not light, silvered the pastures. Today, October 21, a lowering sky promised not much rise in the temperature, which at nine-thirty A.M. hovered at 45°F. No doubt it would climb into the 50s, but those clouds just might hold scent down. Given that the breeze was stiff, this would be desirable.

Tuesday's and Thursday's hunts saw a couple of good runs. The first hunt, held at Skidby, proved bracing. Thursday's hunt at Mousehold Heath was going along just fine until the neighbor's herd of goats managed to break through his fencing. Poor hounds. Goats everywhere. Horses upset and some people now on the ground. Sister and Shaker had no choice but to call hounds together, walk them back to the party wagon, and put the horses back in the trailer. The young couple who owned Mousehold Heath, Lisa and Jim Jardine, were both at work. They didn't have much by way of money, doing most of the work on the old house themselves, including their own fencing—and it wasn't their fence that was breached. But the damned goats would tear up Lisa's garden and God knows what else. The hunt stalwarts—and Thursday's crew was maybe twenty people—set out on foot to round up the goats, herd them back onto their property, and then repair the fence as best they could. Helping landowners, a foxhunting tradition, often tested the ingenuity and muscle power of hunt clubs. Fixing the fence so it would hold had members cutting down tree limbs. Ronnie Haslip kept a small chain saw in his tack room. He swore it upped his butch credentials. Using baling twine, people pieced the breach back together. It would hold until the neighbor fulfilled his responsibility and truly restored the fence. Such things were crystal clear in the country.

After both Tuesday's and Thursday's hunts, all heard the cowhorn call. But as she left the fence on Thursday, Tootie, lagging behind, looked back down the small rise to see Weevil, on his hands and knees, adding to the fence. She stopped and whistled. He looked up, waved, and whistled back.

Back at the farm, Sister called Jim Jardine at work. He worked for a large plumbing company; those skills were very useful at home. He was grateful to the club. Sister liked the young couple, as did everyone, and people hoped the day would arrive when Jim would strike out on his own.

Hounds, having been stymied on Thursday, were eager to go on Saturday. Kasmir wanted everyone back at Tattenhall Station at least one more time before Opening Hunt, which loomed on the horizon, each year taking place at After All Farm, a tradition since 1887.

Sister asked Crawford to join them, but he politely declined as he wanted to be at Old Paradise that afternoon when old, reclaimed lumber would be delivered. He did allow Skiff and Sam to join the hunt, leaving their hounds at Beasley Hall.

"Some of these gusts have to be fifteen miles an hour." Shaker leaned toward Sister before they took off.

"If we get low that will help." She stated the obvious.

"Sure, and the fox will run high the minute we get his scent." Shaker shrugged.

"Oh, I bet we get a run or two."

Tootie waited on the left of the pack while Betty, as usual, covered their right.

As they moved south from the train station over the restored pastures, good orchard grass still green, people ducked their heads due to the wind. Even with gray skies, the vibrant reds, pulsating oranges, clear bright yellows announced high fall. To their right, the Blue Ridge Mountains exploded in color, although the top ridgeline trees were now denuded. Higher and colder, it was already early winter up there.

Hounds, noses down, moved across the pasture. They worked under no illusion that they'd strike a line. Up ahead woods beckoned. Maybe there.

Once in the woods, treetops swayed but lower it wasn't too bad. Riders who wore heavier coats were grateful, and most everyone had slipped on some kind of warm underwear. Sister would pull on an ancient white cashmere sweater, over which she would button her crisp white shirt. Her keeper's tweed coat repelled just about any type of thorn as well as wind blasts. Keeper's tweed, a greenish heathery tightly woven fabric, proved a godsend. She tied a colored stock tie, silk maroon with tiny yellow polka dots. Her gloves were unlined. Usually one didn't need lined gloves until the mercury dipped to the 30s. Her oxblood, highly polished field boots, two pairs of socks on her feet, finished off the kit.

A few riders yanked up their collars to ward off the wind. Once in the woods, though, one could concentrate on hunting, not battling the weather.

Hounds patiently made good the ground. It wasn't until they dipped down toward the swift creek that Pookah spoke.

She'd proven herself last year, so hounds honored her. They all trotted on a line that they and the staff hoped would warm up.

It did.

A wily red foraging in Tattenhall Station Woods heard hounds ten minutes back. Not wishing to work too hard, he took off, leaving a tantalizing signature.

Hounds spoke louder now. The pace quickened. They ran along the path by the creek. Then the line moved up toward the thick woods. Slowed a bit, they pressed on.

A good run followed this, and the pack emerged at the southern end of Kasmir's property. An in-and-out jump divided his land from Beveridge Hundred. Two coops in the fence lines provided one jump, and three strides later, another jump, hence the name in-and-out. Not everyone kept their leg on their horse; some became stranded between the jumps. This rarely added to good fellowship, and Freddie Thomas found herself yelling for Sam Lorillard to give Keith Minor a lead or the whole field would be backed up.

Horses, eager to move forward, gave their riders fits as people had to pull up while Sam tried to get Keith over the second jump.

According to rules, Keith should have ridden down the fence line, allowed everyone else to take the in-and-out, then come back and try again. But he was undone by the task, so Sam took the first jump.

"Keith, slide behind me. Your mare will pop right over. Look up!"

Keith managed it. Freddie cleared the jumps, followed by everyone else. Freddie, too much of a lady to cuss Keith like a dog, simply blew by him once in the open without a backward glance.

Walter Lungrun, riding tail this Saturday, swept up the leavings as he put it. Everyone did get over, but this left Bobby Franklin with a hell of a run alongside the fence, out onto the road, and finally onto Beveridge Hundred. The entire field thundered past Yvonne's tidy rental house as she watched in amazement and decided she'd follow by herself in the car. She thought she'd learned enough to do so. Within minutes she was creeping along the road in the Continental.

Tootie, on the left, waved to her mother as she moved ahead.

The fox knew Beveridge Hundred well. He ducked into a culvert and ran under the road, appearing on the north side. As Old Paradise comprised seven thousand acres, the smart fellow was now on Crawford's land. If he headed farther away from Chapel Cross, the crossroads now four miles behind him along with Tattenhall Station, they would land in Kingswood.

Sister, up ahead, thought like a Master. New people had bought Kingswood. She'd only met them once, and she didn't want to meet them again with the Jefferson pack streaming across their land.

They had seemed nice enough, but why test it?

Fortunately, the red fellow cut hard right, bounced through a fallen-down hay shed, left scent everywhere, and then—*poof!*

Hounds roared into the old shed, one Crawford would eventually tear down or rebuild, then stopped.

"Where did he go?" Trooper moved to the end of the big shed, half the roof sagging.

"Keep your noses down," Cora commanded.

They did but to no avail.

The field, happy for a break, passed around flasks, tightened girths, felt grateful that the wind slowed a bit. It wasn't truly a cold day—mid 40s is a wonderful hunting temperature—but when the wind hit, it just cut. The gusts had diminished to a hard puff every now and then. A breeze, maybe five miles an hour, kept steady, so one still had to compensate for that when a fox was seen or a line found.

Tootie waited away from the shed, her back to the wind, which came from the northwest per usual. Betty, however, felt the breeze right in her face. Wasn't bad, but she somewhat envied Tootie's position.

Shaker let the hounds try, then he picked them up, walking slowly toward Chapel Cross. Surely, somewhere within those four miles they would hit another fox.

While hounds walked away from the hay shed, Binky DuCharme, at his Gulf station, heard a rap on the garage door. He opened it.

"Binky, get in the truck." Weevil held a .38 in his face. "Now!"

Arthur, underneath a car, heard a voice but not much more. "Dad?"

Weevil shoved the barrel in Binky's ribs. "Tell him you'll be back."

"Arthur, be right back."

"Where is your cell?"

Binky patted a pocket of his grease-streaked overalls. Crestfallen, he opened the old truck door and slid in the bench seat.

"Are you going to shoot me?"

"That depends on how cooperative you are. Now call your brother."

"I don't speak to my brother."

"You will now." Weevil pointed the barrel right in Binky's face as with his left hand he turned the steering wheel to leave the station.

Although Binky never spoke to his brother, he knew the number. It had been the same phone number for forty years.

"Alfred."

"What the goddamned hell is this?"

Weevil grabbed the phone. "Alfred, meet us at the stables at Old Paradise. If you aren't there in twenty minutes I will kill your brother and then I'll come for you."

"I hate my brother."

"I know, but if you don't come you're a dead man. If you come, you just might live."

"Who the hell is this?"

"Alfred, you don't recognize my voice?"

"No."

Weevil handed the phone back to Binky.

"It's Weevil Carruthers."

"He's dead!"

"He's sitting here next to me, Alfred. Do as he says."

Weevil drove past Old Paradise, where the very expensive huge timbered beams were being offloaded with a massive logging grappling machine. The claws could grip the beams without harming them just as it could lift stripped heavy logs. Crawford and the crew looked up at Weevil's truck, then back at the job. So many workmen drove up and down that road, this appeared to be one more.

Parking behind the stone stable, Weevil, gun trained on Binky, said, "We will open our doors at the same time. If you run, I'll shoot you. We're going inside to wait for Alfred."

Binky opened the door, and waited. Weevil walked around the truck, dropped the tailgate, pulled out a spade, handed it to Binky.

Then he pulled out another one.

"It's tempting to think about swinging that spade at my head, but I can fire this gun before you can hit me, so let us calmly, carefully walk into the stable. You first."

As the two men walked into the sumptuous stable, three and a half miles away, Earl, the big red who lived in the stable, became careless.

He'd been chasing grouse. He wasn't hungry. He just wanted to hear them tweet and run away, then lift up.

Hounds picked up Sarge's scent, ran to the boulders, tried again as they kept heading toward Old Paradise, then picked up Earl. So he had to move along a bit faster than he intended.

"It's Earl, I know it." Dragon sped, nose down.

"He's got a head start." Zandy kept up.

"Doesn't mean we can't try. There's many a slip 'twixt the cup and the lip," Diana counseled, and she couldn't have known how prophetic she was.

Alfred, driving a new Range Rover, which he didn't need, parked next to the truck. He walked into the stable.

Weevil and Binky waited for him in the center aisle.

Alfred stopped; his jaw dropped. "Weevil."

Binky's lip quivered. He looked at Weevil. "He made me do it. You know he made me do it."

"Shut up!" Alfred stepped toward his sniveling brother.

"Ah, yes, brotherly love. Alfred, here's a shovel. You and Binky are going to dig up Wesley Carruthers's body. If you don't, I will start by shooting your kneecaps and move up your body from there. Well, first maybe I'll shoot your feet. Get to it."

"I don't remember," Alfred lied, and that fast Weevil smashed the gun in his face.

"Do it now!"

Blood running from his eyebrow, Alfred stepped into the next-to-the-last stall, Binky behind him. Weevil stood in the stall door as the first spade bit into the good earth.

Earl sped toward the stable and shot into his home way ahead of any danger, but there were three men in the stable digging next to his stall. From time to time, Earl would loll about in the tack room, but when he needed to disappear, his den was it. Here were humans digging. Rude. Very rude, but his curiosity got the better of him. He tiptoed to the other side of the center aisle and watched through the open stall door. Weevil could smell him, but he'd smelled fox when he entered the stable. He kept his eyes on the two brothers.

"Dig faster."

In the distance, hounds spoke, Shaker blew "Gone Away."

Earl realized the pack was going to charge into the stable very shortly. He hurried to his den, jumped in in the nick of time. The entire pack of Jefferson Hounds roared into the stable and stood in the stall next to the one with the brothers in it.

"He's in here!" Audrey, terribly excited, as this was her first time at a den, hollered.

"Earl, I know it's you!" Parker stared into the opening.

"Oh, Parker, you're a genius," Earl sassed.

Shaker, now outside, dismounted and ran inside. He realized there was commotion, but he blew "Gone to Ground." Then he looked into the next stall.

"Shaker, this man's crazy. He's going to kill us." Alfred spoke as reasonably as he could.

"Shaker, if Ben Sidell is out there, would you bring him inside?" Weevil quietly commanded.

Shaker walked outside, looked up at Sister, and walked by her to Ben Sidell with Second Flight. "Sheriff, please come with me." Ben dismounted, handing Nonni's reins to Bobby Franklin.

The hounds, still in Earl's stall, started digging themselves. Shaker led Ben to Weevil, then returned to Earl's stall.

"Leave it."

"He always gets away with this," Dragon complained.

"Come along." Shaker walked outside, hounds with him. "Sister, Tootie, Betty, come here."

As they did, Sister dismounted. She knew something was up. Tootie and Betty dismounted, too.

"Can you hold the hounds? It might be easier if you're down here with them." Then he called, "Ronnie."

"Yo."

"Will you go get the party wagon?"

"Of course."

Sister turned to the field. "Folks, go on back with Ronnie. We'll meet you at the station."

Everyone wanted to know what was going on, but everyone also knew not to ask. They turned and rode with Ronnie as hounds sat down, lay down, at Sister's, Tootie's, and Betty's feet.

Shaker walked back in.

Alfred pleaded, "Sheriff, he's got a gun on us. He's crazy."

Ben assessed the situation. He didn't know the young man but he did know the brothers, and he knew they never spoke, but they were digging together. Best not to act in haste.

Weevil, without turning his head, said, "Sheriff, if you will be patient, an old murder is about to be solved. Alfred and Binky killed Wesley Carruthers. I wasn't sure what they did with his body. I guessed they'd dig where it would be easy, and then the horse in this stall would pack the earth. I knew if I pulled a gun on them they'd dig to save their sorry skins. And so they are."

Ben stood next to Weevil now while Shaker, wide-eyed, watched through the stall bars.

The two men were knee-deep, mounds of soft stall earth around them. A soft *thunk* was heard.

Ben walked over as a thighbone appeared. He looked at the sweating men, in their seventies. "Keep digging."

They dug enough for part of a skeleton to be clearly seen. Binky fell to his knees sobbing.

Alfred ignored him, disgusted.

"I didn't want to do it. He made me do it."

Alfred backhanded Binky, who fell on his side, on the part of Wesley that was exposed.

Ben walked to the makeshift grave, Binky now in it. "Binky, how did you kill him?"

"Shot him. Alfred shot him first but he said I had to do it, too. I didn't want to do it," he blubbered.

Alfred just glared.

"I arrest you two for the murder of—"

Weevil filled that in. "Wesley Carruthers."

"Do you have a cellphone, sir?" Ben asked Weevil.

"No."

"I do." Shaker stepped up.

"Call the department. Get someone out here immediately and—well, just give me the phone."

Ben punched in the department's number. "Hey, Patty, send the forensics team out to Old Paradise, the stables, and also a squad car. We need to take two men to the jail." He listened a minute. "Okay. No, I don't think they're dangerous anymore, but who is to say. Thanks." He handed the phone back to Shaker.

Sister, Tootie, and Betty talked to the hounds, petted them, and told them to pay no attention to Earl, who was glorying in this situation.

As the field reached Tattenhall Station, they heard two sirens screaming right for them. Horses stood at their trailers as two sheriff's vehicles sped by, one a van, the other a squad car.

Ronnie, now in the party wagon truck, followed them, not knowing what he would find.

As the two county vehicles roared down Old Paradise's drive, Crawford stepped away from the timber and headed for the stables.

Crawford walked into the stables just as the two officers from the squad car did. The forensics team came behind them, needing to see the situation to know what to carry in.

"What's going on here?" Crawford demanded.

Ben turned to him. "Look here."

Crawford slid past Weevil and stood next to Ben as Alfred and Binky were walked out, handcuffed.

"My God!" Crawford's voice rose.

"Murdered in 1954," Weevil quietly stated.

Crawford looked at the handsome man. "Who are you?"

"Wesley Blackford. This was my grandfather."

The three women outside tried to hear what was being said, but to no avail. Ronnie pulled up, so hounds were quietly loaded onto the party wagon. Then the Master and two whippers-in walked into the stables.

Sister came to the open stall door, saw Weevil. "Weevil."

"Yes, Master."

"I'm glad you're not a ghost." She smiled.

Tootie now stood next to her, as did Betty.

He smiled. "So am I."

"This is Weevil?" Sister pointed to the opened grave.

"Yes, ma'am. Alfred and Binky killed him." Weevil took a deep breath. "My grandmother was Margaret DuCharme. She bore my mother in Toronto, where the baby was given to her college roommate, who had protected Margaret during her pregnancy. And she raised my mother as her own."

"How did you figure this out?" Ben asked as he held out his hand for the gun, which Weevil placed in his palm, handle first.

"Mother, who is still alive, in her sixties, had letters from Margaret. They never met, but Margaret loved her, I believe, and sent money. My grandmother suspected either her husband or the boys killed Weevil. Over the years she came to believe it was her sons. Her sons hated Weevil, hated each other. I don't know much more than that, except Margaret told my mother she had given Weevil her mother's and grandmother's jewels. If she could find them, all would be well. I studied those letters, studied maps once Mother allowed me to read it all, which was last year. I devised a plan."

Ben asked, "Were the jewels ever found?"

379

"No, and that was part of the problem, because Alfred and Binky accused my grandfather of trifling with Margaret, then stealing her jewelry."

Tootie started to say something but Sister quickly held her hand, squeezing it.

"Weevil was clever. He left a trail somewhere," Sister simply said.

"I think his horn is a kind of map, but I haven't really figured it out. In one of her letters, Margaret mentioned the scrimshaw. What matters to me is that he be laid to rest, properly buried. I know Mother would want that. She never met him, of course, but Margaret's letters to Beverly, my mom, are filled with love. I know you all must test his bones, do all manner of things, but when all is done, please release him to me."

Sister spoke clearly with warmth. "Weevil, if you would like, you may bury your grandfather at the farm. There is a lovely hound graveyard, and I think he would be pleased to be with old friends. Some of those hounds go back to the late-nineteenth century. The hounds he hunted rest there."

"Thank you. Thank you very much. If Mother likes the idea, I think it would be wonderful. He was an Episcopalian."

"We can take care of that," Betty chimed in.

Tootie looked at this handsome fellow and he looked back. "I am so sorry," she said.

"Tootie, I can lay him to rest. It's done. He

died before his time, but he knew love and loved in return and his hounds loved him, too. In the main, I think he lived a good life."

Crawford, rarely speechless, was.

Weevil turned to him. "Mr. Howard, I got the blueprints for all this off your computer. I apologize, but I had a hunch he was here somewhere. And then I became interested in what you are doing. It's fabulous. Forgive this uproar."

"Don't give it a second thought," Crawford generously replied.

"Well, Ben, if it's all right with you, let's all go to Tattenhall Station. Kasmir will spoil us as always, and this will be a hunt no one will ever forget. Crawford, please come. It won't be a breakfast without you—and you, too, Weevil. Forgive me, I only know you as Weevil."

"Mother calls me that." He grinned, then left the stall, and peeked into Earl's stall. "I'll be along. Let me repair this damage. Won't take a minute."

Sister laughed. "That stinker runs Crawford's stables!"

Crawford peered into the stall and got a strong whiff of Earl. "You know, I've wondered if there was a fox in here."

Weevil quickly patted down the extra earth dug up, and fished in his pocket for a treat. He had an old peppermint there and he unwrapped it, dropping it into the den.

"*Candy. I love candy.*" Earl grabbed the peppermint.

"Well, let's mount up and get there." Sister happily allowed Shaker to give her a leg up. "Weevil, catch a ride with Crawford. We'll meet you at Tattenhall Station."

"Yes, Master." He smiled that dazzling smile.

Within fifteen minutes the riders reached the station. All dismounted, stripped off their tack, wiped down the horses. Weevil quite properly took care of the Master's horse as Crawford did drive him to the Station. Sister was impressed. Then he helped Betty and Tootie.

When they finally walked into the packed breakfast, everyone looked up. Silence.

Kasmir, as the host, walked up to his beloved Master. "If you would like to make an announcement I will fetch you a drink."

That fast, Gray handed her a restorative libation. He'd come back with Sam to help with the hounds, since they would arrive before the rest of the staff.

"Ladies and gentlemen. Your Master has a few words." Kasmir turned to Sister.

"It's wonderful to see you all. I will be mercifully brief. Allow me to introduce Wesley Blackford, Wesley Carruthers's grandson." A murmur went up, especially from those old enough to recall Weevil. "He has solved the mystery of his grandfather's disappearance which

I regret to say was because he was murdered, then buried in a stall at Old Paradise." A rumble followed this. "The mournful cowhorn echo you heard was our new Weevil. Beautiful though it was, I think it unnerved our killers who I am dreadfully sorry to report are Alfred and Binky DuCharme." This really set them off. She held up her hands. "Binky has confessed. Alfred, no. This will all come out in time, but I ask you to welcome a very alive Weevil, and I thank Crawford, first for allowing us to follow the fox onto his land and then for his calm under the current circumstances." She turned to extend her hand to Crawford.

It wasn't that he did but so much, but then again, masters are political creatures, wise, hopefully, and she had done the exact right thing because now Crawford could be praised, questioned, lend his voice to the situation.

Sister raised a glass. "To Wesley Carruthers, Huntsman of The Jefferson Hunt from 1947 to 1954 and member of the Huntsman Hall of Fame. Three cheers."

A riot followed.

People rushed up to Sister, Crawford, Shaker, Weevil, Betty, and Tootie.

Weevil put his hand under Tootie's elbow. "May I get you a drink?"

They were now surrounded.

Tootie laughed. "We'll have to fight our way to the bar."

Weevil declared, "I hope to meet each one of you, but this beautiful whipper-in needs a drink. Allow me to get her one."

The crowd trailed the two to the bar.

"My God, he is a carbon copy!" Tedi exclaimed while those around them listened intently, as the Bancrofts were much older and had hunted behind Weevil.

Edward Bancroft, next to Tedi, with Ronnie Haslip on one side and Alida Dalzell on the other, said, "I know some of you know about my late sister and Weevil. That was a long time ago, and things were different then. Let's give this young man a chance."

Tedi looked at her husband. "Edward, you are the most open-minded man, the biggest heart. Yes, let's give him a chance." She kissed him with feeling.

Red-faced but quite pleased, he mumbled, "Now, now."

The breakfast went on for four hours.

Yvonne, who had followed in the car, was there. She and Sam just raked over everything. People couldn't stop talking, eating, drinking. Foxhunting is convivial as it is. This was over the top.

Sister finally made her way to Weevil, who wasn't going to let Tootie slip away, a fact registered by many. "I need to ask you. How do you know our fixtures so well? And have you a place to stay?"

"I'm staying at the Days Inn in Waynesboro. As for the territory, Mother gave me my grandfather's diaries when I graduated from college. I memorized everything."

"Yes, you did." She smiled. "Pack up. You can stay at Roughneck Farm. There's lots of room, and Gray and I will help you sort things out if you need help. And please, your mother is welcome, too."

"Thank you. I don't want to put you out. I think Mother will come down once the body is released to me or her. I guess there are a lot of decisions to be made."

"You won't put me out. Gray's there and the house is big. I'll put you to work."

He smiled. "All right."

"You can walk hounds with us and work horses."

"Oh, madam, that isn't work. That's paradise."

CHAPTER 32

In the midst of life we are in death. Of whom may we seek for succor, but of Thee, O Lord, who for our sins are justly displeased.

"Yet O Lord God most holy, O Lord most mighty, O holy and most merciful Savior: Suffer us not, at our last hour, for any pains of death, to fall from Thee."

The Reverend Judy Parrish's vestments swayed slightly in the November 12 breeze as she stood over Wesley Carruthers's grave. A small, highly polished walnut casket rested on the side of the grave. When his body was found only bones remained. They were gathered up to be laid in this small casket.

Sister and Gray had helped Weevil with the paperwork and the legal hoops.

Beverly Blackford sat next to her son as the service unfolded. Reverend Parrish, a true shepherd to her flock even if someone wasn't an Episcopalian, avoided bromides. She said she didn't know what was on the other side, but she did trust God's love and Wesley was infolded in that love.

Most of Jefferson Hunt crowded into the calm, lovely hound cemetery with its statue of the great hound Archie in the middle. Few there

386

remembered Weevil, but all were there to honor a Jefferson member and huntsman.

Weevil was not alone, surrounded by hounds he had loved and that had loved him.

Standing behind Beverly and Weevil II, seated under a canopy, holding hands, Sister thought, hoped, the murdered man was now hunting his hounds with George Washington, Teddy Roosevelt, the young Winston Churchill, the Empress of Austria, and the Virginia Astor sisters behind him, thrilled with the chase, with viewing an eternal fox. A fancy perhaps, but since no one does know what comes next, or if there is a next, Sister's dream of heaven was as good as someone else's.

The service concluded, Weevil walked his mother to the house, where Kasmir had taken care of everything, given all Sister needed to do.

Sister walked with Marion Maggiolo and Monica Greenberg, who had driven down together for the service. Betty walked with Bobbie, and Tootie escorted her mother. Everyone had attended, except for Margaret DuCharme, M.D., and Arthur DuCharme. They felt it might be inappropriate, since their fathers were the killers, but they trusted that in time they could offer their condolences and respects to Weevil and his mother.

Kasmir had outdone himself. The table carried American, Indian, and English food considered necessary for after a funeral. His Oxford days served him well. The big bar was in the kitchen, a smaller one in the library where it truly resided, one in the mudroom, given all the kitchen traffic, and another in the hall by the front door.

The shockingly beautiful floral arrangements impressed as much as food and drink. Large calla lilies along with dwarf calla lilies, with a red rose in the middle of each arrangement, made those who loved flowers gasp. Kasmir, being Indian, possessed a sense of color not native to Americans and Europeans. He also understood the absence of color, and he paid for everything no matter how much Sister fought with him.

The creature who most appreciated the lilies was Golly, lurking behind one on the Sheraton side table in the dining room. She knew she couldn't launch onto the table, but she could hide. This unnerved a few guests who, oogling the arrangements, found themselves staring into brilliant green eyes.

"I accept tribute." Golly purred.

She actually received some treats.

The dogs were in the upstairs bedroom, which they hated, especially since Golly had the run of the house and could not have cared less that someone had been buried. They, at least, were sensitive to the occasion.

Seated close to the library door, Aunt Daniella

chatted with everyone as people moved through the house.

Weevil came to her, kissed her hand. "Do you forgive me?"

"You were very convincing and yes, I do forgive you. You brought back vivid memories." She beckoned him closer. "How did you know I was close to your grandfather?"

"There were hints in my grandmother's letters to my step-grandmother, but when I saw you, I knew. You are beautiful."

To be ninety-four, more or less, and be told you are beautiful . . . Aunt Daniella glowed and gave him a kiss.

Hours later, the guests began to leave, most on their own steam, a few with assistance.

Marion and Monica, facing a two-and-a-half-hour drive home if there was traffic, walked over to Weevil.

Monica said, "I must have walked right by you when I was working on my project at the museum."

"I was behind the door to the Huntsman's room," he admitted, then turned to Marion.

"I apologize for breaking into the case." Weevil had had no chance to really talk with her until now. "I knew the scrimshaw meant something, but I didn't know what. I hoped it might help me flush out the killers."

She nodded. "Well, you were right."

"I assume you want the horn back?"

"Yes," she simply answered.

"Hold on." He ran upstairs, grabbed it, came down—acknowledging people as he moved along—and handed her the treasure.

She ran her fingers over it. "Weevil, you were a cheeky devil to make the video for my iPhone."

He smiled his grandfather's smile. "Miss Maggiolo, my mother didn't show me the letters until I was thirty. She felt I needed to know something about my people, as she put it, but I would have been too hotheaded before. So I read the letters, where the horn's design was mentioned. It took me a year to come up with a plan I hoped would work."

"You come up and see me at the store anytime. I'll drive you up to Morven Park if you like, although I know you've seen the exhibit."

"I would like that."

The last guest left. Kasmir's team cleaned up everything, except a few missed tidbits behind Golly's lilies.

Exhausted from the day, and the emotions it stirred, Sister, Gray, Beverly, and Weevil had collapsed in the library. Raleigh and Rooster, finally free, plopped on the floor.

"Weevil, be sensible," Beverly chided him.

"Mother, take the jewelry."

One of the first things Sister did when Beverly arrived from Canada was to give her the silver box, which she had polished. When Beverly read the letter she wept. Weevil, mist in his eyes, comforted his mother. Now he felt, people gone, this should be resolved.

"I don't want the jewelry, and when I die that will be one more complicated thing to figure out and bring here."

He had told his mother he wanted to stay in Virginia.

Gray echoed Beverly. "She's right."

"I feel that the jewelry belongs to Mother. She is Weevil's daughter. I'm the next generation."

Sister spoke. "Margaret left that jewelry for future generations. She was clear about that, and prophesied that it would keep generations of Carruthers. She was right."

"What am I going to do with it?"

Gray, quietly but with authority, for who knew money better than he, said, "You are a rich man and you, Beverly, a rich woman. Divide up as you wish; keep some in a safety deposit box, or purchase a huge vault for your home. Sell a piece—all you each need is one—invest a portion of it and use the rest for living. Neither one of you seems like the spendthrift type. This jewelry is worth a fortune. Beverly, you could also make a claim against the DuCharme estate."

Weevil looked at his mother. She looked back.

With a deep sigh Beverly firmly stated, "They can keep their damned money." She then turned to Weevil. "Son, your future is ahead of you. Mine is past. Keep those jewels here. If I need more than the one piece I will choose, I'll let you know."

"Oh, Mother, I don't know."

"Listen to your mother," Sister ordered nicely.

A long silence followed this.

Finally, Weevil agreed. "All right." He turned to Gray. "Am I really rich?"

"Indeed you are." Gray smiled broadly.

"I told Mom I want to stay here, hunt with Jefferson Hunt. I guess I need a green card, because I'm a Canadian citizen."

"I can help there," Gray offered, and given his connections, he truly could.

A lot of people in Washington owed him favors.

"Madam,"—Weevil addressed Sister now as his Master—"I whipped-in at Toronto and North York. I would like to whip-in here. Since I am rich, I don't need a salary. I don't want to take money that can go to the hounds. Will you have me?"

"That is exceedingly generous and I would be thrilled as will be my other whippers-in."

Weevil smiled at his mother. "Mother, I know I'm not going to change the world. I belong with horses and hounds. I belong outside, and now I can do what I love without working a full-time job. I am so grateful to the grandfather and grandmother I never knew. I'm not even sure I belong in this century, but I belong here."

True mother that she was, a teary Beverly responded, "Son, as long as you're happy."

Sister couldn't resist, she leaned toward Weevil. "If you're going to whip-in for Jefferson Hunt, remember silence is golden."

He replied, "And duct tape is silver."

They all laughed. Sister felt, heard, an echo of her son RayRay, who could shoot from the lip. For the first time in her life, she knew the future of The Jefferson Hunt was secure.

AFTERWORD

Randolph D. Rouse, MFH, mentioned in this book, passed away after it was finished. He knocked out his last win as a horse trainer after his 100th birthday. Obviously, Randy was highly intelligent, fair-minded, physically tough, and great fun. How lucky we were to have had this incandescent presence for so long.

J. Harris Anderson, another writer and hunter, wrote in a remembrance in *In and Around Horse Country*, the official publication of the Virginia Steeplechase Association, Volume XXIX/ Number 3 Summer 2017, that it was always a special moment at a hunt ball when Randy would sing "Young at Heart."

Indeed.

He is survived by his energetic wife, Michele. Everyone notes that Michele was thirty-eight years younger than Randy. She had to be. Who else could keep up with him?

THE MATERNAL GRANDSIRE EFFECT

For centuries this generational hop has been noted by Thoroughbred breeders and hound breeders. The study of this is relatively new. It is not within the scope of this novel to explain what is happening genetically. I can produce this in my kennel with many of my hounds and I have produced it with a horse or two. That doesn't mean I understand it, even though I can often effect it.

Please research The Maternal Grandsire effect if you are curious. I think of it as train signals being switched on and off but gender produces the flip.

You see this in humans, as well, but I have assiduously avoided breeding same.

Ever and Always,
Dr. Rita Mae Brown, MFH

Rita Mae Brown is the bestselling author of the Sneaky Pie Brown series; the Sister Jane series; the Runnymede novels, including *Six of One* and *Cakewalk*; *A Nose for Justice* and *Murder Unleashed*; *Rubyfruit Jungle*; *In Her Day*; and many other books. An Emmy-nominated screenwriter and poet, Brown lives in Afton, Virginia, and is a Master of Foxhounds.

ritamaebrownbooks.com

Books are
produced in the
United States
using U.S.-based
materials

Books are printed
using a revolutionary
new process called
THINKtech™ that
lowers energy usage
by 70% and increases
overall quality

Books are
durable and
flexible
because of
smythe-sewing

Paper is
sourced using
environmentally
responsible
foresting methods
and the
paper is acid-free

Center Point Large Print
600 Brooks Road / PO Box 1
Thorndike, ME 04986-0001 USA

(207) 568-3717

US & Canada:
1 800 929-9108
www.centerpointlargeprint.com